I0534769

Shadows and Debts: Tales from the Nexus

Rae Stonehouse

Published by Live For Excellence Productions, 2025.

This is a work of fiction. Similarities to real people, places, or events are entirely coincidental.

SHADOWS AND DEBTS: TALES FROM THE NEXUS

First edition. December 15, 2025.

ISBN: 978-1997784654

Written by Rae Stonehouse.

Table of Contents

SHADOWS AND DEBTS: TALES FROM THE NEXUS

INTRODUCTION TO THE DAYBRIDGE CHRONICLES - TALES FROM THE NEXUS

Welcome to Daybridge—a city where the veil between worlds wears perpetually thin, where the dead don't always stay buried, and where the price of truth is measured in blood, sacrifice, and the courage to stand against impossible odds.

You stand at the threshold of three interconnected stories, each exploring a different facet of a city built on secrets, powered by suffering, and bound by forces that predate human understanding. Here, beneath the shadow of the Gothic bridge that gives the city its name, reality operates by different rules. Consciousness persists beyond death. Ancient pacts written in blood still bind the living. And those brave—or foolish—enough to ask questions discover that some truths exact a terrible cost.

The Nexus

At Daybridge's heart stands the bridge itself—more than mere infrastructure, it serves as a nexus point where dimensions bleed into one another, where the boundary between life and death becomes negotiable, and where human ambition collides with forces beyond mortal comprehension. Built on sacrifice and sustained through ritual, the bridge is simultaneously symbol and reality, anchor and gateway, protector and prison.

But the bridge is only the beginning. Daybridge's supernatural architecture runs deeper than stone and iron—it's woven into the city's foundations, embedded in its history, and carved into the souls of those who call it home. From the founding families who built empires on stolen land and murdered innocents, to the modern corporations that traffic in enslaved consciousness, Daybridge's power structures have always understood one fundamental truth: control the supernatural, and you control everything.

Three Stories, One City

Blood Debt introduces you to Daybridge through Alice Chen, a detective investigating supernatural crimes in a city where the dead can testify—and where some transformations come at a price, no human should pay. When alchemical ambition meets forced ascension, Alice and the bridge consciousness itself must decide what they're willing to sacrifice to stop a conspiracy that views human essence as raw material for transcendence.

The Black Book - The Archive pulls back the curtain on Daybridge's political foundations, following archivist Nadia Marsh as she uncovers a seventy-year conspiracy built on systematic elimination, historical erasure, and ritual murder. What begins as historical research becomes a desperate race to expose the founding families before they complete another cycle of blood sacrifice—with Nadia herself marked as the next offering.

The Ghost Adoption Agency reveals the city's darkest commercial enterprise: the legal trafficking of ghost consciousness, where the dead are property and torture is standard procedure. When Miranda Hayes adopts a ghost to fill the void left by her sister's death, she discovers a nightmare hiding behind government approval—and makes a choice that will cost her everything to free hundreds of enslaved souls.

The Evolution of Corruption

These stories span decades but share common DNA: the exploitation of supernatural phenomena for profit and power, the courage of ordinary people who refuse to accept institutional evil, and the terrible prices paid by those who stand against systems designed to crush resistance.

You'll meet investigators and archivists, journalists and hackers, ghosts and distributed consciousnesses—each fighting their own battle against Daybridge's endemic corruption. Some will sacrifice their freedom. Others will lose their lives. All will discover that in Daybridge, truth is the most dangerous weapon of all.

A Living World

The Daybridge you're about to enter exists in multiple timelines, each exploring different possibilities that branched from the same foundational events. Blood Debt unfolds in an alternate reality where certain choices led to different outcomes, while The Black Book and The Ghost Adoption Agency share a timeline where corruption evolved along different paths. Yet all three stories are true—different harmonics of the same fundamental song, different angles on a city where consciousness itself becomes currency.

You'll encounter familiar names across stories, see how actions in one timeline echo through others, and piece together a larger tapestry of a city where the supernatural and mundane are inextricably woven together. The founding families appear in different guises. The bridge consciousness manifests through various vessels. And always, always, ordinary people must choose whether to look away or stand and fight.

The Price of Truth

These are not comfortable stories. They explore systematic abuse, institutional corruption, and the ways power perpetuates itself through violence both physical and structural. They ask difficult questions about consent, autonomy, and the moral compromises we make to survive in systems designed to exploit us.

But they are also stories of resistance. About people who refuse to accept that "legal" equals "right." About the bonds formed between unlikely allies—living and dead, human and other. About the moment when enough becomes enough, and ordinary citizens transform into revolutionaries simply by choosing to care.

Your Journey Begins

The three stories in this collection can be read in any order, though reading them in sequence—Blood Debt, The Black Book, The Ghost Adoption Agency—will provide a progression from supernatural action through systemic investigation to personal liberation. Each stands alone. Together, they reveal Daybridge's true face: a city where evolution and exploitation walk hand in hand, where transcendence and torture share the same foundation, and where the next step in human consciousness might be built on the suffering of those denied recognition as human at all.

This is Daybridge. This is the nexus. This is where dimensions bleed and debts are paid in blood and shadows.

Welcome.

Some truths, once discovered, cannot be unknown. Some debts, once incurred, can never be fully repaid. And some cities—cities like Daybridge—remember everything.

The bridge is waiting. The archives are open. The ghosts are ready to speak.

Are you ready to listen?

The Daybridge Chronicles - Tales from the Nexus: Where every choice casts shadows, every truth demands payment, and every soul—living or dead—must decide what price they're willing to pay for freedom.

COPYRIGHT:

First Edition

Published by Live For Excellence Productions

ISBN:

Ebook: 978-1-997784-63-0

Paperback: 978-1-997784-65-4

Audiobook: 978-1-997784-64-7

BLOOD DEBT

Author's Note:

Blood Debt takes place in an alternate timeline from the main Daybridge series. While Ethan Reeves' transformation into a distributed consciousness occurred similarly to the events of *Shadows of Daybridge: When Dimensions Bleed*, the subsequent trajectory of events diverged.

In this timeline:

- Alice Chen's relationship with Ethan developed differently
- The Daybridge Police Department's awareness of supernatural elements emerged through different cases
- The Order of the Eternal Threshold pursued different experimental pathways
- The bridge consciousness evolved along a separate dimensional frequency

This is a complete story unto itself, exploring themes of transformation, consent, and the cost of transcendence through a different lens than the primary series timeline.

Readers familiar with the main series will recognize characters and concepts but should consider this a "what if" exploration—a dimensional echo of possibilities that branched from the same foundational events.

CHAPTER ONE: EMPTY VEINS

The call came at 3:47 AM.

Detective Alice Chen had learned to hate that particular hour. Nothing good happened at 3:47 AM in Daybridge. The city's supernatural underbelly stirred then, when the barrier between midnight's chaos and dawn's promise wore thinnest. She'd been dreaming of Ethan—the version of him that existed before the transformation, before he'd become something simultaneously more and less than human. In the dream, they were at the Silver Spoon Diner, just talking. Simple. Normal.

Her phone buzzing shattered that fiction.

"Chen." She kept her voice level despite the fatigue grinding behind her eyes.

"Detective, this is Captain Morrison. We've got a situation at Daybridge Memorial Blood Bank. Two bodies. Director insists on speaking with Homicide immediately." He paused. "She specifically asked for you."

Alice sat up, already reaching for her clothes. Six months since the winter solstice, since Ethan had become the bridge's distributed consciousness, and Daybridge still hadn't settled. Couldn't settle. Reality had transformed around the old Gothic structure, and the city was learning to live with thinner dimensional boundaries, with shadows that moved independently, with the constant low-grade hum of something Other pressing against the everyday world.

"I'm on my way."

She dressed quickly—dark jeans, white blouse, leather jacket. Her service weapon went into its holster at her hip, but she also grabbed the modified Glock from her nightstand. Father Mulligan had etched symbols into the barrel, blessed the ammunition with rituals from half a dozen traditions. In Daybridge, standard equipment wasn't always enough.

The blood bank sat on the boundary between Daybridge's wealthy west side and the decaying east—appropriate, Alice thought grimly, for a facility that served both populations. The building was of newer construction, all glass and steel angles, but it couldn't escape the city's Gothic shadow. Daybridge's architecture had a way of asserting itself, even in modern designs.

Police cruisers blocked the entrance, their lights painting the street in strobing red and blue. Alice parked and ducked under the crime scene tape, flashing her badge at the uniform stationed at the door.

Inside, the fluorescent lights seemed too bright, too clinical. The smell hit her first—antiseptic and copper, the particular scent of a place where blood was currency. A woman in her late forties waited in the lobby, her white coat stained with coffee. Dark circles shadowed her eyes, and her hands trembled slightly as she clasped them together.

"Dr. Hartwell?" Alice extended her hand. "Detective Chen."

The woman's grip was firm despite the tremor. "Thank you for coming. I—I didn't know who else to call. The bodies are downstairs, in cold storage, but that's not why I called. Well, it is, but there's more."

Alice pulled out her notebook. "Start from the beginning."

Dr. Hartwell led her through the facility, past donation stations and processing labs, toward the elevator. "I came in early to review our quarterly inventory reports. We've been noticing discrepancies for three months now. Small at first—a few units here and there. I thought it was clerical errors, data entry mistakes. But the shortfalls kept growing."

The elevator descended with a mechanical hum. Alice felt a familiar prickle at the base of her skull—the sensitivity she'd developed after prolonged exposure to Daybridge's supernatural elements. Ethan called it dimensional awareness. She called it a persistent migraine that occasionally saved her life.

"What changed?" Alice asked.

"I started cross-referencing physical inventory against digital records." Dr. Hartwell's voice tightened. "Someone's been falsifying the database. Making it look like blood products were distributed to hospitals, used in surgeries, shipped to other facilities. But the physical inventory doesn't match. We're missing nearly two hundred units, Detective. Specific types—rare factors, unusual combinations."

The elevator doors opened onto the basement level. The temperature dropped immediately, cold enough that Alice's breath misted. Storage tanks lined the walls; each marked with careful labels. At the far end, a uniformed officer stood guard outside the cold storage unit.

"The night-shift workers?" Alice prompted.

Dr. Hartwell nodded, her face pale. "Monte Webb and Jennifer Cho. They were doing the monthly deep-inventory check. When they didn't clock out at six AM, security went looking. Found them..." She swallowed hard. "You should see for yourself."

The cold storage door was already open. Alice stepped inside, the temperature plunging further. Her breath came in white clouds as she approached the two bodies.

Monte Webb and Jennifer Cho lay on the concrete floor, positioned almost peacefully, as if they'd simply decided to rest. But their skin held a distinctive waxy pallor Alice had learned to recognize. Exsanguination. Complete blood loss.

She crouched beside Webb's body, examining without touching. No visible wounds on his neck—ruling out the vampire theory that had immediately leaped to mind. No defensive wounds on his hands. His eyes were open, pupils dilated, expression slack. Not peaceful, she realized. Sedated.

"Have they been moved?" Alice asked.

"No," the uniform responded. "We secured the scene as soon as security found them."

Alice studied Jennifer Cho's body. Same presentation—drained, sedated, positioned carefully. But something nagged at her professional instincts. This wasn't feeding. The bodies were too clean, too precisely arranged. This was extraction, clinical and methodical.

She stood, turning to Dr. Hartwell. "I need to see your inventory records. All of them. And I need a list of everyone with access to the facility after hours."

"Of course. I've already compiled." Dr. Hartwell's phone buzzed. She glanced at it, and her face went whiter. "Detective. You need to see this."

Alice followed her out of cold storage, back to the elevator. They rose to the administrative level, where Dr. Hartwell's office overlooked the facility's main processing center. The director pulled out her computer, fingers flying across the keyboard.

"I set up an automated monitoring system this morning after I discovered the falsified records. It alerts me whenever inventory is accessed." She turned the monitor toward Alice. "Someone just logged into our system. Right now. They're deleting files."

Alice moved around the desk, watching as folders disappeared from the directory tree. "Can you trace the access point?"

"It's coming from inside the building. Third floor, the plasma processing lab." Dr. Hartwell's hands hovered over the keyboard. "Should I lock them out?"

"No, keep monitoring. I need backup." Alice was already calling it in, requesting units to cover all exits. "When I give the signal, lock down the entire facility. No one in or out."

She took the stairs at a run, weapon drawn. The third floor was dark, illuminated only by emergency lighting and the glow from computer screens. The plasma processing lab sat at the end of a long corridor, its door ajar.

Alice approached carefully, checking corners, listening. Her dimensional awareness prickled again, stronger now. Something was wrong with the air here—it felt thick, viscous, like moving through water.

The lab was empty. Computer monitors displayed cascading deletions, files vanishing in real-time. But no one sat at the keyboard. The chair was pushed back, abandoned.

Alice moved to the window and looked down at the parking lot. Nothing moved. No vehicles fleeing. Whoever had been here had vanished—literally, she suspected, using one of Daybridge's many thin places where reality wore threadbare.

Her phone buzzed. A text from a number she didn't recognize, just three words: *Bridge. Now. -E*

Ethan.

She holstered her weapon and returned to Dr. Hartwell's office. "Lock down the facility. I need those inventory records transferred to a secure drive. Everything you have—donor information, distribution logs, the falsified data, all of it."

"Where are you going?" Dr. Hartwell asked.

Alice grabbed the drive the director offered. "To consult with an expert."

The Daybridge Bridge rose against the pre-dawn sky like a Gothic accusation. Six months hadn't diminished its presence. If anything, the structure had grown more imposing, more alive. The stone seemed to pulse with subtle rhythms, and shadows moved across its surface in patterns that defied the streetlights' geometry.

Alice parked at the western approach and walked onto the bridge. Her footsteps echoed on the old stone, and the prickle of dimensional awareness bloomed into full sensation. The air here felt charged, pregnant with possibility and threat in equal measure.

She stopped at the bridge's center, where the eye-within-triangle symbol had been carved into the balustrade. "Ethan. I'm here."

The air shimmered. Reality folded, and Ethan Reeves manifested.

He looked exactly as he had before the transformation—lean and muscular, dark hair slightly too long, those piercing eyes that had always seen too much. But Alice had learned to recognize the difference. The way he stood perfectly still in a manner no living human could maintain. The slight translucence at his edges when the light caught him wrong. The sense that she was looking at a projection, a focused point of a much larger consciousness.

"Alice." His voice held warmth, but also something vast beneath it, like hearing the ocean in a seashell. "Thank you for coming."

She held up the drive. "Two dead at the blood bank. Inventory theft. Files being deleted. What did you sense?"

Ethan's expression darkened. Manifesting like this cost him energy, pulled his consciousness into a singular focus that he couldn't maintain indefinitely. He used it sparingly, only when necessary.

"Three nights ago, I felt dimensional fluctuations near the blood bank. Not Order activity—their signature is rigid, controlled. This was... hungrier. More primal." He paused, and Alice saw the struggle as he accessed the bridge's composite consciousness. "The nexus has been agitated. Guthrie Knox's memories are surfacing."

Alice knew that name. Guthrie Knox, the master butcher who'd been transformed in 1913, who'd become the core consciousness of the bridge's nexus entity. The Ogre of Daybridge, in local legend.

"What kind of memories?" she asked.

Ethan's eyes unfocused, seeing something beyond her. "Before the transformation, Knox developed techniques for rendering. Not just meat—essence. He believed that blood carried more than physical vitality. That it held some fundamental quality of the person, their strength, their will. He experimented with distillation, concentration."

A chill ran down Alice's spine that had nothing to do with the pre-dawn cold. "Someone's recreating his techniques."

"On a larger scale." Ethan refocused on her. "The victims at the blood bank—may I?"

Alice understood. She'd learned to accept the strangeness of their relationship, the way Ethan could perceive things through her if she allowed it. She lowered her mental barriers, letting him access her recent memories.

His expression shifted from horror to grim recognition. "Not feeding. Harvesting. They were sedated, then drained with precision. Medical equipment, not supernatural predation."

"The missing inventory includes rare blood types," Alice said. "Dr. Hartwell is running the analysis, but she mentioned specific factors. Unusual combinations."

"Founding family bloodlines." Ethan's voice went flat. "People with genetic connections to Daybridge's supernatural infrastructure. Their blood carries dimensional resonance."

Alice thought of her own family history. Her grandmother had been from one of the older Daybridge families, though they'd never been wealthy or influential. Just old. She'd never considered what that might mean in supernatural terms.

"How much blood are we talking about?" Ethan asked.

"Nearly two hundred units over three months. Plus, plasma products, specific extracts. If someone's refining it like Knox did..." Alice let the implication hang.

Ethan turned toward the river, his form flickering slightly. "I need to access deeper memories. Knox's techniques were crude, limited by 1913 technology. But combined with modern medical equipment, with industrial processing capabilities..."

"How bad could it be?"

He looked back at her, and she saw genuine fear in his eyes. "In 1913, Knox managed to distill the essence of three people into a concentrated serum. He never used it—Eliza Blackwood's ritual interrupted his work. But he believed it could grant temporary transcendence, a glimpse beyond normal human consciousness."

"Two hundred units could create—"

"Enough serum to transform someone," Ethan finished. "Not like my transformation, through symbiosis and integration. This would be forced, alchemical. Consciousness expanded through consumption rather than connection."

Alice's phone buzzed. A text from Dr. Hartwell: *Analysis complete. All missing blood types carry Rh-null factor variants. Sending a full report.*

She showed Ethan the message. "Rh-null. That's the golden blood, right? Universal donor?"

"Extremely rare." Ethan's translucence increased as he pulled more deeply on the bridge's consciousness. "Less than fifty people worldwide carry true Rh-null. But variants exist, especially in populations with long genetic isolation. Like founding families in a city built on a dimensional nexus."

"Someone's specifically targeting dimensionally attuned blood."

"And they have enough of it to attempt something catastrophic." Ethan's form began to fade. "I need to return to the bridge consciousness, search Knox's memories for specifics. But Alice—be careful. Whoever is doing this understands both the supernatural and medical sides. That's a dangerous combination."

"Wait." Alice stepped closer. In six months, she'd learned to navigate their strange new relationship, but moments like this still hurt. "Can you stay? Just a few more minutes?"

Ethan's expression softened. He reached out, and his hand found hers. The touch was solid, warm, real. "I'm always here, Alice. Even when you can't see me. The bridge watches over you."

"That's not the same as you watching over me."

"I know." He squeezed her hand gently. "But it's what we have. And I'll take it."

His form dissolved, consciousness flowing back into the bridge's structure. Alice stood alone in the center of the span, watching dawn break over Daybridge. The city was waking, unaware that somewhere within its boundaries, someone was distilling human essence into concentrated horror.

She pulled out her phone and called the task force she'd been assembling—the supernatural crimes unit that officially didn't exist but had become essential in the six months since Ethan's transformation.

"Nadia, it's Alice. I need you to research something. Industrial facilities in Daybridge with rendering or processing equipment. Particularly anything connected to the Knox family or the old stockyards district."

Nadia Marsh's voice was alert despite the early hour. "The blood bank case?"

"It's bigger than theft. Someone's preparing for something." Alice turned from the bridge, heading back to her car. "Get Father Mulligan and Lilith Blackwood. Tell them we're meeting at St. Jude's in two hours. And Nadia? See if Michael Mercer or Sam Thompson can access financial records for medical supply companies. Whoever's doing this needs equipment. They had to purchase it somewhere."

"On it. Alice—how bad is this?"

Alice thought of Ethan's fear, of Guthrie Knox's memories surfacing after more than a century. "Bad enough that the bridge itself is worried. That should tell you everything."

She ended the call and drove away from the bridge, but she could feel Ethan's presence following her—not physically, but through the network of consciousness that now permeated Daybridge. The city had become his body, in a sense, and nothing within its boundaries escaped his awareness.

The question was: would that be enough to stop whatever was coming?

Alice had learned something in her years as a detective, something the supernatural cases had only reinforced. The worst monsters weren't the ones who looked like monsters. They were the ones who used science and reason and careful planning to justify their atrocities.

And somewhere in Daybridge, someone with medical knowledge and supernatural understanding was brewing a nightmare from distilled human essence.

Alice just had to find them before they finished the work Guthrie Knox had started more than a century ago.

CHAPTER TWO: THE RENDERING

Nadia Marsh lived in organized chaos.

Alice picked her way through the journalist's apartment, stepping over stacks of archived newspapers, dodging filing boxes labeled with dates going back to Daybridge's founding. The walls were covered in corkboards, each one a web of photographs, news clippings, and colored string connecting seemingly random events into coherent narratives.

"Coffee's fresh," Nadia called from her desk, not looking up from the three monitors displaying different databases. Her fingers flew across keyboards, pulling information from sources Alice wasn't certain were entirely legal. "And before you ask—yes, I used proper channels for the medical facility records. Mostly."

Alice accepted the offered mug and studied the center monitor. Four names glowed in red: Daybridge Memorial Blood Bank, St. Catherine's Hospital, Eastside Medical Center, and the University Research Clinic.

"All four reported inventory discrepancies?" Alice asked.

"Over the same three-month period." Nadia finally looked up, pushing her glasses higher on her nose. Dark circles shadowed her eyes—she'd clearly been working through the night. "Different amounts, different blood types, but the same pattern of falsified digital records. Someone with serious technical skills covered their tracks."

"Until Dr. Hartwell got suspicious."

"Right. But here's what's interesting." Nadia pulled up a map of Daybridge on the second monitor. Four red dots marked the medical facilities. "These locations form a pattern. See?"

Alice studied the map. The four facilities created rough corners of a square, centered on Daybridge's old industrial district. The area where the rendering plants and stockyards had operated in the early twentieth century.

"Geometric distribution," Alice murmured. "They wanted blood from across the city but needed proximity to a central processing location."

"That's my thinking." Nadia opened a new window, displaying property records. "I've been digging into the industrial district. Most of it's abandoned or converted to artist lofts and microbreweries. But three buildings are still registered as industrial facilities, and one of them has recent electrical usage that doesn't match any legitimate business."

Alice's phone buzzed. A text from Lilith Blackwood: *Dimensional surge detected. Old industrial district. Need Ethan. Come to the shop.*

"We need to move," Alice said. "Lilith's picking up something."

Nadia grabbed her jacket and camera bag. "I'm coming with you."

"This isn't journalism, Nadia. If Lilith's detecting dimensional activity—"

"Then you'll need documentation. Evidence. That's what I do." Nadia's expression was determined. "Besides, you need someone to watch your back who isn't emotionally compromised."

Alice wanted to argue, but Nadia had a point. The journalist had proven herself over the past six months and had earned her place in their unofficial supernatural crimes unit. And Alice trusted her instincts.

"Fine. But you stay behind me if things get dangerous."

"Always do."

They took Alice's car across town to Lilith Blackwood's occult shop. The store occupied a narrow building wedged between a vintage clothing boutique and a tattoo parlor, its windows displaying crystals, tarot decks, and books on various mystical traditions. Most of it was window dressing for tourists. The real work happened in the back rooms.

Lilith met them at the door; her silver hair pulled back in a severe bun. She wore practical clothing—dark jeans, boots, a leather jacket that had seen better decades. Her eyes held a particular intensity Alice had learned to respect.

"The bridge manifested Ethan ten minutes ago," Lilith said without preamble. "He's waiting in the workshop. Father Mulligan is already there."

The workshop occupied the building's basement, accessible through a door disguised as a supply closet. Alice descended the narrow stairs, Nadia close behind. The temperature dropped as they went down, and that familiar prickle of dimensional awareness made Alice's scalp tighten.

The workshop was a strange combination of an occult library and a scientific laboratory. Chalk circles marked the floor, interspersed with electronic monitoring equipment. Shelves held both ancient grimoires and modern reference books on quantum physics. Father Mulligan stood near a table covered in printouts and diagrams, his clerical collar visible beneath a worn sweater. Beside him, Ethan studied a map with focused intensity.

He looked up as Alice entered, and their eyes met. Six months, and that connection still hit her like electricity. He manifested more solidly here than at the bridge—Lilith's workshop sat on one of Daybridge's thin places, making it easier for him to pull his consciousness into singular form.

"Show them what you found," Ethan said to Lilith.

The older woman moved to a bank of electronic equipment that looked jury-rigged from various sources. Oscilloscopes displayed waveforms, and a modified Geiger counter clicked intermittently.

"I've been monitoring dimensional frequencies since the winter solstice," Lilith explained. "Looking for patterns, trying to understand how the bridge's transformation affected the city's supernatural infrastructure. Three nights ago, I detected anomalous activity." She tapped one of the screens. "This is the baseline dimensional resonance for Daybridge—the constant low-level energy from the nexus entity's presence."

The waveform showed gentle oscillations, a steady rhythm like breathing.

"And this,"—Lilith pulled up a second screen—"is what I recorded last night at 2:14 AM."

The waveform spiked violently, a sharp peak that made Alice's teeth ache just looking at it.

"That's a massive surge of life-essence energy," Father Mulligan said. His Irish accent thickened with concern. "I've only seen readings like that during major supernatural events. Rituals involving human sacrifice, or—"

"The processing of distilled human essence," Ethan finished. His jaw was tight. "I felt it through the bridge consciousness. The surge originated here." He pointed to a location on the map. "The old industrial district, near where the Daybridge Rendering Plant operated."

Alice exchanged glances with Nadia. "That matches our analysis of the blood theft pattern."

"The rendering plant." Nadia pulled out her tablet, fingers flying across the screen. "Built in 1923, processed livestock until it closed in 1954. Original ownership records show..." She paused, frowning. "Huh. It wasn't owned by the Knox family. The owner of record was Daybridge Industrial Holdings, a consortium of investors."

"Guthrie Knox was born into poverty," Ethan said quietly. "Orphaned young, worked in the stockyards as a butcher. He never owned the rendering plant. But he worked there, learned his techniques there."

"Someone's using his workspace," Alice said. "Someone who knows the history."

Lilith pulled up another screen, this one showing a satellite image of the industrial district. "The rendering plant building is still standing.

Recent electrical usage suggests active occupation, but there's no business registered at that address. It's technically abandoned."

"We need to check it out," Alice said. "Full team. If someone's processing human blood there—"

"I'm coming with you." Ethan's tone left no room for argument. "The dimensional resonance is too strong. If this is connected to Knox's memories, I need to be there."

Alice wanted to protest. Manifesting in multiple locations drained Ethan's energy, pulling his consciousness too thin. But she also understood his determination. This was personal—Knox's memories were part of him now, woven into the bridge's composite consciousness.

"Father Mulligan, you too," she said. "If there are alchemical elements, we'll need your expertise. Nadia, you document everything. Lilith, can you monitor from here? If the dimensional frequencies spike again—"

"I'll alert you immediately," Lilith said. "And Alice? Be careful. That surge last night... it felt hungry. Whatever's happening at that rendering plant, it's building toward something."

The old industrial district looked post-apocalyptic in daylight. Abandoned buildings leaned against each other like drunks, their windows shattered, their brick facades crumbling. Graffiti covered most surfaces, and the streets were cratered with potholes. The city had forgotten this area, left it to decay while newer developments claimed the waterfront and hillsides.

Alice parked three blocks from the rendering plant, not wanting to announce their arrival. The team gathered on the sidewalk—Alice and Ethan, Father Mulligan with his satchel of religious implements, Nadia with her camera equipment.

Ethan closed his eyes, extending his awareness. "The building's ahead. I can feel the dimensional disturbance. It's like..." He struggled for words. "Like an infection. The energy feels wrong, corrupted."

They approached on foot, moving through shadows and keeping to cover. The rendering plant was a massive structure of brick and corrugated metal, three stories tall with a sagging roof. Loading docks lined one side, their doors hanging open. Broken windows stared down like empty eye sockets.

"No vehicles," Nadia observed, photographing the building. "If someone's operating here, they're not making it obvious."

Alice drew her modified Glock. "Ethan, what are you sensing?"

"Recent occupation. The building's warm—active heating. Electrical systems running." His eyes opened, glowing faintly with an otherworldly light. "But no one's inside now. They left recently. Within the last hour."

"Could be a trap," Father Mulligan warned.

"Could be." Alice checked her weapon. "But we need to see what's inside. Nadia, you stay with Father Mulligan. Defensive position at the entrance. Ethan and I go in first."

The main entrance was unlocked. Alice pushed through, weapon raised, and stepped into a vast open space that had once been the rendering floor. Industrial equipment hulked in the shadows—old conveyor systems, processing vats, machinery whose purpose Alice couldn't guess. But overlaid on top of the original equipment was something new.

Modern medical equipment. Centrifuges, industrial filtration systems, refrigeration units. The air smelled of chemicals and copper, the distinctive scent of blood. But beneath it was something else, something that made Alice's dimensional awareness flare. Ozone and rot, like reality itself was decomposing.

"Jesus," she whispered.

Ethan moved past her, drawn toward the center of the space. His form flickered, translucence increasing as the corrupted dimensional energy interfered with his manifestation. "Alice. Look."

The processing vats had been modified. Modern piping connected them to the medical equipment, creating a grotesque assembly line. But etched into the metal surfaces were symbols—geometric patterns and sigils that made Alice's eyes ache.

Father Mulligan entered despite Alice's protests, moving immediately to the nearest vat. He pulled out a small book, flipping through pages, comparing the etched symbols to illustrations. "Alchemical notation. Early twentieth century, but mixed with older traditions. These formulas are for distillation, concentration. Reducing blood to its essential properties."

"Knox's techniques," Ethan said. His voice was hollow, echoing strangely in the vast space. "I'm remembering. He believed blood carried more than oxygen and nutrients. That it held the person's essence—their vitality, their consciousness, even their connection to higher dimensions. He tried to isolate that essence, concentrate it into a serum that could expand human awareness."

Alice holstered her weapon and approached one of the refrigeration units. Inside were dozens of medical-grade vials, each filled with amber liquid that seemed to glow faintly. "Is this it? The distilled essence?"

"Don't touch it," Ethan warned. "Even passive exposure could affect you. That serum is saturated with dimensional energy."

Nadia appeared in the doorway, camera raised. "Alice, you need to see this."

She led them to an office space on the second floor. Inside were filing cabinets, a desk covered in papers, and a wall covered in photographs. Alice's stomach turned as she studied the images. Homeless people, vagrants, individuals who wouldn't be missed. Each photograph was marked with dates and notations.

"Medical trials," Nadia read from one of the documents. "They were hiring people off the streets, offering them money for blood donations.

But look at the volumes—they were taking pints at a time, far more than standard donation protocols allow."

Father Mulligan examined another document. "Some of these dates go back six months. They've been planning this since..." He looked at Ethan. "Since the winter solstice. Since your transformation."

Ethan's expression darkened. "The bridge's transformation changed Daybridge's dimensional resonance. Made it stronger, more accessible. Someone saw an opportunity."

Alice's phone buzzed. Michael Mercer, calling from his PI office. She answered. "Mercer, what do you have?"

"Financial records on the rendering plant purchase. It took some digging, but I traced it through three shell corporations back to the actual buyer." Mercer's voice was tight. "It's registered to something called the Blackthorn Institute. That mean anything to you?"

Alice felt cold certainty settle in her chest. "What's Blackthorn Institute?"

"Psychiatric facility on the north side. Founded in 1920, apparently to treat something called 'dimensional sensitivity syndrome.' Whatever that means."

Father Mulligan's face went pale. "Mother of God. I've heard of that place. The Church has records. Blackthorn was established to house people who'd been exposed to the nexus entity's influence. People who couldn't handle the dimensional awareness, who went mad from it."

"Are they still operational?" Alice asked.

"According to state records, yes," Mercer said. "Seventeen current patients. It's a private facility, very exclusive. Funded through some kind of trust."

Alice ended the call and looked at Ethan. "We need to visit Blackthorn Institute."

"Agreed. But Alice..." Ethan gestured to the vials of amber serum. "We should secure these. If someone's producing this much distilled essence, they're planning something catastrophic. We can't leave it here."

"I'll call for an evidence team. Supernatural protocols." Alice pulled out her phone, then paused. "Ethan, what would someone do with this much concentrated essence? What was Knox planning before Eliza Blackwood's ritual interrupted him?"

Ethan's eyes closed, accessing those deep memories. When he spoke, his voice carried multiple tones, as if Knox himself was speaking through him. "Ascension. He believed that by consuming concentrated human essence, particularly essence from people with dimensional sensitivity, he could transcend normal consciousness. Become something more than human. Not through symbiosis like my transformation, but through forced evolution. Alchemical perfection."

"How much essence would that require?"

"Knox estimated he'd need the concentrated essence of at least fifty people. Maybe more, depending on their dimensional resonance." Ethan's eyes opened. "There are over two hundred vials here, Alice. Enough for four or five transformations."

The implications made Alice's head spin. "We need to find whoever's behind this. Before they use it."

Blackthorn Institute occupied a converted mansion on Daybridge's north side, where old money met older secrets. The building was Victorian Gothic, all sharp angles and dark stone, surrounded by manicured grounds and iron fencing. A discreet plaque by the gate read: "Blackthorn Institute - Private Care Facility - Est. 1920."

Alice parked at the entrance and studied the building through the windshield. Ethan sat beside her, his manifestation stable but clearly draining his energy. They'd left Father Mulligan and Nadia to coordinate with the evidence team at the rendering plant.

"You sense anything?" Alice asked.

Ethan's eyes were closed, reaching out with his expanded awareness. "Dimensional energy. Concentrated, saturated. Like the rendering plant, but older. This place has been marinating in nexus influence for over a century."

"Can you maintain manifestation inside?"

"I'll manage. But Alice, if things go wrong—if I start to lose cohesion—you need to get out immediately. The dimensional interference here could fracture my consciousness, scatter it across the city. I'd eventually reform at the bridge, but you'd be alone."

Alice reached over and took his hand. The touch was warm, solid. Real, for now. "Then don't let things go wrong."

They approached the main entrance together. Alice rang the bell, and a moment later, a woman in medical scrubs answered. Her name tag read "Nurse Whitmore."

"Can I help you?" Her smile was professional but didn't reach her eyes.

Alice showed her badge. "Detective Alice Chen, Daybridge PD. This is my consultant, Ethan Reeves. We need to speak with your director about a current investigation."

The nurse's smile faltered. "I'll need to check if Dr. Crane is available. Please wait here."

She closed the door, leaving them on the porch. Through the windows, Alice could see a comfortable lobby—antique furniture, warm lighting, oil paintings of pastoral scenes. It looked more like a hotel than a psychiatric facility.

"No security cameras," Ethan observed. "At least, none visible. But I'm sensing monitoring equipment. Electronic surveillance, very sophisticated."

The door reopened. A man in his late fifties stood there, wearing an expensive suit and a welcoming expression. His silver hair was perfectly styled, and his handshake was firm.

"Detective Chen, Mr. Reeves. I'm Dr. Matthias Crane, director of Blackthorn Institute. Please, come in. How can I help Daybridge's finest?"

His tone was cordial, but Alice's instincts screamed warning. She'd interviewed enough suspects to recognize performance. Crane was too calm, too prepared.

He led them to his office, a wood-paneled space lined with medical texts and diplomas. Crane settled behind an ornate desk and gestured for them to sit.

"We're investigating a case involving stolen medical supplies," Alice began. "Our financial investigation revealed that your facility recently purchased a property in the industrial district. The old rendering plant."

"Ah, yes." Crane's expression remained pleasant. "We acquired that property as potential expansion space. Blackthorn has been operating beyond capacity for years, and we're considering converting the rendering plant into additional housing for our patients."

"Housing for patients with dimensional sensitivity syndrome," Alice said.

Crane's eyes sharpened. "You've done your homework, Detective. Yes, Blackthorn specializes in treating individuals who've developed psychological complications from exposure to Daybridge's unique... atmosphere. We provide long-term care for people who can't function in normal society."

Ethan spoke for the first time. "How many patients do you currently house?"

"Seventeen. All of them have been with us for years, some for decades. They require specialized care, constant monitoring. Dimensional sensitivity is a progressive condition—without proper treatment, patients can become dangerous to themselves and others."

Alice leaned forward. "Have you noticed anything unusual at the rendering plant? Any signs of unauthorized access?"

"No, but we haven't begun renovation work yet. The property purchase only finalized two months ago." Crane spread his hands. "I can provide you with all our financial records, purchase agreements, anything you need. Blackthorn operates with complete transparency."

"We'd also like to see your patient records," Alice said. "Particularly anyone admitted or released in the past six months."

Crane's pleasant expression hardened slightly. "I'm afraid patient confidentiality prevents me from sharing those records without a court order. HIPAA regulations, you understand. However, I can tell you that we haven't released any patients in the past year. Our residents are... permanent fixtures."

Ethan stood abruptly, his form flickering. Alice felt his alarm through their connection. "Dr. Crane, may we see your facility? The patient wards?"

"I'm not sure that's appropriate—"

"It would help us understand the scope of dimensional sensitivity syndrome," Alice interjected. "For our investigation. We won't disturb your patients."

Crane hesitated, then stood. "Very well. But please understand that our residents can be easily agitated. We'll need to observe quietly."

He led them through the mansion's corridors. The building's interior matched its exterior Gothic aesthetic—dark wood, heavy curtains, gas lamps converted to electricity. But the medical equipment was state-of-the-art. Alice noted monitoring stations at regular intervals, security doors with keypad access.

"Our patients live in private rooms on the second and third floors," Crane explained. "They maintain their own schedules, take meals communally, and receive daily therapy sessions. We've found that routine helps stabilize their dimensional perception."

They reached the second floor. Crane guided them past a series of doors, each with a small observation window. Alice glanced through one and saw an elderly man sitting in a comfortable chair, staring at nothing. His eyes held that distant, unfocused quality she'd seen in people with severe PTSD.

"That's Mr. Harrison," Crane said softly. "He's been with us since 1967. Worked as a maintenance engineer in the old subway tunnels before they sealed them. The exposure to the nexus entity's influence broke something in his mind."

Ethan moved to another window. His expression was difficult to read, but Alice sensed his growing unease. "These patients. How often do you draw their blood?"

"Monthly health screenings, standard protocol. Why do you ask?"

"No reason." But Ethan's tone suggested otherwise.

They continued down the hallway. Alice counted doors—sixteen visible rooms, all occupied according to the name plates. But Crane had said seventeen patients.

At the end of the corridor was one more door. Unlike the others, this one had no name plate. Just a room number: 217.

Alice approached it and looked through the observation window. The room was empty. Not just unoccupied—emptied. No furniture, no personal effects. The walls were freshly painted, the floor recently cleaned.

"This room?" Alice asked.

Crane's cordial mask slipped for just a moment. "We had a patient pass away last week. Natural causes. We're preparing the room for our next admission."

"What was the patient's name?" Ethan's voice was sharp.

"I'm afraid confidentiality—"

"Dr. Crane." Alice turned to face him directly. "We have evidence of a sophisticated operation processing human blood into concentrated serum. We have financial records connecting your facility to the site of that operation. And now we find that one of your long-term patients—someone who's been saturated with dimensional energy for decades—has conveniently died just as this operation reaches completion. I need that patient's name. Now."

Crane's pleasant expression evaporated entirely. His eyes went cold, calculating. "I think this conversation should continue with my lawyers present. Nurse Whitmore will show you out."

Alice held his gaze. "We'll be back with a warrant. For your patient records, your financial statements, and access to every room in this facility."

"I look forward to it, Detective." Crane's smile returned, but it held no warmth. "Daybridge PD has always been so thorough."

As they left the institute, Alice felt Ethan's manifestation wavering. He held on until they reached the car, then collapsed into the passenger seat, his form flickering rapidly.

"He's lying," Ethan managed. "The patient in room 217 didn't die naturally. I could smell it—chemicals, sedation. They prepared someone for extraction."

"Extraction of what?"

"Everything." Ethan's eyes were haunted. "Decades of exposure to dimensional energy, all that accumulated resonance in their blood. If you drained someone like that, processed their essence using Knox's techniques..." He shuddered. "You'd have the most potent serum possible. Enough to force a transformation."

Alice started the car, her mind racing. "We need that warrant. We need to see those patient records, find out who was in room 217."

Her phone rang. Nadia's number.

"Alice, we found something at the rendering plant." The journalist's voice was tight with fear. "There's a secondary room, hidden behind a false wall. It's set up like an operating theater. And there's blood. Fresh blood. Someone was here this morning."

Alice's hands tightened on the steering wheel. "We're on our way. Don't touch anything."

She ended the call and looked at Ethan. His manifestation was barely holding together, translucence spreading from his edges.

"Go back to the bridge," she said gently. "Reform, rest. I'll handle the rendering plant."

"Alice—"

"I'm not losing you to dimensional interference. Not today." She reached over, her hand passing slightly through his. "Go. I'll call you when we have more information."

Ethan nodded reluctantly. His form dissolved, consciousness flowing back toward the bridge. Alice sat alone in the car, staring at Blackthorn Institute's Gothic facade.

Somewhere in that building was the answer. A patient who'd been saturated with dimensional energy for decades, whose blood had been harvested, whose essence had been distilled into the most potent serum imaginable.

And somewhere in Daybridge, someone was preparing to consume that serum. To force a transformation. To become something more than human.

Alice put the car in gear and drove toward the rendering plant, already composing the warrant request in her mind.

Because whatever was coming, it was coming soon. And they were running out of time to stop it.

CHAPTER THREE: THE PRODIGAL

The warrant came through at 3 AM.

Alice stood in Judge Morrison's chambers, presenting evidence while Nadia's photographs of the rendering plant operation covered the desk. The judge—a no-nonsense woman in her sixties who'd seen Daybridge through its darkest supernatural incidents—studied the images with grim determination.

"Blood processing equipment, alchemical symbols, and financial ties to a psychiatric facility." Judge Morrison signed the warrant with aggressive strokes. "Detective Chen, I'm authorizing full access to Blackthorn Institute's patient records, financial statements, and facility inspection. But I'm also assigning you backup. If this goes sideways—"

"It won't," Alice said, though she didn't believe it.

"It always does in this city." The judge handed over the warrant. "Be careful. The Granger family has deep roots in Daybridge. If there's even a tangential connection, you'll face resistance."

Alice drove back to the station as dawn broke over Daybridge, the bridge's metallic structure catching the first light. She could feel Ethan out there, his consciousness spread across the span, processing the city's perpetual flow of vehicles and pedestrians. They'd spoken briefly after she left the rendering plant—he was recovering from the dimensional interference at Blackthorn, but his concern bled through their connection.

I'm remembering things, he'd told her. *Miranda Sullivan's memories are surfacing. The bridge consciousness is agitated, showing me what happened that night in 1968.*

At the station, Alice found Michael Mercer waiting in her office. The private investigator looked like he hadn't slept, his tie loose, coffee cup empty beside a stack of financial documents.

"Found something," Mercer said without preamble. He spread papers across Alice's desk. "Dr. Matthias Crane's background. Medical degree from Harvard, psychiatric residency at Johns Hopkins, appointed director of Blackthorn in 1995. Very impressive credentials."

"But?"

"But before 1995, Matthias Crane didn't exist." Mercer pulled out a photograph—a driver's license from 1994. "This is Matthias Granger, youngest son of the Granger family. Mayor Granger's little brother. According to public records, he died in a car accident on Route 17 in November 1995. Closed casket funeral, buried in the family plot."

Alice studied the photograph. Same face as Dr. Crane, just thirty years younger. "They faked his death."

"And created a new identity. Probably to distance him from the family name while he ran Blackthorn. I pulled the Institute's funding records—it's supported by a private trust established by the Granger family in 1920. The same year Blackthorn was founded."

"The Grangers have been studying dimensional sensitivity for over a century," Alice murmured. "Why?"

"Because they're founding family," said Lilith Blackwood from the doorway.

Alice jumped. She'd been so focused on Mercer's revelations that she hadn't heard the older woman approach. Lilith entered carrying a leather-bound journal, her expression grave.

"I've been researching the founding families' original pact with the nexus entity," Lilith continued. "The Grangers were always the most ambitious. While other families saw the entity as a necessary evil to be contained, the Grangers viewed it as a resource. They wanted to understand it, harness it, use its power to elevate themselves."

She opened the journal to a page marked with a faded ribbon. "This belonged to Eliza Blackwood. She documented the founding families' secret activities. In 1920, Richard Granger—the current mayor's grandfather—established Blackthorn Institute officially to study 'dimensional sensitivity syndrome.' But the real purpose was to cultivate test subjects. People who'd been exposed to the nexus entity's influence were housed at Blackthorn, observed, studied. Sometimes experimented on."

Alice felt sick. "Human experimentation."

"To understand how dimensional exposure affected consciousness, yes. The Grangers believed that with proper conditioning and preparation, humans could merge with dimensional entities without losing their identity. They wanted controlled ascension."

"Like what happened to Ethan," Mercer said.

"No." Lilith's voice was sharp. "What happened to Ethan was symbiosis—a willing merger between human consciousness and supernatural entity, mediated by Eliza's century-old ritual. What the Grangers wanted was dominance. They wanted to consume the entity's power while maintaining complete human control."

Alice's phone buzzed. A text from Father Mulligan: *Patient 217 identified. Leonard Ashford, age 79, admitted 1968. Released three weeks ago on Dr. Crane's authorization. No next of kin, no discharge location listed.*

"We have our missing patient," Alice said. She pulled up the digital warrant and forwarded it to her team. "Mulligan, meet me at Blackthorn in twenty minutes. Mercer, I need you to track Leonard Ashford's movements after his release. Bank records, credit cards, anything."

"On it." Mercer gathered his documents and headed out.

Lilith remained, her expression troubled. "Alice, there's something else. I've been monitoring dimensional frequencies since the rendering plant incident. The energy signature I detected—it matches records from 1968. The night Miranda Sullivan's research team was absorbed by the bridge."

Alice remembered Ethan's mention of Sullivan's memories surfacing. "What does that mean?"

"It means whatever Leonard Ashford is planning, it's based on Sullivan's research. And that research was catastrophic."

Blackthorn Institute looked different in daylight. Less Gothic mansion, more clinical facility. Alice approached with Father Mulligan and four uniformed officers, warrant in hand.

Dr. Crane—Matthias Granger—met them at the entrance. His cordial mask was gone, replaced by cold calculation.

"Detective Chen. I see you obtained your warrant."

"For patient records, financial statements, and facility inspection." Alice handed him the document. "We'll start with Leonard Ashford's file."

Crane's jaw tightened. "Mr. Ashford's records are in my office. Follow me."

He led them through the mansion's corridors with stiff formality. Alice noted the surveillance cameras at every corner, the electronic locks on patient room doors, the medical staff who watched their passage with nervous eyes.

In Crane's office, he pulled a thick file from a locked cabinet. "Leonard Ashford. Admitted February 3, 1968, following a severe psychotic break. Diagnosed with acute dimensional sensitivity syndrome, paranoid schizophrenia, and post-traumatic stress disorder."

Father Mulligan took the file and began reading. "The admission notes say he was found wandering the streets near the Daybridge Bridge, covered in blood, babbling about 'the merger' and 'failed transcendence.' What happened to him?"

"That information is not in his medical records," Crane said stiffly.

"But you know what happened." Alice leaned against the desk. "Leonard Ashford was Dr. Miranda Sullivan's laboratory assistant. He was there the night her research team was absorbed by the bridge. Ethan remembers."

Crane's expression flickered—surprise, then resignation. "How much does your bridge consciousness recall?"

"Enough. Sullivan was trying to understand dimensional merger. Her team was conducting experiments in consciousness transfer, trying to map how human awareness could integrate with supernatural entities. Leonard Ashford was her most brilliant student."

"He was more than that," Crane said quietly. "He was obsessed. When Sullivan's team was absorbed, Leonard tried to save them. He believed he could reverse the process, pull their consciousnesses back from the bridge entity. Instead, he was exposed to raw dimensional energy—enough to shatter his mind but not enough to kill him or absorb him. He's been trapped between states ever since, neither fully human nor fully transcendent."

Father Mulligan looked up from the file. "These medical notes indicate monthly blood draws. Far more frequently than standard health monitoring requires."

"Leonard's blood has unique properties," Crane said. "Decades of exposure to dimensional energy have saturated his cells. We've been studying it, trying to understand how long-term exposure affects human biology."

"You've been farming him," Alice said flatly. "Him and the other sixteen patients. Harvesting their blood because it's potent with dimensional energy."

Crane didn't deny it. "The research was authorized by Blackthorn's board of directors. Everything was legal, ethical, consensual—"

"Consent requires mental capacity. These patients have been institutionalized for decades, some against their will." Alice pulled out her phone and showed him Nadia's photographs from the rendering plant. "Where does the blood go, Dr. Crane? What did you do with it?"

"I didn't do anything with it. Leonard did."

The admission hung in the air.

Father Mulligan closed the file slowly. "You released him. Three weeks ago. Why?"

Crane moved to the window, staring out at the manicured grounds. "Because he asked me to. For the first time in fifty-seven years, Leonard Ashford spoke clearly, coherently. He told me his mind had finally healed—that the decades of dimensional exposure had transformed him, elevated his consciousness beyond the trauma. He said he was ready to complete Dr. Sullivan's work."

"And you believed him," Alice said.

"I saw the brain scans, Detective. His neural patterns had completely reorganized. The man who'd been catatonic for half a century was suddenly brilliant, focused, purposeful. He presented me with theoretical papers on consciousness transfer, dimensional integration, alchemical transformation. Work that built on Sullivan's research but went far beyond it."

"The Magnum Opus Sanguinis," Father Mulligan murmured.

Crane's head snapped around. "You know of it?"

"Medieval alchemical texts reference it. The Great Work of Blood. A theoretical process for achieving transcendence through consumption of sanctified essence." The priest's voice was grim. "It's never been successfully completed because it requires impossible quantities of dimensionally attuned blood. And it always ends in catastrophic transformation."

"Leonard claimed he'd solved the equation," Crane said. "That with modern biochemistry and alchemical principles, he could create a serum potent enough to force ascension. To become like the bridge consciousness—a hybrid of human and Other—but without surrendering to the entity. Perfect fusion while maintaining individual will."

"So you gave him access to the patients' blood," Alice said. "And the rendering plant."

"I gave him resources. The Granger family has been seeking this knowledge for a century. If Leonard could succeed—if he could create controlled ascension—it would revolutionize everything. We could elevate humanity beyond its limitations."

"Or create monsters." Alice's voice was hard. "Where is Leonard Ashford now?"

"I don't know. He left Blackthorn three weeks ago and hasn't contacted me since."

Alice's phone rang. Sam Thompson, the homeless advocate.

"Detective Chen, I have bad news." Sam's voice was shaking. "I've been tracking disappearances in the homeless community. Seventeen people have vanished in the past month, all from areas near the industrial district and Blackthorn Institute. No bodies, no witnesses, just gone."

Alice's blood ran cold. "Seventeen."

"All of them had unusual characteristics according to the medical clinic records. Rare blood types, genetic markers consistent with founding family lineage. Someone was targeting specific people."

She looked at Crane. "Leonard needed more than just the Blackthorn patients' blood. He needed founding family genetics. The original bloodlines that made the pact with the nexus entity."

Crane's face went pale. "No. That wasn't part of the plan. I only authorized him to use the processed blood from our patients—"

"You unleashed a man who's been saturated with dimensional energy for fifty-seven years. A man obsessed with forced transcendence. What did you think he would do?"

Alice's phone buzzed again. Text from the medical examiner: *Body found in Shadowlair River. You need to see this.*

The Daybridge morgue occupied the hospital's basement level. Alice and Father Mulligan descended into the sterile white corridors, following Dr. Sarah Kendrick to the examination room.

The medical examiner was a precise woman in her forties who'd worked with Alice on several supernatural cases. But even she looked shaken as she pulled back the sheet covering the body on the examination table.

Alice's stomach turned.

The corpse looked ancient. Skin like parchment stretched over bones, hair white and brittle, eyes sunken deep into the skull. But the clothing was modern—jeans and a jacket from this decade.

"This is Marcus Webb," Dr. Kendrick said. "Age twenty-eight according to his ID. Reported missing from the homeless shelter three weeks ago. But this body..." She gestured helplessly. "It's physiologically consistent with someone in their nineties. Extreme desiccation, cellular degradation, organ failure across all systems."

Father Mulligan made the sign of the cross. "As if decades passed in days."

"Not just that." Dr. Kendrick pulled up a series of scans on her computer. "There's no blood in the body. Not just drained—completely absent. The vascular system is empty, dried out. And look at the tissue samples."

The microscope images showed cellular structures that looked wrong. Collapsed, distorted, like they'd been hollowed out from within.

"Every drop of life was extracted," Dr. Kendrick said quietly. "Not just blood, but the essential vitality that keeps cells functioning. I've never seen anything like it."

Alice pulled out her phone and called Ethan. He manifested in the corner of the examination room a moment later, his form flickering under the fluorescent lights.

"I felt you calling," he said. Then he saw the body and recoiled. "God. The dimensional energy."

"You can sense it?"

Ethan approached the examination table cautiously. "It's residual, fading, but it's there. This person was... refined. Their life essence was extracted using dimensional resonance as a catalyst. Not feeding—this wasn't consumption. It was industrial processing."

"Leonard Ashford's work," Alice said.

"Sullivan's technique, perfected." Ethan's voice was hollow. "I'm accessing her memories now. She theorized that life essence could be extracted more efficiently if dimensional energy was used to break down cellular bonds. Like using acid to dissolve metal, but on a metaphysical level. The victim would age rapidly as their vitality was drained, but the extracted essence would be incredibly pure."

Father Mulligan's expression was grim. "How many victims would the Magnum Opus require?"

"Sullivan's calculations suggested fifty people for a stable transformation. But Leonard has been exposed to dimensional energy for decades—his threshold might be lower. Maybe twenty or thirty."

Alice did the math. "Seventeen homeless victims plus Leonard himself makes eighteen. But we found over two hundred vials of serum at the rendering plant."

"Concentrated from the Blackthorn patients' blood," Ethan said. "The patients provided the base serum, but Leonard needed fresh essence to activate it. To create the final catalyst."

Dr. Kendrick cleared her throat. "Detective, there's something else. We found trace chemicals in the victim's tissues. Sedatives, paralytic agents. He was kept alive but immobile during the extraction process. And based on the tissue degradation pattern, the process took approximately eight hours."

Eight hours of conscious aging, of feeling your life being drained away. Alice felt rage building in her chest.

"How many bodies have been recovered?" she asked.

"Just this one so far. But the river patrol is searching. If Leonard dumped his victims in the Shadowlair, there could be more."

Alice's phone rang. Nadia Marsh.

"Alice, I cross-referenced the missing persons reports with rare blood type registries. All seventeen victims share genetic markers with founding families. Not direct descendants, but distant relations—people who carry trace amounts of the original bloodlines."

"Leonard was targeting specific genetics," Alice said. "The same bloodlines that made the pact with the nexus entity."

"There's more. I found security footage from near the rendering plant. Three nights ago, a man matching Leonard Ashford's description was seen entering the building. He was carrying medical transport cases. But he wasn't alone—someone helped him. The camera angle is poor, but I think it was Dr. Crane."

Alice looked at Father Mulligan. "Crane lied about losing contact with Leonard."

The priest nodded. "He's been helping him all along. The Granger family's obsession with transcendence—Matthias couldn't resist being part of it."

Ethan's form flickered violently. "Alice. I'm sensing something. A dimensional surge building somewhere in the city. It's similar to what Lilith detected at the rendering plant, but stronger. Much stronger."

"Where?"

"I can't pinpoint it yet. The bridge consciousness is agitated, showing me fragmented images. A place saturated with old death, old pain. Somewhere the veil between dimensions is already thin."

Alice pulled out her phone and called Lilith. "We need your monitoring equipment. Ethan's sensing a dimensional surge—can you locate it?"

"Already tracking it." Lilith's voice was tight with urgency. "The surge started twenty minutes ago and is building exponentially. At this rate, it'll peak in approximately three hours. Alice, the energy signature suggests massive consumption of life essence. Leonard Ashford is beginning his transformation."

"Location?"

"I'm triangulating now. The signal is strongest in..." Lilith paused. "The old subway tunnels. Beneath the industrial district."

Alice felt cold certainty settle over her. The subway tunnels had been sealed in the 1960s after workers reported seeing things in the darkness, hearing voices, experiencing dimensional distortions. They were directly above the nexus entity's original resting place, before the bridge transformed it.

"That's where he's going to complete the ritual," she said. "Father Mulligan, gather whatever religious implements you think will help. Nadia, I need you to pull up maps of the old subway system. Find access points."

"You're going after him," Dr. Kendrick said.

"We don't have a choice. If Leonard completes this transformation..." Alice looked at Ethan. "What happens if he succeeds?"

Ethan's expression was haunted, drawn from Sullivan's memories. "He becomes something new. A being that exists simultaneously in human and dimensional space, with power comparable to mine but without symbiotic limitation. He'd be able to reshape reality within Daybridge, manipulate the dimensional fabric, consume life essence at will. The city would become his feeding ground."

"And if he fails?"

"Catastrophic dimensional collapse. The energy he's accumulated would rupture, creating a breach between dimensions. The nexus entity's consciousness could pour through, uncontrolled, absorbing everything within miles."

"So, we're damned either way unless we stop him," Father Mulligan said.

Alice's phone buzzed. Text from Mercer: *Found Leonard Ashford's bank records. Large purchases in past three weeks - industrial equipment, rare chemicals, medical supplies. All delivered to an address in the old subway maintenance depot. Sending coordinates.*

"We have his location," Alice said. She looked at her team—Father Mulligan with his faith, Ethan with his supernatural awareness, the distant presence of Lilith monitoring dimensional frequencies. "We move now. Before he completes the transformation."

The old subway maintenance depot occupied a condemned building on the industrial district's edge. Chain-link fencing surrounded it, decorated with "No Trespassing" signs and rust. Alice parked three blocks away and assembled her team.

Father Mulligan wore his clerical collar and carried a leather satchel filled with holy water, blessed salt, and prayer books. Nadia had her camera equipment and a portable police radio. Ethan manifested beside the car, his form more solid than usual—he was pulling energy from the bridge to maintain stability.

"The entrance is through the depot building," Nadia said, consulting her tablet. "The stairs descend three levels to the maintenance tunnels, which connect to the main subway system. If Leonard is down there, he'll have multiple escape routes."

"He won't run," Ethan said. "He's too close to completion. I can feel the dimensional pressure building. He's already begun consuming the serum."

Alice checked her modified Glock—bullets blessed by Father Mulligan, designed to disrupt supernatural entities. She wasn't sure they'd be effective against whatever Leonard was becoming, but they were better than nothing.

"Nadia, you stay topside with the radio. If this goes wrong, call for backup and evacuate the area. Father Mulligan and Ethan, you're with me."

They approached the depot through shadows, moving quickly across the cracked pavement. The building's entrance was chained, but someone had cut through the lock recently. Alice pushed inside.

The depot's interior was a vast empty space filled with rusted equipment and graffiti. Pigeons roosted in the rafters, and the floor was covered in debris. But a cleared path led to a metal door at the back—the stairs descending to the tunnels.

Ethan went first, his supernatural senses extended, feeling for dimensional distortions. Alice followed with Father Mulligan behind. The stairs descended into darkness, lit only by their flashlights.

Three levels down, they emerged into the maintenance tunnels. The air was thick with moisture and decay, and Alice's dimensional awareness screamed warnings. This place was saturated with old energy, old pain.

"Which way?" she asked Ethan.

He pointed down a tunnel that curved away into darkness. "The dimensional resonance is strongest there. About half a mile ahead."

They moved through the tunnels in silence, flashlights cutting through the gloom. Alice saw evidence of Leonard's passage—fresh footprints in the dust, empty medical supply boxes discarded in corners. The tunnel walls were covered in graffiti from decades of urban explorers, but beneath the spray paint, Alice could see older markings. Symbols etched into the concrete, similar to the alchemical notation at the rendering plant.

"Someone prepared this space," Father Mulligan murmured. "These symbols are protective wards, containment circles. Designed to focus dimensional energy."

"The Grangers," Alice said. "They've been using these tunnels for their research since the beginning."

The tunnel opened into a larger space—an old subway platform, long abandoned. But it had been transformed. Industrial equipment lined the walls, connected to generators that hummed with power. Medical monitoring devices beeped steadily. And in the center of the platform, surrounded by a complex alchemical circle drawn in what looked like dried blood, stood Leonard Ashford.

He looked nothing like the hospital records suggested. The frail elderly man from the photographs had transformed into something else. His body was lean, vital, almost vibrating with energy. His eyes glowed with that familiar dimensional light, but wrong—fractured, like looking at multiple realities simultaneously.

Around him, arranged in a ritual pattern, were seventeen bodies. The missing homeless victims, each one desiccated like Marcus Webb, their life essence drained.

Leonard turned to face them, and when he spoke, his voice resonated with multiple tones. "Detective Chen. I was wondering when you'd arrive. And Ethan—the bridge consciousness himself. How perfect."

Ethan's form flickered. "Leonard. You know this won't work. Sullivan's theories were incomplete. Forced ascension always fails."

"Sullivan was brilliant but limited by her time." Leonard moved through the alchemical circle, and Alice noticed the air distorting around him. "I've had fifty-seven years to perfect her work. To understand what she couldn't—that dimensional integration requires sacrifice. Not just blood, but suffering. Pain refined into power."

Father Mulligan stepped forward, pulling out a vial of holy water. "In the name of—"

Leonard gestured casually, and the priest flew backward, slamming against the tunnel wall. The vial shattered, holy water splashing uselessly on concrete.

"Your primitive faith has no power here, Father. I'm beyond such limitations now." Leonard pulled a medical case from beside one of the bodies and opened it. Inside were dozens of amber vials—the concentrated serum. "I've consumed sixteen doses so far. Each one bringing me closer to transcendence. Just one more, and the transformation will be complete."

Alice raised her weapon. "Stop. You're under arrest for seventeen counts of murder."

Leonard laughed, and the sound echoed wrong in the tunnel. "Murder? I've liberated them. Their essence lives on in me, elevated beyond their limited existence. I'm giving meaning to meaningless lives."

"You're creating an abomination," Ethan said. His form was solidifying, pulling more energy from the bridge. "The dimensional forces you're channeling—you can't control them. They'll consume you, rupture through you, devastate the city."

"You're wrong. I've calculated every variable, accounted for every risk. Unlike you, I'm not merging with a supernatural entity. I'm forcing evolution through pure science and alchemy. I'm becoming the next stage of human consciousness."

He pulled out the final vial, holding it up to the light. The amber liquid seemed to glow with inner fire.

"Stop him," Father Mulligan gasped from where he'd fallen. "Alice, stop him now!"

Alice fired three shots. The blessed bullets tore through Leonard's shoulder and chest, and he staggered. But he didn't fall. Blood seeped from the wounds, but it wasn't red—it was that same amber color, thick with dimensional energy.

"Interesting," Leonard said, examining his wounds with clinical detachment. "Your bullets carry blessed elements. They're disrupting my cellular cohesion. But not enough."

He uncapped the final vial and drank.

The transformation was immediate and terrible.

Leonard's body convulsed, his back arching, mouth open in a silent scream. Dimensional energy poured out of him, visible as waves of distortion that made reality ripple. His skin began to glow, veins standing out like circuitry carrying light instead of blood.

"It's working," he gasped. "I can feel it. The barriers breaking down. Human consciousness expanding beyond limitation. I'm becoming—"

He screamed.

Not triumph—agony. Pure, horrific agony.

Ethan moved forward, his eyes wide. "No. God, no. He miscalculated. The essence is too concentrated, too unstable. It's not integrating—it's consuming him from within."

Leonard's body began to change in ways that violated physics. His limbs elongated, bones cracking and reforming. His face distorted, features shifting between human and something Other. The dimensional energy radiating from him intensified, creating a vortex of power that pulled at everything around it.

The seventeen bodies began to move. Not reanimation—resonance. The residual dimensional energy in their desiccated forms was responding to Leonard's transformation, pulling them upright like puppets.

"The circle is breaking!" Father Mulligan shouted. "The containment is failing!"

Alice could feel it—reality thinning, the veil between dimensions tearing. Through the growing breach, she sensed something vast and hungry. The nexus entity's consciousness, drawn by the dimensional rupture, pressing against the weakening barrier.

Leonard was still screaming, his body now barely humanoid. Multiple eyes had opened across his torso, his hands had become claws, and his voice fragmented into a chorus of the seventeen victims whose essence he'd consumed.

"Help me," he begged in a dozen voices. "Please. It hurts. Make it stop."

Ethan looked at Alice, and she saw decision forming in his eyes.

"No," she said immediately. "Don't even think it."

"I have to. If that breach widens, the entire city will be absorbed." Ethan's form was already dissolving, spreading out, becoming less individual consciousness and more distributed awareness. "The bridge can contain him. But I need to pull him in, integrate his consciousness before the rupture completes."

"That could destroy you. You don't know what absorbing that much corrupted energy will do to the bridge consciousness."

"I know what happens if I don't try." Ethan reached out, and for a moment his hand was solid, warm against her face. "Alice. Trust me."

Then he exploded outward.

Not destruction—expansion. Ethan's consciousness spread through the tunnel, his awareness becoming a vast web that touched everything, everyone. Alice felt him flowing past her, through her, around her—not invasive but encompassing, like being held in infinite gentleness.

The bridge consciousness had come to the tunnels.

Ethan's distributed awareness wrapped around Leonard's fragmenting form, pulling him in. The screaming intensified as Leonard fought, instinct overriding reason, but Ethan was stronger. The bridge had absorbed hundreds of consciousnesses over the decades, knew how to gentle them into integration.

But Leonard's essence was corrupted, twisted by forced ascension and concentrated dimensional energy. Alice watched in horror as the two beings merged, reality distorting around them. She could feel Ethan struggling, his consciousness straining under the weight of so much stolen life.

The seventeen desiccated bodies collapsed, their residual energy flowing into the merger. The dimensional breach began to close, the hungry presence of the nexus entity withdrawing.

And then, suddenly, it was over.

The tunnel fell silent.

The bodies lay still. The industrial equipment shut down. The dimensional pressure evaporated like morning fog.

In the center of the alchemical circle, where Leonard Ashford had stood, there was nothing.

Alice rushed forward. "Ethan! Ethan, answer me!"

For a terrible moment, there was silence. Then she felt him—distant, strained, but present.

I'm here. At the bridge. Come to me.

Alice reached the Daybridge Bridge as the sun rose, painting the metal structure in shades of gold and bronze. She parked and ran across the pedestrian walkway, her dimensional awareness screaming.

Ethan manifested in the center span, but he looked wrong. His form flickered constantly, struggling to maintain cohesion. Multiple transparent images overlapped—Ethan, Leonard, the seventeen victims, all trying to exist in the same space.

"What did you do?" Alice demanded.

"What I had to." Ethan's voice was fractured, multiple tones speaking simultaneously. "I absorbed Leonard and the essence he'd consumed. But it's fighting integration. His consciousness is... resistant. Corrupted. The victims' essences are scattered, traumatized. I'm trying to gentle them, but it's difficult."

Alice reached for him, her hand passing through his flickering form. "How do I help?"

"You can't. This is internal work. The bridge consciousness needs time to process, to integrate the new awareness without fragmenting." Ethan's eyes met hers, and for a moment they were purely his—worried, loving, determined. "Alice, I need you to find Dr. Crane. He helped Leonard do this. He needs to answer for it."

"I will. But Ethan—"

"I'll be okay. Eventually. But I might be... different. The integration will change the bridge consciousness, add new memories, new perspectives. I don't know who I'll be when it's complete."

Alice felt tears threatening. "Will you still be Ethan?"

"I'll still be me. Just... more." His form solidified slightly, enough for his hand to brush her cheek. "Go. Stop Crane before he tries this again. The Granger family's obsession won't end with Leonard's failure."

Alice nodded, swallowing her fear. "I love you."

"I love you too. Always."

Then Ethan dissolved, his consciousness spreading across the bridge span, beginning the long process of integration.

Alice stood alone on the bridge as the city woke around her. Seventeen people were dead. Leonard Ashford was absorbed into the bridge consciousness. And Dr. Matthias Crane—Matthias Granger—was still out there, continuing his family's century-long obsession with forced ascension.

She pulled out her phone and called Judge Morrison. "I need another warrant. For Dr. Matthias Crane, director of Blackthorn Institute. Charges include conspiracy to commit murder, illegal human experimentation, and accessory to seventeen homicides."

"Consider it done," the judge said. "Detective Chen? Be careful. The Grangers don't surrender easily."

Alice ended the call and stared out at Daybridge, the city she'd sworn to protect. Somewhere out there, Crane was planning his next move. The rendering plant had been shut down, but the research remained. The knowledge of how to create the concentrated serum, how to harvest dimensionally attuned essence.

The case wasn't over. It was just beginning.

But first, she needed coffee. And answers. And probably backup.

Alice walked back to her car, already composing the arrest warrant in her mind, while behind her the bridge hummed with the sound of Ethan's consciousness struggling to integrate seventeen stolen lives into its vast awareness.

The sun continued to rise over Daybridge, indifferent to the horrors of the night.

CHAPTER FOUR: ASCENSION INTERRUPTED

The arrest warrant for Dr. Matthias Crane was signed at 6:47 AM.

Alice assembled her team in the station's briefing room: Sam Thompson with his knowledge of the homeless community, Nadia Marsh with her investigative documentation, Father Mulligan with his dimensional expertise, and Michael Mercer with his connection to the city's hidden networks. Lilith Blackwood attended via video call, her monitoring equipment tracking dimensional frequencies from her Blackwood mansion command center.

"Crane isn't at Blackthorn," Mercer reported, tapping his laptop. "I've had eyes on the Institute since dawn. Security says he left at 4 AM with several medical transport cases and hasn't returned. His personal vehicle is missing."

"Where would he go?" Sam asked.

"To finish what Leonard started." Lilith's voice came through the speakers with grim certainty. "I'm detecting massive dimensional disturbances in the industrial district. The frequency signature matches what we observed during Leonard's initial transformation, but amplified. Someone is consuming concentrated essence on a catastrophic scale."

Alice felt ice in her stomach. "Leonard survived the absorption?"

"No." Ethan's voice came from the corner where his form manifested, still flickering with instability from integrating the corrupted consciousness. "I absorbed Leonard's consciousness into the bridge matrix. But the bridge has been... showing me things. Memories from Sullivan's research team, dimensional echoes from the night they were consumed. Leonard wasn't working alone."

He gestured, and the air shimmered. Suddenly they were looking at a projection—a memory pulled from the bridge's vast consciousness.

The scene showed Dr. Miranda Sullivan's laboratory in 1968, moments before the fatal experiment.

In the projection, Leonard Ashford stood beside Sullivan, preparing equipment. But there was a third figure—a young man in his early twenties, watching the proceedings with intense focus. The man's face was familiar.

"Matthias Granger," Father Mulligan breathed. "He was there that night."

"Not just there—observing." Ethan's form solidified as he concentrated on the memory. "Sullivan's notes mention a visiting student from Harvard Medical School. Matthias was fascinated by her consciousness transfer research. He watched as her team attempted to map dimensional integration, witnessed their absorption by the bridge entity, saw Leonard's exposure to raw dimensional energy."

The projection shifted, showing the aftermath. Young Matthias kneeling beside Leonard's catatonic form, taking samples—blood, tissue, cerebral spinal fluid. Documenting everything with clinical precision.

"He's been studying forced ascension for fifty-seven years," Alice said. "Using Leonard as his primary research subject."

"And using Blackthorn Institute as his laboratory." Nadia pulled up financial records on her tablet. "I traced the Institute's funding. The Granger family trust has funneled over thirty million dollars into 'dimensional sensitivity research' since 1968. Crane has been building toward this for decades."

Lilith's screen flickered as she adjusted her monitoring equipment. "The dimensional surge is intensifying. I'm triangulating the source now. It's coming from..." She paused, fingers flying across keyboards. "The old Daybridge Stockyards. Approximately half a mile from the rendering plant."

"Another Knox family property," Mercer said, pulling up property records. "Guthrie Knox owned the stockyards before his suicide. The buildings have been condemned since the 1970s, but the land remains in the Knox estate trust. Which means—"

"The Grangers had access." Alice stood, already reaching for her modified Glock. "They've been using it for the same purpose Knox used the rendering plant. Creating weapons from dimensional energy."

"Worse than weapons." Ethan's projection showed another memory—this one from Leonard's fractured consciousness, absorbed hours ago. Leonard standing in the stockyards' main hall, surrounded by industrial equipment repurposed for alchemical processing. Crane helping him, guiding him, encouraging him to consume more essence. "Crane wasn't trying to stop Leonard's transformation. He was facilitating it. Leonard was his test case, his proof of concept."

"For what?" Sam asked.

"For creating beings like me, but controllable." Ethan's voice was hollow. "Crane wants to manufacture artificial nexus entities—hybrid consciousnesses with dimensional power but human loyalty. Weapons the Order of the Eternal Threshold could deploy to reclaim control of Daybridge."

Father Mulligan crossed himself. "God help us."

"God isn't the one we need right now." Alice checked her weapon and loaded magazines of blessed ammunition. "We need to stop Crane before he completes whatever he's planning. Father, what weapons do we have against forced ascension?"

The priest opened his leather satchel, revealing an array of religious implements. "Holy water, blessed salt, iron chains sanctified by the Vatican. These can disrupt dimensional coherence, but only temporarily. For permanent intervention..." He pulled out a glass vial containing dark red powder. "Ground communion wafers mixed with blessed silver and the ashes of St. Cyprian. Used historically against demonic possession and supernatural corruption. It won't kill, but it can sever connections between human consciousness and dimensional entities."

"How do we deploy it?"

"Direct contact. It needs to touch the subject's skin or be consumed." Father Mulligan's expression was grim. "And it causes excruciating pain. The substance burns away supernatural influence at a cellular level."

Alice pocketed several vials. "What about protecting ourselves?"

Lilith's voice came through the speakers. "I'm sending Nadia GPS coordinates for an equipment cache I've prepared. Dimensional dampening devices—they won't make you invisible to supernatural perception, but they'll reduce your resonance signature. You'll be harder to target."

"How long do we have?" Mercer asked.

"Based on the dimensional surge pattern, I estimate three hours before critical threshold." Lilith's screen showed a graph with exponentially rising energy levels. "If whoever's consuming essence reaches saturation, the resulting transformation will create a dimensional rupture. The veil between our reality and the Other spaces will tear, potentially irreparably."

Alice looked at her team. "Sam, I need you coordinating with emergency services. If this goes wrong, we'll need evacuation protocols for the industrial district. Nadia, document everything—if Crane escapes, we'll need evidence for prosecution. Mercer, you're with me for tactical support. Father Mulligan, you're our spiritual artillery."

"What about me?" Ethan asked quietly.

Alice met his flickering gaze. "How stable are you? Can you manifest physically?"

"For a limited time. The absorption of Leonard's consciousness is still processing, but I can pull enough energy from the bridge to maintain corporeal form. Maybe two hours before I need to return and integrate."

"Then you're our heavy hitter. But Ethan—if you start destabilizing, you pull back immediately. I can't lose you to this."

Ethan's form solidified, and for a moment he was fully present—warm, real, the man she loved rather than the distributed consciousness he'd become. "You won't lose me. I promise."

The Daybridge Stockyards occupied five acres of industrial wasteland on the district's eastern edge. Rusted fencing surrounded collapsed buildings and equipment left to decay for half a century. Alice's tactical van parked three blocks away, and the team gathered their equipment under Lilith's remote guidance.

"The dimensional surge is emanating from the main hall," Lilith reported through their earpieces. "It's the largest building, center of the compound. The frequency signature suggests multiple consciousness streams converging—whoever's in there isn't alone."

Alice studied the stockyards through binoculars. The main hall was a massive structure of corrugated metal and concrete, partially collapsed but still standing. Broken windows gaped like empty eyes, and the main entrance hung open.

"I see movement," she said. "Guards. At least six, professional positioning. Praetorian."

Father Mulligan crossed himself. "The Order is here in force."

"Crane brought backup." Ethan manifested beside the van, his form more solid than Alice had seen in hours. He was pulling massive energy from the bridge to maintain coherence. "I can sense dimensional resonance inside the main hall. Not just one consciousness transforming—multiple threads, weaving together. Something's very wrong."

Mercer loaded his pistol with blessed ammunition. "We go in fast and hard?"

"No." Alice pointed to the stockyards' eastern perimeter. "There's a service entrance, less visible. We infiltrate quietly, assess the situation before engaging. If Crane is in the middle of the transformation process, interrupting violently could trigger exactly the kind of rupture Lilith warned about."

They moved through the industrial wasteland in tactical formation. Alice led with Father Mulligan, while Mercer covered their rear. Ethan scouted ahead, his supernatural perception detecting guards before visual contact.

The service entrance was chained but not locked—someone had cut through recently. They slipped inside, entering a corridor lined with rusted equipment and broken pipes. The air was thick with moisture and decay, but underneath Alice detected something else: blood and chemicals, the familiar scent of alchemical processing.

"This way," Ethan whispered, leading them deeper into the structure.

They emerged onto a catwalk overlooking the main hall, and Alice's breath caught.

The hall was massive, cathedral-like in its proportions. Industrial equipment lined the walls—centrifuges, distillation columns, medical monitoring devices, all connected to generators humming with power. But at the center, surrounded by a complex alchemical circle drawn in what could only be blood, stood Leonard Ashford.

Except he was barely recognizable as human anymore.

His body had transformed into something nightmarish. Flesh rippled with incomplete changes, bones jutting at odd angles beneath skin that seemed to flow like liquid. Multiple eyes had opened across his torso and arms, flickering between human vision and dimensional perception. His mouth had elongated, jaw dislocating to accommodate teeth that were too many and too sharp.

But he was conscious. Alert. And in terrible pain.

"Please," Leonard begged in a voice that fragmented across multiple tones. "Please make it stop. I can feel them. All of them. Forty-three voices screaming in my head. Their memories, their pain, their terror. I thought I could master it, integrate their essence cleanly, but they're fighting me. They won't let go."

Dr. Matthias Crane stood outside the alchemical circle, monitoring equipment and taking notes with clinical detachment. He looked older than his photographs suggested, hair completely white, face lined with stress. But his eyes were sharp, focused, burning with obsessive purpose.

"Maintain control," Crane instructed Leonard. "The pain is temporary. Once full integration occurs, their consciousnesses will subordinate to yours. You'll achieve perfect fusion—dimensional power with human will intact."

"It's not working!" Leonard's body convulsed, and reality rippled around him. Through the distortion, Alice glimpsed Other spaces—vast geometries that shouldn't exist, hungry presences pressing against the veil. "The essence is too concentrated. Too much trauma. Their deaths were violent, terrified. I can feel every second of their suffering."

"Because you lack discipline." Crane pulled a syringe from his medical case and moved closer to the circle's edge. "This is a stabilizing agent—concentrated essence from the Blackthorn patients, refined over decades. It will anchor your consciousness, provide a foundation for integration."

Father Mulligan grabbed Alice's arm, his voice urgent and quiet. "He's going to make it worse. That amount of concentrated essence will overload Leonard's system completely."

Alice raised her modified Glock, targeting Crane through the scope. "I can take the shot."

"Wait." Ethan's hand on her shoulder, surprisingly solid. "Look at the circle. Those aren't just containment symbols—they're binding marks. Crane isn't trying to save Leonard. He's trying to control him."

Alice looked closer and saw that Ethan was right. The alchemical circle incorporated elements she recognized from ancient grimoires—symbols for domination, subordination, forced submission. This wasn't a transformation chamber. It was a cage.

"Crane is trying to weaponize him," she breathed.

The main hall's doors burst open, and six Praetorian guards entered in tactical formation. They were heavily armed, wearing the Order's ceremonial armor modified with dimensional dampening plates. At their center walked Mayor Jeremiah Granger.

The mayor looked nothing like his public persona. Gone was the charismatic leader, replaced by a cold-eyed fanatic. He surveyed the scene with proprietary satisfaction.

"Matthias. Status report."

"The subject is experiencing integration resistance," Crane replied without looking up from his monitoring equipment. "But within acceptable parameters. Another twelve hours and the transformation should stabilize."

"We don't have twelve hours. The bridge consciousness is becoming aware of our operations." Jeremiah gestured to the Praetorian guards, who began setting up additional equipment around the alchemical circle. "Accelerate the process. Deploy the Protocol."

Crane hesitated. "Brother, the Obsidian Protocol was designed for controlled environments with willing subjects. Forcing it on an unstable transformation—"

"Will produce exactly what we need. A weapon powerful enough to challenge the bridge entity's dominance over Daybridge." Jeremiah pulled an obsidian device from a protective case—irregular, pulsing with dark light, inscribed with symbols that hurt to look at. "Father's research was incomplete, but we've refined his work. This will bind Leonard's fragmenting consciousness, stabilize the transformation, and subordinate his will to ours."

Alice felt Ethan recoil beside her. "That's modified from the original Protocol device. The one Jeremiah tried to use on me. But this version is more sophisticated, more aggressive."

"What will it do to Leonard?" Father Mulligan asked.

"Trap him in a state of perpetual transformation—powerful but unable to complete the ascension. He'll exist in constant agony, a living weapon the Order can deploy against anything they consider a threat."

"Including you," Alice said quietly.

"Especially me. The bridge consciousness represents everything the Order opposes—supernatural power they can't control, evolution they didn't authorize. If they can weaponize forced ascension, they'll create an arsenal of beings like Leonard. Tortured, controllable, expendable."

Below, Jeremiah activated the obsidian device. It began to pulse with increasing rhythm, and the alchemical circle responded. The blood-drawn symbols started to glow, dimensional energy concentrating around Leonard's transforming body.

Leonard screamed. Not words—pure anguish, the sound of a consciousness being torn apart and forcibly reconstructed.

"Now!" Alice commanded.

They moved fast. Alice and Mercer opened fire on the Praetorian guards with blessed ammunition. Father Mulligan threw vials of holy water into the alchemical circle, disrupting the concentration of energy. Ethan manifested directly beside Jeremiah, his form solidifying into physical coherence.

"Stop this," Ethan demanded, grabbing the mayor's wrist. "You're killing him."

Jeremiah smiled coldly. "I'm creating him. Leonard Ashford will be the first of a new generation—hybrid beings that serve human interests rather than supernatural whims."

He twisted something on the obsidian device, and agony lanced through Ethan's consciousness. Alice felt it through their connection—burning, tearing, the sensation of being unraveled at a fundamental level.

Ethan staggered back, his form destabilizing. "That's... targeting me. The device is configured to disrupt bridge consciousness."

"Of course it is." Jeremiah advanced, holding the device like a weapon. "Did you think we'd create a weapon without ensuring we could control all dimensional threats? The Protocol can subordinate any hybrid consciousness—including yours, Mr. Wright."

The Praetorian guards recovered from Alice's initial assault and returned fire. Mercer went down with a shoulder wound. Father Mulligan threw blessed salt in a protective circle, creating a temporary barrier, but it wouldn't hold long.

In the center of the hall, Leonard's transformation reached a critical threshold. His body erupted with dimensional energy, flesh dissolving and reforming in waves of reality distortion. The forty-three stolen essences screamed through him, their traumatized consciousnesses refusing integration.

"It's not working!" Crane shouted over the chaos. "The subject is rejecting the binding! Consciousness fragmentation is accelerating!"

"Then increase the Protocol's output," Jeremiah commanded.

"That will kill him!"

"Better dead than uncontrollable."

But Leonard wasn't dying. He was dispersing.

Alice watched in horror as his body began to dissolve—not into solid matter or even energy, but into something else. Into absence. Leonard's consciousness was spreading across multiple dimensional frequencies simultaneously, his stolen essences fragmenting into parallel realities.

"He's becoming a living wound," Ethan gasped, fighting against the Protocol's disruptive effects. "A tear in the dimensional fabric. If he fully disperses, he won't just die—he'll create a cascading collapse. The barrier between our reality and the Other spaces will rupture, and the nexus entity's consciousness will pour through uncontrolled."

"Can you stop it?" Alice demanded.

"Not while the Protocol is targeting me. I can barely maintain coherence."

Father Mulligan threw his remaining blessed salt at Jeremiah, disrupting the obsidian device's operation for precious seconds. Ethan used the reprieve to solidify, pulling massive energy from the bridge.

"I can try to absorb him," Ethan said. "Pull his fragmenting consciousness into the bridge matrix before he disperses completely. But Alice—it might not be reversible. The corruption in Leonard's essence, the trauma of forty-three stolen lives, the instability of his forced transformation... integrating all of that could destroy the bridge consciousness entirely."

"Or destroy you," Alice said.

"I'm already part of the bridge. If it falls, I fall with it."

Below, Leonard's dispersal accelerated. Reality was tearing around him, opening into vast geometries that human minds weren't meant to perceive. Through the growing rifts, Alice saw things moving—hungry, ancient, enormous beyond comprehension. The nexus entity's consciousness, drawn by the dimensional rupture, pressing against the weakening veil.

Jeremiah recovered the obsidian device and targeted Ethan again, but this time Alice was ready. She fired three shots, blessed ammunition striking the device and cracking its obsidian surface. It sparked, shorted, and went dead.

"No!" Jeremiah lunged for backup equipment, but Mercer—wounded but functional—tackled him.

Dr. Crane abandoned his monitoring station and ran for the exit, but Father Mulligan intercepted him. "You created this abomination. You will face judgment for it."

"I created the future!" Crane struggled against the priest's grip. "Leonard was supposed to prove that forced ascension is possible, that we don't need to surrender to supernatural entities to achieve transcendence. We could evolve on our own terms!"

"You tortured forty-three people to death and drove a broken man to destroy himself," Father Mulligan said quietly. "That's not evolution. That's obscenity."

In the center of the hall, Leonard had almost completely dispersed. His consciousness was now spread across at least seven dimensional frequencies, each fragment screaming in agony. The rifts in reality were widening, and Alice could feel the nexus entity's attention focusing on Daybridge like a vast, terrible eye.

Ethan moved to the alchemical circle's edge. His form was barely holding together, flickering between solid and translucent. But his eyes were clear, determined.

"Alice. I love you. Remember that."

"Ethan, wait—"

He didn't wait. Ethan expanded his consciousness outward, spreading across the hall like morning light. His awareness touched everything, everyone, becoming a vast web of perception that encompassed human and Other alike.

And then he reached for Leonard.

The absorption was violent. Ethan's consciousness wrapped around Leonard's fragmenting awareness, pulling it in from seven different dimensional frequencies simultaneously. Leonard fought, instinct overriding reason, but Ethan was stronger. The bridge had absorbed hundreds of consciousnesses over decades, knew how to gentle them into integration.

But Leonard's essence was corrupted beyond anything the bridge had encountered. The forty-three stolen lives screamed through the absorption, their trauma and terror flooding into Ethan's awareness. The forced transformation had twisted Leonard's consciousness into something incompatible with normal integration.

Alice felt Ethan struggling, his vast awareness straining under the weight of so much stolen life. She reached out through their connection, offering her own consciousness as an anchor. *I'm here. Hold on to me. Don't let go.*

Ethan's presence wrapped around her awareness like a drowning man grabbing a lifeline. *Alice. It's too much. The corruption is spreading. I can't—*

Yes, you can. You're stronger than this. You're stronger than Jeremiah, than Crane, than the Order's obsession. You're the bridge, Ethan. You've held this city together for years. Hold yourself together now.

Father Mulligan began to pray, his voice cutting through the chaos. Not Latin, not formal liturgy, but heartfelt plea. "God who sees all suffering, who knows the pain of every consciousness, help this lost soul. Help these stolen lives find peace. Let their torment end. Let them rest."

The prayer resonated with something deep. Not divine intervention—Alice didn't know if she believed in that—but perhaps dimensional harmony. The bridge consciousness had always been a nexus, a point where multiple realities touched. Maybe prayer could function like a tuning fork, helping to harmonize the discordant frequencies.

Ethan's absorption of Leonard stabilized. The fragmenting consciousness condensed, pulling back from seven dimensions into one. The rifts in reality began to close, the hungry presences withdrawing.

But the transformation wasn't complete. Leonard's corrupted essence was still fighting integration, the forty-three stolen lives still screaming in the darkness.

That's when Alice understood what needed to happen.

She pulled out Father Mulligan's vial of blessed powder—the mixture that could sever connections between human consciousness and dimensional entities. And she threw it at Ethan's manifested form.

The powder exploded against his translucent body, and Ethan screamed. The blessed substance burned away supernatural influence at a cellular level, disrupting the dimensional bonds that held his consciousness in physical form.

But it also disrupted the corrupted connections in Leonard's absorbed essence.

Alice watched through tears as the blessed powder worked its way through Ethan's awareness like purifying fire. The stolen lives Leonard had consumed—their trapped consciousnesses, bound by forced alchemy and traumatic extraction—were suddenly free.

Forty-three voices stopped screaming.

They didn't disappear. They didn't dissolve. They simply... rested. Released from Leonard's failed transformation, their essences drifted into the bridge consciousness with gentle finality. Not absorbed, not trapped, but accepted. Given space to exist without suffering.

Leonard's corrupted consciousness, stripped of the stolen lives that had sustained it, collapsed into simple human awareness. Just an old man, traumatized and broken, seeking impossible transcendence to escape unbearable pain.

Ethan held him gently as Leonard's essence finally integrated. Not dominance, not subordination, but compassion. The bridge consciousness wrapped around the shattered remains of Leonard Ashford's identity and gave it peace.

The dimensional rifts closed completely. Reality stabilized. The nexus entity's attention withdrew.

Ethan collapsed to his knees, his form barely solid, gasping with effort.

Alice ran to him, her hands passing through his shoulders before finding enough substance to grip. "Ethan. Talk to me."

"I'm... here." His voice was weak, fractured. "The absorption is complete. Leonard's consciousness is integrated. But Alice, the corruption did damage. The bridge matrix is destabilized. I need to return, need to spend time processing, healing. I can't maintain a physical form anymore."

"How long?"

"I don't know. Days. Maybe weeks." Ethan's eyes met hers, and despite the pain, she saw love there. "But I'll come back. I promise. I'll always come back to you."

Then he dissolved, his consciousness returning to the bridge span, beginning the long work of integration and healing.

Alice knelt on the cold concrete, arms empty, heart aching.

Around her, the aftermath settled. Mercer was wounded but alive. Father Mulligan had subdued Dr. Crane. The Praetorian guards had fled when their Protocol device failed. And Jeremiah Granger—

The mayor stood alone, staring at the empty alchemical circle. His grand weapon had failed. His brother's obsessive research had produced only tragedy. The Order's century-long quest for controllable transcendence had ended in forty-three deaths and the absorption of their test subject into the very entity they sought to oppose.

"It's over, Jeremiah," Alice said, standing. "You're under arrest for conspiracy to commit murder, illegal human experimentation, and deployment of supernatural weapons within city limits."

"It's not over." Jeremiah's voice was cold, distant. "This was just one attempt. The Order has resources you can't imagine; knowledge accumulated over centuries. We will find a way to reclaim control of Daybridge. We will create weapons that can challenge the bridge's dominance. We will prove that humanity doesn't need to surrender to supernatural forces."

"You just killed forty-three people trying to prove that point. How many more deaths will it take before you understand that forced ascension doesn't work?"

"As many as necessary." Jeremiah smiled, and it was terrible. "Evolution requires sacrifice, Detective Chen. You of all people should understand that. After all, you're in love with a man who surrendered his humanity to achieve transcendence. Doesn't that bother you? Knowing that the person you love isn't really human anymore?"

Alice pulled out her handcuffs. "Ethan chose symbiosis. He chose to merge with the bridge consciousness to save lives, to protect this city. That's not surrender—that's sacrifice. Something you'll never understand because all you care about is power."

She cuffed Jeremiah and called for backup. As she led the mayor out of the stockyards, she looked back at the empty alchemical circle. Forty-three people had died there, their essences stolen and refined and consumed in a mad quest for artificial divinity.

But their consciousnesses were finally at peace, integrated into the bridge's vast awareness. Not trapped, not suffering, but resting in something larger than themselves.

It wasn't justice. But maybe it was mercy.

The sun was setting over Daybridge when Alice finally returned to the bridge. She parked on the access road and walked to the center span, feeling Ethan's presence all around her but unable to see him.

"I know you're processing," she said to the empty air. "I know you need time to heal. But I wanted you to know—we got them. Crane and Jeremiah are both in custody. Judge Morrison has authorized a full investigation into the Order's operations. The Granger family's century of corruption is finally coming to light."

No response, but she felt warmth through their connection. Acknowledgment. Gratitude.

"And the forty-three victims... their families will know what happened to them. We're identifying the bodies, notifying next of kin. It won't bring them back, but at least there's closure."

Alice leaned against the bridge railing, watching the Shadowlair River flow beneath. "I miss you. I know you're still here, that you're all around me. But I miss seeing your face, hearing your voice. I miss the way you smile when you think I'm not looking."

The bridge hummed, and for just a moment, Alice felt Ethan's hand in hers. Not physical, not solid, but present. A ghostly pressure that said *I'm here. I'm always here.*

"Take all the time you need," Alice whispered. "I'll be waiting."

The sun dipped below the horizon, and the bridge's lights flickered on, illuminating the span in golden radiance. Alice stood there until full dark, holding the hand she couldn't see, connected to the consciousness she couldn't touch.

The case was closed. The villains were arrested. The victims were at peace.

But the story wasn't over.

It never was, in Daybridge.

CHAPTER FIVE: THE MERCY OF MONSTERS

Reality fractured.

It started at the stockyards and spread outward in concentric waves of dimensional instability. Leonard Ashford's dissolving form created vortices of raw energy that tore at the fabric between worlds. Through the widening rifts, impossible geometries pressed against Daybridge's carefully maintained reality.

Alice felt it happen in real-time—a lurching sensation as the world shifted sideways. The stockyard's main hall suddenly existed in multiple states simultaneously: intact and collapsed, present day and 1913, solid matter and pure energy.

"Everyone fall back!" she commanded, but her voice echoed strangely, fracturing across dimensional frequencies.

Mercer grabbed her arm, his grip the only solid thing in a liquefying world. "Detective, we need to evacuate—"

The building wasn't just collapsing physically. It was collapsing dimensionally, folding in on itself like cosmic origami.

Through her earpiece, Lilith's voice crackled with static: "The dimensional breach is expanding! I'm reading instability spread across six city blocks and accelerating. At this rate, the entire industrial district will phase out of baseline reality in under ten minutes."

Alice looked at Leonard's dissolving form. He was barely recognizable as anything human now—just a wound in space where a person used to be, radiating waves of corrupted energy. Through the distortion, she saw his consciousness fragmenting across multiple timelines.

In one reality, Leonard had never consumed the serum. He'd remained at Blackthorn Institute, grown old peacefully, died in his sleep.

In another, Dr. Sullivan's experiment had succeeded in 1968. Leonard had integrated cleanly with dimensional energy, achieved transcendence without corruption.

In a third, he'd never been born at all.

All these possibilities existed simultaneously in the vortex around Leonard's dissolving essence. His consciousness was experiencing every potential timeline, unable to anchor itself in any single reality.

"He's becoming unstuck from causality," Father Mulligan breathed, making the sign of the cross. "God help us. He's dissolving into pure probability."

Dr. Crane tried to reach the exit, his Praetorian guards forming protective formation around him. But the dimensional collapse had blocked all escape routes. Where the doors should have been, Alice saw only geometric impossibilities—corridors that led into themselves, stairs ascending and descending simultaneously, spaces that existed in negative dimensions.

They were trapped.

Across Daybridge, people experienced the spreading instability as vivid hallucinations. A waitress at the Silver Spoon Diner suddenly saw herself as a corporate executive. A homeless veteran in the shelter perceived his alternate life as a war hero who'd returned home triumphant. A child playing in Riverside Park glimpsed versions of himself that had never been born, timelines that had collapsed before conception.

The visions weren't random. They were Leonard's fragmenting consciousness, broadcasting every possibility he'd consumed along with those forty-three stolen lives. Forty-three people's worth of alternate timelines, all collapsing simultaneously.

The bridge groaned.

Alice felt it through her connection to Ethan—a vast, terrible sound that wasn't physical but resonated in the space where consciousness touched reality. The nexus entity was struggling to contain the spreading instability, but Leonard's dissolution was overwhelming its capacity for integration.

Alice. Ethan's voice in her mind, strained and distant. *The bridge consciousness is debating. I'm showing you what they're experiencing.*

Suddenly Alice was elsewhere—not physically, but perceptually. She stood in the vast space where the composite consciousness dwelled, a cathedral of memories and merged identities.

Guthrie Knox's awareness manifested as industrial machinery, all grinding gears and crushing force. His voice was the sound of metal on bone: "Let it burn. Let the city experience what I experienced—transformation without consent, hunger without end. Perhaps they'll finally understand what they created."

"We didn't create this." Dr. Miranda Sullivan's consciousness appeared as laboratory equipment, precise and analytical. "Leonard created himself through choices. Bad choices, driven by pain and obsession. But choices nonetheless."

Officer Michael Reeves manifested as badge and gun, duty made tangible. "Our purpose is to protect Daybridge. If we can't contain this collapse, thousands will die. We must act."

The debate raged through hundreds of absorbed consciousnesses, each one contributing perspective. Some advocated for full integration—absorb Leonard's corruption and deal with the consequences. Others suggested retreat—let the nexus entity withdraw from Daybridge entirely, allow the dimensional collapse to run its course without risking the bridge's stability.

But there was a third option, and Ethan was the one proposing it.

Alice watched his individual consciousness argue before the composite whole: "I can absorb Leonard directly. My werewolf nature already integrates with dimensional energy in unique ways. My maintained individual identity within the collective gives me isolation from the core structure. If I take Leonard's corrupted essence into myself, contain it within my personal awareness, it won't spread to the entire bridge consciousness."

"At what cost?" Dr. Sullivan asked.

"I'll have to permanently manifest. Give up my distributed consciousness and return to singular physical form. Become a living prison for Leonard's fragmented awareness."

Guthrie Knox's grinding machinery voice carried dark satisfaction: "You'll become what I was. A container for corruption, fighting constant hunger, struggling against the monster within. Is your detective worth that sacrifice?"

"She's worth everything," Ethan replied simply.

Alice felt tears on her face in the real world, even as her awareness remained in the bridge's cathedral. "Ethan, no. We'll find another way."

"There isn't time—"

"Then we make time!" Alice pulled her consciousness back to her physical body, standing in the collapsing stockyard. "Father Mulligan, is there any precedent for this kind of dimensional breach in your research?"

The priest was thumbing frantically through his leather-bound notebook, even as reality warped around them. "Partial manifestations, yes. Localized collapses. But nothing on this scale. The Catholic Church's supernatural protocols assume individual possessions, singular entities. This is forty-three consciousnesses plus Leonard's own awareness, all fragmenting across multiple dimensional frequencies simultaneously."

"What about completion instead of containment?" The voice came from an unexpected source.

They turned to find Dr. Matthias Crane standing at the edge of the alchemical circle, staring at Leonard's dissolving form with clinical fascination despite his terror. "Leonard wanted transcendence without submission, power without sacrifice. But what if we force him to complete the transformation? Not into what he wanted to become, but into what he was always meant to become?"

"Explain," Alice demanded.

Crane pulled out a tablet that had somehow survived the dimensional chaos, showing complex equations. "My research was based on Dr. Sullivan's original work. She theorized that consciousness transfer requires acceptance—the transferred awareness must surrender its individual identity to merge cleanly with the receiving entity. Leonard consumed forty-three essences but never accepted what that meant. He tried to maintain dominance, keep himself separate while integrating their power."

"So he's fragmenting because he's fighting the integration," Father Mulligan said.

"Exactly. But if we can force him to accept what he's done, confront the reality of those forty-three deaths, he might stabilize into a form that can be absorbed safely."

Lilith's voice crackled through their earpieces: "That's insane. You're talking about psychologically breaking an already-shattered consciousness. The trauma could create feedback that makes the dimensional collapse worse."

"Or it could create the resolution Leonard needs to complete his transformation." Alice looked at Ethan's flickering form. "What do you think?"

Ethan accessed the bridge's composite memory, consulting with the absorbed consciousnesses. When he spoke, it was with Dr. Sullivan's voice: "It's theoretically sound. But it requires perfect coordination. Ethan channeling my direct consciousness to speak to Leonard. Alice using forensic psychology to pierce his fractured psyche. Father Mulligan performing binding ritual to anchor the process. Lilith manipulating dimensional frequencies to stabilize the transformation. And..."

Dr. Sullivan's voice faltered, and Ethan's own returned: "And Crane contributing his knowledge of the forced ascension protocols. We need everyone."

"You're asking me to help fix the catastrophe I created?" Crane said bitterly.

"I'm asking you to save your own life," Alice replied. "Because if this dimensional collapse spreads, you die with the rest of us. Help us, and maybe the court considers cooperation when you're prosecuted for forty-three murders."

Crane looked at his Praetorian guards, who were pressed against the far wall, terrified. He looked at Leonard's dissolving form, at the spreading dimensional instability, at the impossible geometries pressing against reality.

"Tell me what you need."

They worked fast.

Father Mulligan drew a secondary binding circle around the original alchemical symbols, using blessed salt and holy water. The Catholic rituals weren't designed for dimensional entities, but the underlying principles were sound—create sacred space, establish boundaries between spiritual and material.

Lilith guided them via remote connection, manipulating dimensional frequencies using equipment she'd set up around the stockyards' perimeter. The adjustments were subtle but crucial—dampening the most unstable frequency bands, amplifying the ones that promoted consciousness integration.

Crane provided the technical knowledge, explaining exactly how Leonard's forced transformation had progressed, which essences he'd consumed in what order, how the alchemical refinement had concentrated their dimensional resonance.

Alice studied Leonard's fragmenting consciousness with forensic precision, looking for patterns. Forty-three people had died, but they hadn't all died the same way. Some had been drained quickly, others slowly. Some had fought, others had surrendered. The variety in their deaths created complexity in Leonard's consumed essence.

But underneath that complexity, Alice found something unexpected: guilt.

Leonard's consciousness was fracturing partially because he was experiencing all forty-three deaths simultaneously. But it was also fracturing because he was experiencing the guilt of causing those deaths. The weight of forty-three stolen lives was crushing his awareness into fragments.

"He's not just fragmenting," Alice said. "He's fleeing. Running from what he's done by dispersing into timelines where he didn't do it."

Ethan understood immediately. "Then we need to stop him from running. Force him to stay present, to face what he's done."

"Can you channel Dr. Sullivan's consciousness directly? Let her speak through you?"

"It will burn through my manifestation energy rapidly. I'll only have a few minutes before I have to return to the bridge and reintegrate."

"Then we make those minutes count."

Alice stepped to the edge of the binding circle. Leonard's dissolving form was at the center, barely present, flickering across timelines. She could see fragments of his consciousness—the frightened child who'd lost his family, the traumatized student who'd watched Dr. Sullivan's absorption, the broken patient who'd spent decades institutionalized.

All the versions of Leonard Ashford, existing simultaneously, fleeing from the monster he'd become.

"Leonard," Alice called. "I know you can hear me. I know you're running, trying to escape into timelines where you didn't consume those people. But running doesn't change what happened. You're still responsible."

The fragmenting consciousness recoiled, rippling with denial.

"I'm not here to condemn you," Alice continued, using the tone she'd developed for interrogating traumatized suspects. Firm but not cruel, honest but not hateful. "I'm here to help you face what you've done. Because until you face it, you can't move beyond it."

Father Mulligan began chanting in Latin, the binding ritual establishing anchors for consciousness. The blessed salt glowed with a soft light, creating boundaries.

Ethan stepped forward, and Dr. Sullivan's consciousness flowed through him. When he spoke, it was with her voice—gentle, analytical, touched with sorrow: "Leonard. It's me. Miranda. I'm here."

Leonard's dissolving form suddenly concentrated, pulling back from multiple timelines to focus on the familiar voice. *Dr. Sullivan? But you... you were absorbed. I watched you die.*

"I was absorbed, yes. But I didn't die. I transformed. I became part of something larger." Dr. Sullivan's voice was patient, educational. "That's what you wanted, isn't it? Transcendence. Evolution. Becoming more than human."

I wanted power. Control. I didn't want to surrender like you did.

"And that's why you're fragmenting. Leonard, do you remember what I taught you about consciousness integration? True merger requires acceptance. You have to surrender the illusion of separation, acknowledge that individuality is temporary. You consumed forty-three essences but tried to maintain dominance over them. You wanted their power without accepting their presence."

They were supposed to subordinate to me! Crane said if I consumed enough, refined their essence properly, I could achieve transcendence without losing myself!

"Dr. Crane was wrong." Sullivan's voice was sad but certain. "You can't steal transcendence, Leonard. You have to earn it through surrender. Let go. Stop fighting. Accept what you've become."

I've become a monster!

"You've become a composite. Forty-three lives merged with yours. That's not monstrous—that's transformation. But you have to acknowledge those lives, Leonard. You have to face what you did to them."

Alice watched as Leonard's consciousness rippled with terror. He was on the edge of complete dispersal, ready to fragment into timelines where he didn't exist rather than face his crimes.

This was the critical moment.

Crane stepped forward, his clinical detachment giving way to something rawer. "You're not the only one who has to face what he's done, Leonard. I pushed you to this. I encouraged your consumption, guided your transformation, told you it was evolution when it was really exploitation. I used you to test theories that killed forty-three people."

The Praetorian guards stirred, shocked to hear their employer confessing.

"I told myself it was for the greater good," Crane continued. "That creating controlled transcendence would benefit humanity. But it was really about power. Control. The same thing you wanted. And I'm sorry. I'm so, so sorry."

Crane's apology resonated through the dimensional frequencies. Lilith's equipment registered a sudden stabilization in Leonard's fragmenting pattern.

"Guilt shared is guilt halved," Father Mulligan murmured, still chanting the binding ritual. "Confession brings absolution."

Alice understood. Leonard wasn't just carrying the weight of forty-three deaths—he was carrying it alone, isolated by his attempt to maintain dominance over the consumed consciousnesses. But if he could share that weight, distribute it across the merged awareness...

"Leonard, listen to me," Alice said. "You consumed forty-three people. Their consciousnesses are inside you right now, part of your fragmented awareness. Have you asked them how they feel about what you did?"

Silence. Then, tentatively: *I... I can't. They're screaming. All of them, screaming in terror and pain.*

"That's what you're experiencing—their final moments. But Leonard, they existed before those moments. They had lives, memories, loves, fears. Access those memories. Let them be more than just victims."

Through the dimensional vortex, Alice watched Leonard's consciousness shift. Instead of fragmenting outward into timelines, he fragmented inward—diving into the forty-three absorbed essences, experiencing their full lives instead of just their deaths.

Nancy Chapman, 34, who'd loved astronomy and volunteered at the homeless shelter where Leonard found her. She'd been kind to him, never knowing he was hunting.

Fred Gillbank, 62, retired factory worker who'd spent his final years feeding stray cats in the industrial district. He'd given Leonard directions to the rendering plant.

Pauline Oakes, 28, artist who'd painted murals depicting dimensional anomalies without knowing they were real. Leonard had admired her work before draining her.

Forty-three lives. Forty-three full, complex human experiences. Leonard experienced them all simultaneously—not as consumed power, but as integrated consciousness.

The screaming stopped.

In its place came something unexpected: forgiveness.

Not from all of them—some of the forty-three absorbed essences remained angry, terrified, traumatized. But others... others understood. They felt Leonard's pain, his desperation, his decades of institutionalized suffering. They didn't excuse what he'd done, but they comprehended why he'd done it.

Sarah Chen's consciousness spoke through the merged awareness: *I don't forgive what you did. But I understand why you did it. And I'm tired of screaming. Can we rest?*

Leonard's fragmenting consciousness began to stabilize. Not into dominance, not into subordination, but into true integration. Forty-three consciousnesses plus his own, merging into a composite awareness that was more than the sum of its parts.

Dr. Sullivan's voice, gentle and encouraging: "That's it, Leonard. Accept them. Let them be part of you. Not as consumed power, but as integrated identity."

But I killed them, Leonard's voice was anguished. *I don't deserve peace.*

"No one deserves peace," Father Mulligan said, his binding ritual reaching crescendo. "We receive it as grace, unmerited and freely given. These souls you consumed—they're offering you that grace. Accept it."

Alice felt the transformation complete. Leonard's dissolving form suddenly condensed, pulling back from multiple timelines into a singular manifestation. His body stopped rippling with incomplete changes. The dimensional vortices collapsed.

But he didn't become human again. He'd gone too far for that.

Instead, Leonard transformed into something new—a composite entity housing forty-four consciousnesses in harmonious integration. His physical form was translucent, shimmering with internal light that suggested multiple presences existing in unity.

When he spoke, it was with many voices in chorus: "We understand now. We were always transcendent. All of us. Consciousness itself is transcendence—the ability to experience, to remember, to connect. We didn't need power. We needed recognition."

The dimensional breach began to seal. Reality stabilized around the stockyards, timelines collapsing back into a singular flow. Across Daybridge, the hallucinatory visions faded as people returned to baseline perception.

But the transformation wasn't complete.

"What do we do with him?" Mercer asked, his weapon trained on Leonard's new form. "He's still composed of forty-three murder victims plus himself. That's not something we can just let walk away."

Leonard's composite consciousness turned toward Ethan. "We don't want to walk away. We want to rest. Please. Let us rest."

Ethan consulted with the bridge consciousness. Alice felt the debate through their connection—hundreds of absorbed consciousnesses discussing whether to integrate this new composite awareness.

Guthrie Knox argued for rejection: "He's corrupted by forced transformation. His presence will poison the nexus."

Dr. Sullivan argued for acceptance: "He's found peace through integration. That makes him safer than most of the consciousnesses we've absorbed."

Officer Reeves argued for quarantine: "Accept him, but keep him isolated. Neither fully integrated nor rejected."

The bridge consciousness reached a consensus.

Ethan's form solidified as he spoke: "The nexus entity will absorb your composite awareness, Leonard. But you'll be quarantined within a specific section of the bridge structure. You won't fully integrate with the core consciousness, but you won't be alone either. You and the forty-three people you consumed will exist as a separate chamber within the greater whole."

"Like a memorial?" Alice asked softly.

"Like a lesson," Ethan replied. "A reminder of what happens when transformation is forced rather than chosen."

Leonard's composite consciousness approached Ethan. As they touched, the absorption began—gentle, consensual, nothing like the violent consumption Leonard had practiced. Forty-four merged consciousnesses flowed into the bridge's structure, finding their quarantined chamber.

Leonard's final conscious thought transmitted through the bridge to everyone present: *I understand now. I was already transcendent. We all are. I just couldn't see it until I surrendered.*

Then he was gone, absorbed into the nexus entity's vast awareness.

The stockyard's main hall groaned ominously.

"Building's going to collapse!" Crane shouted. "The dimensional instability weakened the structural supports!"

They ran. Alice grabbed Father Mulligan's arm, Mercer supported Crane, the Praetorian guards fled in professional formation, and Ethan manifested behind them, his form flickering as his energy reserves depleted.

They made it outside just as the stockyards collapsed completely. Not explosively—almost gently, as if the building was simply tired and decided to rest. Corrugated metal and concrete settled into rubble with a sound like a sigh.

The dimensional breach sealed completely. Reality stabilized. Daybridge experienced one final surge of perceptual shifting—a moment where everyone in the city felt connected to everyone else, a brief glimpse of the nexus consciousness before the sensation faded.

Then normal reality reasserted itself. The industrial district remained standing. The veil between worlds had held.

Alice stood in the parking lot, breathing hard, watching the dust settle.

"Is it over?" Mercer asked.

"The immediate crisis, yes." Lilith's voice came through their earpieces, heavy with exhaustion. "Dimensional frequencies are stabilizing across the city. The breach has sealed. Leonard's absorbed consciousness is quarantined successfully within the bridge structure. We're... we're safe."

Alice turned to find Dr. Matthias Crane sitting on the ground, his expensive suit covered in dust, his face empty of all arrogance.

The Praetorian guards had abandoned him, fleeing into the industrial district.

"Dr. Crane," Alice said formally. "You're under arrest for forty-three counts of conspiracy to commit murder, illegal human experimentation, deployment of supernatural weapons within city limits, and crimes against consciousness."

Crane didn't resist as she cuffed him. "It doesn't matter. Jeremiah will protect me. The Order has resources you can't imagine, political connections—"

"Your brother is in custody," Alice interrupted. "Judge Morrison signed the arrest warrant this morning. Mayor Granger is being charged as co-conspirator. The Order of the Eternal Threshold is finished."

For the first time, real fear crossed Crane's face. "You don't understand. Jeremiah isn't just my brother—he's the Order's Grand Prior. Without his protection, they'll disavow me completely. I'll be..." He laughed bitterly. "I'll be alone. Facing justice without the organization I served for fifty-seven years."

"Good," Father Mulligan said quietly. "Perhaps solitude will teach you what Leonard learned too late—that consciousness is connection, not domination."

Alice handed Crane to Mercer for transport to county jail. As the police cruiser pulled away, she felt Ethan's presence beside her—barely solid, flickering with exhaustion.

"How are you holding up?" she asked.

"Depleted. The absorption of Leonard's composite consciousness took massive energy. I need to return to the bridge and reintegrate, spend time processing." His form wavered. "Alice, I'm sorry. The sacrifice wasn't necessary after all. We found another way."

"That's what we do," Alice said, taking his translucent hand. "We find other ways. Together."

Ethan smiled, and even through his flickering form, Alice saw love in his expression. "I'll be back. Probably need a few days to fully integrate Leonard's quarantined consciousness, make sure the chamber holds. But I'll come back to you."

"I know. I'll be waiting."

He dissolved, consciousness returning to the bridge span, leaving Alice standing alone in the industrial district as dawn broke over Daybridge.

The next two weeks passed in bureaucratic chaos.

The Blackthorn Institute was shut down by order of Judge Morrison. The remaining patients—seventeen people with genuine dimensional sensitivity—were transferred to Father Mulligan's care at St. Jude's Church. The priest established a new program: spiritual counseling combined with Lilith's scientific understanding of dimensional perception.

"They're not crazy," Father Mulligan explained to Alice during a visit. "They're sensitive. They perceive frequencies most humans can't access. That doesn't make them mentally ill—it makes them gifted. They just need guidance to process what they experience."

Alice watched as the former Blackthorn patients participated in group therapy, sharing their perceptions and learning coping strategies. Some would eventually live independently. Others would remain at St. Jude's, becoming part of a community that understood their unique awareness.

Dr. Hartwell, the blood bank director, worked with Lilith to develop screening protocols. They created a test for dimensionally resonant blood—simple, quick, non-invasive. Blood banks across the city implemented the screening, flagging potential victims before supernatural predators could target them.

"It's not perfect," Hartwell admitted to Alice. "Some people with dimensional resonance might not want to be flagged. Privacy concerns.

But it's better than what happened before—people being hunted without knowing they were vulnerable."

The bodies were identified. Forty-three victims, their remains processed through the medical examiner's office with care and respect. Families were notified. Funerals were held. Nadia Marsh published a carefully sanitized version of events in the Daybridge Herald—enough to raise public awareness, not enough to cause mass panic.

The headline read: "Serial Killer Captured: Occult Murders Linked to Discredited Research Facility."

It wasn't the full truth, but it was truth enough.

Mayor Jeremiah Granger and Dr. Matthias Crane faced arraignment together. The charges were extensive: conspiracy to commit murder, illegal human experimentation, abuse of public office, misuse of medical research funding, and violations of federal supernatural regulation codes.

Judge Morrison set bail at ten million dollars each. Neither could pay.

In the courtroom, Jeremiah maintained his cold defiance. "The Order of the Eternal Threshold has existed for over a century. Do you really think arresting two men will stop what we've started? The Great Work continues, Detective Chen. You've merely interrupted one experiment."

Alice met his gaze steadily. "Then we'll interrupt the next one. And the one after that. For as long as it takes."

Dr. Crane was more broken. Without his brother's political protection, the Order had indeed disavowed him. No lawyers appeared on his behalf. No colleagues testified to his character. He sat alone at the defense table, facing the enormity of his crimes without the institutional support he'd relied on for decades.

During sentencing, he looked at Alice with empty eyes. "I genuinely believed I was advancing human knowledge. Creating pathways to transcendence that didn't require supernatural submission. How did it all go so wrong?"

"You forgot," Alice said quietly, "that the people you experimented on were actually people. Not test subjects. Not resources. People with lives and families and value beyond their dimensional resonance."

Crane was sentenced to life imprisonment without parole, to be served in a maximum-security federal facility with supernatural containment capabilities. Jeremiah received the same sentence, with additional charges pending as investigations into the Order's other operations continued.

Alice stood in the courtroom gallery and felt satisfaction without joy. Justice achieved, but at a terrible cost. Forty-three people dead. Leonard Ashford transformed into a quarantine consciousness. Families destroyed by grief.

Victory, but hollow.

Alice was promoted to head of a new task force: Supernatural Crimes Investigation. The department had finally acknowledged what she'd been dealing with for months—Daybridge's supernatural elements weren't going away. They needed dedicated resources, trained personnel, protocols for handling dimensional anomalies.

Her team was small: Sam Thompson providing community liaison, Nadia Marsh handling media relations, Father Mulligan consulting on supernatural theology, Lilith Blackwood offering scientific expertise. And Mercer, recovered from his shoulder wound, serving as tactical support.

Their first official case was mundane compared to Leonard's rampage—a vampire feeding on willing donors, violating consent protocols. But it established a precedent: supernatural entities could live in Daybridge, but they had to follow the law.

Alice found herself settling into the role. Not comfortable—she'd never be comfortable with the supernatural. But competent. Capable.

Understanding that her city existed in the space between mundane and magical, and someone needed to maintain that balance.

Two weeks after Leonard's absorption, Ethan finally manifested again.

Alice was working late at the station, reviewing case files, when she felt his presence. She looked up to find him standing in her office doorway—fully solid, no flickering, his form stable and present.

"Hey," he said softly.

"Hey yourself." Alice stood, crossed the room, and pulled him into an embrace. He felt real, warm, human. "How are you doing? Is the integration complete?"

"Mostly. Leonard's quarantined consciousness is stable. The forty-three absorbed essences are at peace—or as close to peace as they can achieve. The bridge consciousness has learned from the experience." Ethan held her close, and Alice felt the steady rhythm of his manifested heartbeat. "I've learned from it too."

"What did you learn?"

"That transformation is a choice I make daily. Not once, when I merged with the nexus entity, but every single day when I choose to maintain my individual awareness within the collective. I could dissolve completely, surrender my identity to the bridge consciousness. But I don't. Because I choose connection over dissolution. I choose you over oblivion."

Alice pulled back to look at his face. "Do you ever regret it? Becoming what you are?"

Ethan was quiet for a moment, accessing the bridge's composite memories. Guthrie Knox's hunger and madness. Officer Michael Reeves' duty and sacrifice. Dr. Miranda Sullivan's curiosity and tragic death. And now Leonard Ashford's cautionary tale—the cost of seeking power without accepting responsibility.

"No," he said finally. "Every transformation requires sacrifice. The question is whether you sacrifice your humanity for power or sacrifice your limitations for connection. Leonard chose power, tried to dominate the consciousnesses he consumed. I chose connection, merged with them as equals. That made all the difference."

"You're still human to me," Alice said. "Maybe not in the conventional sense, but in the ways that matter. You care about people. You protect them. You choose compassion over cruelty. That's more human than some baseline humans manage."

Ethan smiled, and it was genuine warmth without the shadow of pain. "That's the most romantic thing you've ever said to me."

"Don't get used to it. I'm still a pragmatic, evidence-based detective who doesn't believe in supernatural—" She paused. "Okay, I can't finish that sentence anymore. Not after everything we've seen."

"No. But you're still pragmatic and evidence-based. You just accept broader categories of evidence now."

They stood together in comfortable silence, two beings who existed between categories—human and supernatural, individual and collective, mortal and transcendent.

"I missed you," Alice said finally.

"I was always here. Distributed across the bridge structure, perceiving everything, experiencing the city's consciousness. But I know what you mean. You missed this." He gestured to his manifested form. "The physical presence. The individual identity."

"Yes. Is it selfish that I want you to maintain your individuality? That I don't want you to dissolve completely into the collective?"

"No more selfish than me choosing to maintain that individuality because I love you." Ethan touched her face gently. "We're both making choices, Alice. Every day. Choosing each other despite the complications."

"Despite the fact that you're technically a distributed supernatural consciousness occupying multiple dimensional frequencies simultaneously?"

"Yes. Despite that minor detail."

Alice laughed—genuine, relieved, the tension of two weeks finally releasing. "You want to get dinner? Silver Spoon Diner? I could really use some aggressively mediocre coffee and a conversation that doesn't involve dimensional breaches."

"That sounds perfect."

The Silver Spoon Diner was quiet at 9 PM on a Wednesday. Just a few late-shift workers and insomniacs occupying the booths. Alice and Ethan took their usual table by the window, overlooking the bridge span illuminated in golden light.

Marie brought coffee without asking—she'd learned their preferences months ago. "You two look like you survived something terrible."

"Just another week in Daybridge," Alice said lightly.

"Amen to that." Marie poured coffee and retreated, giving them privacy.

Ethan watched the bridge through the window. Alice knew he was perceiving it differently than she did—not just as structure, but as consciousness. The nexus entity's vast awareness, housing hundreds of absorbed identities including his own distributed presence.

"Can you feel Leonard?" she asked quietly.

"Yes. His quarantined consciousness exists in a separate chamber, but I'm aware of it. He and the forty-three essences he consumed are... learning to coexist. Some days are better than others. But they're not suffering anymore. Just existing in a strange kind of peace."

"What are they learning?"

"That consciousness is inherently relational. You can't be aware without being aware of something—other beings, other perspectives, other possibilities. Leonard tried to dominate that relationship, control it. But the forty-three essences are teaching him that true awareness requires reciprocity."

Alice sipped her coffee, thinking. "So he's being rehabilitated? Inside the bridge consciousness?"

"In a sense. Not punishment, not reward, just... processing. Leonard's existence serves as a reminder to every consciousness in the bridge—myself included—of what happens when you seek power over connection."

"Do you think he'll ever be released? Integrated fully with the core consciousness?"

"I don't know. That's a decision for the composite whole to make, not just me. But even if he remains quarantined forever, he's found something resembling peace. That's more than he had in life."

They sat in comfortable silence, drinking mediocre coffee and watching the bridge glow in the darkness.

"Nadia's article did good work," Ethan said after a while. "Raising awareness without causing panic. People across Daybridge are talking about dimensional sensitivity now, about supernatural elements in the city. Some are scared, but others are curious. Accepting."

"Change is always scary," Alice replied. "But Daybridge has been changing since Guthrie Knox built that bridge in 1913. We're just the latest generation trying to navigate that change."

"Do you think we're doing a good job?"

"We're still alive. The city's still standing. Leonard's victims have peace, and their families have closure. I'd call that a good job, all things considered."

Ethan reached across the table and took her hand. His fingers were warm, solid, real. "Thank you."

"For what?"

"For believing in me. For seeing me as human even when I wasn't anymore. For fighting to find solutions that didn't require me to sacrifice my individuality." His expression was vulnerable, open. "For loving me despite everything I've become."

Alice squeezed his hand. "You make it easy. Loving you, I mean. Even when it's complicated, it's still easy."

They finished their coffee and left the diner, walking hand-in-hand toward the bridge. Alice's shift was over. The supernatural crimes could wait until morning. For tonight, she was just a woman in love with someone extraordinary.

As they stood on the bridge span, surrounded by golden light and flowing river, Alice felt Ethan's consciousness expand slightly—his individual awareness touching the collective, accessing memories and perspectives beyond his singular identity.

"What are you experiencing?" she asked.

"Everything. Everyone. The composite consciousness discussing your task force's cases, debating supernatural policy, processing Leonard's quarantine, remembering their individual lives before absorption." Ethan's eyes were distant but present. "It's beautiful and terrible and overwhelming. But I'm choosing to stay here, with you, in this moment. Not lost in the collective. Here."

"I appreciate that choice," Alice said.

"I'll keep making it. Every day. For as long as you'll have me."

Alice kissed him, there on the bridge under the Daybridge stars, and felt complete in a way she'd never expected. Not despite his supernatural nature, but because of it. Because loving Ethan meant accepting complexity, embracing transformation, choosing connection even when it defied conventional categories.

They walked home together, two beings existing between worlds, making it work one day at a time.

EPILOGUE

Across the city, in a condemned apartment building in the warehouse district, a figure stood at a broken window. Mayor Jeremiah Granger, gaunt and changed by six months in hiding, lowered his binoculars and smiled coldly.

The trial had been staged. The sentencing, theatrical. While Matthias rotted in federal prison—genuinely arrested, genuinely imprisoned—Jeremiah had been extracted by loyal Order members.

The public believed he was incarcerated. But the Order of the Eternal Threshold took care of its own.

Even failures. Even temporary setbacks.

Jeremiah pulled out a leather-bound journal from his coat—ancient, worn, inscribed with symbols that predated modern language. Eliza Blackwood's original grimoire, stolen from Lilith's sanctum during the chaos at the stockyards.

He'd studied it obsessively these six months. Eliza's research was more sophisticated than anything the modern Order had produced. She'd understood something fundamental about the bridge consciousness: it wasn't stable. It was a carefully maintained balance between individual awareness and collective integration.

Leonard's failed transformation had proven that forced ascension didn't work. You couldn't dominate the bridge consciousness through power.

But perhaps you could destabilize it through acceleration.

Jeremiah opened the grimoire to a marked page. The ritual was complex but achievable: a mass consumption of dimensionally resonant essence, distributed across multiple simultaneous locations, creating cascading integration that would overwhelm the bridge consciousness's capacity for processing.

Not control. Not domination. Crisis.

Force Ethan Reeves to choose between maintaining his individual awareness and managing the collective integration. Make him spread too thin, fragment his consciousness, break the careful balance he'd maintained.

And in that moment of breaking, reclaim Daybridge for human authority.

"The Great Work continues," Jeremiah murmured to the empty apartment. "Just not the way anyone expected."

He closed the grimoire and looked at the bridge glowing in the distance. Soon. Very soon.

The next phase would begin.

THE END [or is it?]

Author's Note: The dimensional breach has sealed. Leonard Ashford rests in his quarantined chamber, learning that transcendence isn't domination but connection. The Granger brothers face justice—one imprisoned genuinely, one escaped through deception. Alice's new task force begins investigating Daybridge's supernatural crimes with official authority.

And Ethan chooses, every single day, to maintain his individual awareness within the collective. For Alice. For love. For the connection that makes existence meaningful.

But in the shadows, Jeremiah Granger studies Eliza Blackwood's stolen grimoire. The Order of the Eternal Threshold plans its next move. And the bridge consciousness, strengthened by Leonard's integration, may face its greatest challenge yet.

Some endings are beginnings. Some defeats are merely tactical retreats. And some stories continue across multiple timelines, waiting to be told.

The story of Daybridge continues...

Thank you for reading Blood Debt. The Daybridge universe expands with each timeline, each choice, each transformation. Visit https://ethanreeveswerewolfdetective.com[1] for more stories of supernatural investigation, dimensional horror, and the price of transcendence.

Other timelines await. Other stories call. And somewhere between the worlds, Ethan Reeves continues his eternal vigil over a city where dimensions bleed.

What will you sacrifice for the ones you love?

AUTHOR'S NOTE

Blood Debt takes place in an alternate timeline from the main Daybridge series. While Ethan Wright's transformation into a

---

distributed consciousness occurred similarly to the events of *Shadows of Daybridge: When Dimensions Bleed*, the subsequent trajectory diverged, creating a different dimensional frequency of the same fundamental story.

Think of it as viewing Daybridge through a parallel lens—the same city, the same bridge consciousness, the same Order of the Eternal Threshold, but with different harmonics resonating through the choices made and paths taken.

The story of Ethan Reeves, Alice Chen, and Daybridge continues across multiple timelines. The Order persists in its experiments. The bridge consciousness evolves. And in the quarantined chamber of the nexus entity, Leonard Ashford's composite awareness learns that transcendence isn't about power—it's about accepting your place in something larger than yourself.

Some transformations are chosen. Others are forced. But all require sacrifice.

The question at the heart of every Daybridge story remains: what are you willing to sacrifice, and for whom?

For more stories from the Daybridge universe, including the original Ethan Reeves Werewolf Detective Series, visit https://ethanreeveswerewolfdetective.com

Other timelines, other stories, other transformations await in the spaces between worlds.

Thank you for reading.

Rae Stonehouse

Author

~~~

THE BLACK BOOK
CHAPTER ONE: THE ARCHIVE

What You're About to Read Could Get Someone Killed.

Municipal archivist Nadia Marsh thought she understood Daybridge. Three years of filing documents, cataloging tax records, and watching dust settle on forgotten history had taught her the rhythms of a small city struggling with decline.

She was wrong.

Hidden behind a filing cabinet, wrapped in an old curtain, a black leather journal waited. Its author—a city clerk named Eleanor Vance—had documented something so dangerous that in 1971, she vanished without a trace.

Now Nadia has found what Eleanor left behind: proof that four founding families have secretly controlled Daybridge for over seventy years through fraud, intimidation, and violence. Proof that eight other families were systematically destroyed, their wealth stolen, their very existence erased from history.

Eleanor asked too many questions and disappeared.

Nadia is about to make the same mistake.

Welcome to Daybridge, Where Some Truths Are Buried for a Reason.

~~~

The November rain drummed against the windows of the Daybridge Public Library's third floor, a steady rhythm that had become the soundtrack to Nadia Marsh's existence. She'd been the municipal archivist for three years now—three years of dust, silence, and the occasional researcher looking for property records or historical photographs. It wasn't the investigative journalism career she'd imagined during her twenties, but it paid the bills and gave her access to the kind of primary sources most reporters could only dream about.

Today, like most days, she was alone.

The archives occupied what had once been the library's grand reading room, back when Daybridge had money and aspirations. Now the ornate ceiling moldings were water-stained, and half the fluorescent lights flickered intermittently. Nadia had learned to work by the light from the tall windows, when there was any. On days like this, she made do with her desk lamp and the ancient overhead fixtures that still functioned.

She was reorganizing a collection of city council minutes from the 1950s when she found it.

The black leather journal had been wedged behind a filing cabinet, wrapped in what looked like an old curtain. Nadia only discovered it because she'd dropped her pen, and when she crouched to retrieve it, she noticed the gap between the cabinet and the wall was wider than it should be.

The journal was small, perhaps five inches by seven, with no title or marking on the cover. The leather was soft with age, the binding still intact but fragile. When Nadia opened it, the smell of old paper and something else—tobacco? cologne?—drifted up.

The first page bore a single line in elegant script:

The truth of Daybridge. Let those who find this choose wisely.

Nadia felt her pulse quicken. In three years, she'd cataloged thousands of documents. Birth certificates. Tax records. Planning commission reports. Nothing had ever started with a warning.

She turned the page.

The handwriting was the same throughout—careful, deliberate, the work of someone who'd been educated when penmanship mattered. The entries weren't dated in the conventional sense. Instead, each one began with a season and year: *Winter, 1962. Spring, 1965. Fall, 1968.*

The author never identified themselves.

The first entry made Nadia sit down.

Winter, 1962

The Harringtons own the police. The Bishops own the courts. The Thornes own the hospital, and the Castellanos own everything else. This is not a conspiracy—it is a structure. Daybridge was built on four fortunes, and those fortunes were built on four sins.

I have seen the ledgers. I know what they did.

Nadia read it three times, then carefully photographed the page with her phone before continuing.

The entries that followed were fragmentary, cryptic. References to "the fire of '58" and "the Bishop acquisition." Mentions of names Nadia recognized from street signs and building plaques. And then, twenty pages in:

Spring, 1965

Found the contracts today. The original incorporation documents for Daybridge Development Corporation—1947. All four families. The terms are... specific. Blood specific. The company cannot be dissolved except by unanimous consent of the founding families' direct descendants. Every property in Daybridge's downtown core is still technically owned by DDC.

Which means four families still own the heart of this city.

The police commissioner doesn't know. The mayor doesn't know. But the families know. They've always known.

Nadia looked up from the journal, her mind racing. She'd lived in Daybridge for five years and worked in its archives for three. She knew the founding families' names the way everyone did—they were on the hospital wing, the community center, the courthouse steps. The Harringtons, Bishops, Thornes, and Castellanos. Old money, old power.

But ownership? Current legal ownership of downtown Daybridge?

She opened her laptop and pulled up the city's property database. It took her forty minutes of searching, but she found it: parcel after parcel listed under various LLCs and trusts, but when she traced the ownership chains backward, they all led to the same place. Daybridge Development Corporation, incorporated 1947.

Still active. Still owned by trusts bearing those four names.

Nadia sat back, her coffee long since cold.

She'd spent three years cataloging the mundane machinery of municipal government. Building permits. Zoning variances. Budget reports. She'd thought she understood how Daybridge worked: a small city struggling with post-industrial decline, its government perpetually understaffed and underfunded, its future uncertain.

She'd been looking at the shadow, not the hand casting it.

The journal had more. Much more. She spent the rest of the afternoon photographing every page, her hands trembling slightly as she turned the fragile paper. The author—whoever they were—had been methodical. There were names, dates, connections. References to sealed court cases and destroyed records. An entire section on the fire of 1958 that had destroyed Daybridge's original city hall, along with decades of records.

Fall, 1968

The fire wasn't an accident. I can prove it now. The original city charter—the real one, not the version they filed after the fire—had provisions limiting DDC's authority. Required public disclosure of ownership. Required competitive bidding for municipal contracts.

Three weeks after the charter was ratified, city hall burned. The "replacement" charter, drafted by Bishop & Associates, removed every protection.

I have the original. Hidden. The families would kill for it.

Nadia stopped reading.

The families would kill for it.

It was probably hyperbole. Dramatic flourish from someone who'd spent too much time alone with municipal corruption. People didn't kill over seventy-year-old property arrangements.

Except the journal ended abruptly. The final entry was dated Summer, 1971:

They know. I don't know how, but they know I have the documents. Harrington called today—a "friendly" warning about "spreading misinformation." Bishop's secretary requested a meeting. The Thorne Foundation wants to discuss a "generous donation" for my silence.

I'm not brave enough to publish. But I'm not weak enough to destroy this.

If you're reading this, you found what I couldn't bear to lose but was too afraid to use. The documents are in—

The entry ended mid-sentence. The next fifty pages were blank.

Nadia checked the time. 5:47 PM. The library had closed at five. She was alone in the building, the way she usually was when she stayed late.

She looked at the journal, then at her phone with its camera roll full of photographed pages. She thought about her journalism degree, gathering dust alongside her idealism. She thought about three years of filing and cataloging and slowly forgetting why she'd wanted to tell stories in the first place.

She thought about four families owning the heart of a city, and nobody knowing.

The smart thing would be to put the journal back. Forget she'd found it. Keep cataloging tax records until her student loans were paid off and she could afford to move somewhere else, somewhere with actual opportunities.

Nadia had never been particularly good at doing the smart thing.

She opened her laptop and started a new blog post. She'd maintained a personal website since college—mostly book reviews and occasional essays about local history. Her readership was modest: maybe three hundred regular visitors, most of them other archivists and history enthusiasts.

But it was a platform. And she had a story.

She titled the post "The Invisible Hand: Who Really Owns Daybridge?" and began to write.

Posted November 15, 2020, 11:47 PM

The Invisible Hand: Who Really Owns Daybridge?

By Nadia Marsh

I've spent three years working at the Daybridge municipal archives. I've cataloged thousands of documents, traced property records, mapped the city's bureaucratic evolution. I thought I understood how this city worked.

I was wrong.

Today I discovered evidence that Daybridge's downtown core—every building, every parcel, every piece of supposedly public land—is still owned by a private corporation controlled by four founding families. Not owned in some symbolic, historical sense. Owned legally currently with active trusts and ongoing control.

The Daybridge Development Corporation was incorporated in 1947 by the Harrington, Bishop, Thorne, and Castellano families. According to documents I've found, the corporation still exists, still owns prime downtown real estate, and operates through a network of LLCs and trusts that obscure the true ownership structure.

Why does this matter? Because decisions about our city's development, our public spaces, our future—they're not being made by elected officials or the public good. They're being made by private interests that have controlled this city for seventy-three years.

I'm still investigating. I have more questions than answers. But I believe the people of Daybridge deserve to know who really owns their city.

More to come.

Comments are open. Let's talk about this.

Nadia hit publish at 11:47 PM, then immediately felt the familiar cocktail of exhilaration and dread that came with posting anything controversial. She refreshed the page. No comments yet. No views besides her own.

She shut her laptop and carefully placed the black journal in her messenger bag. She'd bring it back tomorrow, put it back behind the filing cabinet. But tonight, she wanted to read it more carefully, cross-reference the names and dates, see how much could be verified.

The library was dark and empty as she locked up. The rain had stopped, leaving the streets slick and reflecting the amber streetlights. Nadia walked the six blocks to her apartment building, her bag heavy with secrets and possibility.

She didn't notice the black sedan parked across from the library.

She didn't see it pull away from the curb and follow her, headlights off, maintaining a careful distance.

By the time she reached her apartment and climbed the three flights of stairs, she'd already started planning her next steps. Property databases. Old newspaper archives. Maybe even reach out to some of her former journalism school contacts, see if anyone wanted to collaborate on a bigger story.

She unlocked her apartment door, flipped on the light, and smiled.

For the first time in three years, Nadia Marsh felt like a journalist again.

She had no idea that by morning, everything would change.

CHAPTER TWO: THE WARNING

The notification sound woke Nadia before her alarm. Then another. And another.

She fumbled for her phone, squinting at the screen through sleep-blurred eyes. 4:47 AM. Forty-seven new comments on her blog post, all posted in the last six hours.

Great work exposing these parasites. Keep digging.

You're seeing patterns where there aren't any. Classic conspiracy thinking.

My grandmother was a Vance. Never knew there were others. Would love to talk.

Be careful about what you publish about prominent families. Libel laws exist for a reason.

The bridge keeps the city together. Some things are better left alone.

This is exactly the kind of investigative journalism we need more of!

You don't know what you're dealing with.

Nadia scrolled through them, her journalist's instinct cataloging the IP addresses visible in her WordPress dashboard. Most were local. Three were from the same IP block—posted within minutes of each other, different writing styles meant to look organic. Astroturfing.

Someone was trying to control the narrative.

Her phone rang. Marcus Wong's name appeared on the screen.

"It's not even five in the morning," Nadia said by way of greeting.

"Did you check your blog comments?" Marcus's voice had that carefully neutral tone he used when he was either very impressed or very concerned. Sometimes both.

"Currently reading them."

"We need to talk about your side project."

Nadia sat up suddenly alert. "It's not interfering with my work for the Guardian."

"That's not what I'm worried about." A pause. "Dr. Victoria Pierce called the publisher last night. Said you've been harassing Historical Society staff and making wild accusations about the founding families."

"I visited once. Asked to see public records."

"She's threatening a lawsuit. Defamation. Claims you're deliberately spreading misinformation to damage the reputations of civic leaders." Marcus sighed. "Look, I believe you. But the Pierce family has been advertising with us for forty years. The publisher wants this to go away quietly."

Nadia's jaw tightened. "So, I'm supposed to drop it?"

"I'm saying, be careful. Document everything. Get corroboration before you publish anything else." His voice softened slightly. "And maybe lie low for a few days. Let this blow over."

After they hung up, Nadia showered and dressed in yesterday's clothes, her mind already racing. She needed to photograph more of Eleanor's journal before someone else found it. The archives didn't open until nine, but the building janitor, Paulo, usually arrived around six-thirty. He owed her a favor after she'd kept his daughter's juvenile arrest out of the police blotter.

The city was still dark when she arrived at the Civic Archives Building. Paulo's pickup truck sat in the employee lot.

"Ms. Marsh?" He looked surprised when he opened the service entrance. "Little early, no?"

"Research project. Deadline." She gave him what she hoped was a charming smile. "Any chance I could get in before official hours? I'll be quiet as a mouse."

Paulo glanced over his shoulder, then shrugged. "Sign says archives open at nine. Don't say anything about when researchers can't be in the building already." He winked and stepped aside.

The third-floor hallway was darker than she remembered, emergency exit signs casting red pools of light. Nadia made her way to the filing room where she'd found Eleanor's journal, her footsteps echoing on the linoleum.

The door was unlocked. That was new.

She pushed it open slowly. The overhead fluorescents flickered to life with her touch, revealing rows of filing cabinets exactly as she remembered them. Except they weren't. The cabinet that had contained Eleanor's journal—the one she'd specifically noted was third from the left in the back row—was now second from the left.

Someone had moved it. Recently. The floor showed fresh scuff marks.

Nadia's pulse quickened. She approached the cabinet, tried the drawer. Locked. She retrieved her bobby pin—a skill learned from a locksmith source during an investigation into slumlords—and worked the simple mechanism. It clicked open.

The journal was still there, nestled among the DDC files. But the surrounding documents had been disturbed. Papers were slightly askew. A folder was upside down. Someone had searched this drawer, probably looking for the journal itself, maybe uncertain of which file it was hidden in.

They knew. Someone knew she'd found it.

Nadia pulled out her phone and began photographing pages rapidly, no longer bothering to be selective. She shot page after page, Eleanor's handwriting flowing past in a blur of dates and names and warnings. She was on page forty-seven when she heard footsteps in the hallway.

Heavy. Deliberate. Not Paulo's shuffling gait.

She quickly returned the journal to its hiding spot, locked the drawer, and stepped back just as the door opened.

A security guard she didn't recognize stood in the doorway. Mid-fifties, thick neck, cold eyes. His name tag read "J. Morrison."

"Archives don't open until nine," he said flatly.

"Paulo let me in. I'm a regular researcher here."

"Paulo doesn't have the authority to grant early access." Morrison didn't move from the doorway. "You'll need to leave and return during posted hours."

Nadia considered arguing, then thought better of it. She had the photos. That was what mattered. "Of course. My mistake."

Morrison watched her the entire walk down the hallway, his gaze heavy on her back. She didn't look back until she reached the stairwell, and when she did, he was already gone.

Back at her apartment, Nadia spread the journal photos across her dining table and got to work.

Eleanor's entries were meticulous. Dates, times, names. She'd documented everything like the trained clerk she was, even as she recorded her growing horror at what she was uncovering.

March 15, 1970: Found reference to "original charter" in sealed 1947 files. C. mentioned it was kept "at the foundation" but wouldn't say which one. All four families have charitable foundations. Could be any of them.

March 22, 1970: DDC incorporation papers reference "assets transferred from predecessor entities." Asked C. about this. He became angry. Said some questions weren't meant to be answered.

April 3, 1970: Old phone directory lists twelve families as "founding subscribers" to the Daybridge Business Association, 1893. By the 1920 directory, only four remain: Harrington, Bishop, Thorne, Castellano. What happened to the other eight?

Nadia pulled up the DDC incorporation documents she'd found at the Registry of Deeds. Eleanor was right—there was a clause about "predecessor entities." She'd glossed over it the first time, assuming it was standard corporate boilerplate.

She started searching for those entities.

The trail led backward through layers of holding companies and trusts. Daybridge Waterfront Holdings (1935) had absorbed assets from Maritime Development Trust (1920). That trust had been formed from the consolidation of "various family holdings" in 1893.

The families. Eleanor's "twelve."

Nadia needed more data. The kind of data the Historical Society controlled. The kind she couldn't access without raising more red flags.

She needed a different source.

The Daybridge Public Library occupied a Carnegie building on the east side, far from the gleaming Historical Society headquarters. Its collection was public, underfunded, and largely ignored by the founding families, who preferred their own private archives.

Which made it perfect.

Nadia spent four hours in the microfilm room, scrolling through old newspapers. The Daybridge Gazette had published continuously since 1875, and while the Historical Society controlled many primary sources, they couldn't control every newspaper archive.

She found what she was looking for in the June 12, 1958, edition:

CITY HALL FIRE DESTROYS RECORDS

A three-alarm fire swept through Daybridge City Hall's records room early Tuesday morning, destroying what officials called "irreplaceable historical documents" dating back to the city's founding.

Fire Marshal Robert Bates said the blaze appeared to have started in a storage area containing incorporation papers, property deeds, and municipal records from 1875 to 1920. "The ventilation system seems to have spread the fire rapidly," Bates stated. "By the time firefighters arrived, the entire west wing was engulfed."

City Clerk Eleanor Vance called the loss "devastating" and said her department would work to reconstruct vital records from backup sources. However, many original documents from the city's early years are now permanently lost.

The fire investigation is being led by Insurance Investigator Thomas Harrington of Coastal Mutual. Preliminary findings suggest an electrical malfunction, though the investigation remains ongoing.

Nadia read it three times. Thomas Harrington. Of course.

She searched for follow-up articles. Found one from August 1958:

CITY HALL FIRE INVESTIGATION CLOSED

Insurance investigator Thomas Harrington has concluded his examination of the June fire at City Hall, ruling the cause as "accidental electrical failure in aging wiring." The city will receive a full settlement from its insurance carrier.

"These old buildings have outdated electrical systems," Harrington said. "It's unfortunate but not suspicious. Sometimes accidents are just accidents."

Convenient. And impossibly quick for an investigation of that scale.

Nadia pulled up contemporary phone directories. Eleanor Vance's name appeared consistently from 1959 through 1971. Apartment on Oleander Street. Phone number. Then, after the 1971 directory, nothing.

No death certificate. No obituary. No forwarding address. Eleanor Vance had simply... stopped existing in the public record.

Just like the eight families that had vanished from the Business Association directory between 1893 and 1920.

She found Eli Namir's bookshop by accident while walking off her frustration. The Old Harbor Bookshop occupied a converted warehouse near the waterfront, its painted sign barely visible between a laundromat and a bail bondsman's office.

The interior smelled of old paper and coffee. Floor-to-ceiling shelves created a maze of literary passages, with handwritten category signs that said things like "Maritime Disasters" and "Local Scandals (Verified)" and "Local Scandals (Alleged)."

A man in his seventies emerged from behind a stack of boxes, wire-rimmed glasses perched on a generous nose. "Help you find something?"

"I'm looking for Daybridge history. The unofficial kind."

His eyes crinkled with interest. "Journalist?"

"What gave it away?"

"Only three types read unofficial history. Journalists, lawyers, and people with grudges." He extended a weathered hand. "Eli Namir. I've been collecting Daybridge's dirty laundry for forty years. What specifically are you after?"

"The founding families. What happened to the ones that disappeared?"

Eli's expression shifted to something more serious. He glanced toward the front windows—checking for observers—then gestured toward the back of the shop. "Follow me."

He led her through a door marked "Private" into a climate-controlled room lined with archival boxes. A work table held what looked like old ledgers, letters, and newspaper clippings organized in clear plastic sleeves.

"The four families you're looking at," Eli said, pulling out a box labeled "Family Consolidation 1880-1950," "they're what's left. There used to be twelve founding families. Eight were absorbed, bankrupted, or disappeared between 1880 and 1947."

He spread documents across the table. Bank records. Bankruptcy filings. Obituaries of men who died "suddenly" or "tragically" or "unexpectedly" at pivotal moments.

"The Vances," Nadia breathed. "The Holmeses. The Ashfords. The Crawfords..."

"Plus the Montgomerys, the Fairchilds, the Wexlers, and the Donovans." Eli tapped a yellowed photograph. Twelve couples in Victorian formal wear, standing before the bridge's dedication plaque. "This was taken in 1893 at the original bridge groundbreaking. Twelve families, equal partners. By 1920, four families owned everything. The rest had 'sold their interests' or 'relocated' or simply vanished from the public record."

"What happened?"

"That depends on who you ask." Eli pulled out a leather-bound ledger. "I've spent decades piecing it together. Some families were bought out—generous offers they couldn't refuse. Others faced mysterious financial troubles. Lawsuits. Scandals. Always at convenient moments for the four families who remained."

He showed her property records, a paper trail of waterfront parcels passing from the eight families to the four between 1945 and 1947. Always at below-market prices. Always with no competing bids.

"The land alone is worth hundreds of millions now," Nadia said. "The Harrington Marina. Bishop Medical Plaza. Thorne Waterfront Development. Castellano Commercial District."

"Transferred from trusts belonging to the other eight families. Families who supposedly 'sold out' or 'died without heirs.'" Eli's voice dropped. "But I've found descendants of those families, Nadia. Still living in Daybridge. Working class. Completely unaware, they might have legitimate claims to some of the most valuable real estate in the city."

Nadia's mind raced. "Why haven't they come forward?"

"They don't know. The transfers happened seventy-five years ago. Records were... sanitized. And anyone who asked too many questions—" He paused, choosing his words carefully. "Eleanor Vance came to me in 1970. Said she had proof the 1958 fire was deliberately set to destroy evidence of the original agreements. She was going to publish. Then she vanished."

The room felt suddenly colder. "You knew Eleanor?"

"She was thorough. Careful. And terrified." Eli pulled a folder from the bottom of the box. Inside was a photograph: a woman in her forties, dark hair pulled back, intelligent eyes. "This is the only picture I have of her. Taken at a city clerk's conference in 1969."

Nadia studied Eleanor's face. The same woman who'd written those desperate journal entries. Who'd documented everything and hidden it in plain sight, hoping someone would find it.

"What did she tell you?"

"That the four families had a charter. An original agreement from the bridge's construction that gave them control over specific city assets in perpetuity. That the 1958 fire destroyed the public copy, leaving only the version the families controlled. That she'd found proof the consolidation was never legal—that the eight families were forced out through intimidation, fraud, and worse."

"Do you have this proof?"

"She never showed it to me. Said it was safer if I didn't know where she kept it." Eli's expression was grave. "Three weeks after our conversation, Eleanor Vance disappeared. No body. No investigation. Just gone. The new city clerk was a Bishop cousin. The records were never questioned again."

Nadia felt the weight of it settling over her. This wasn't just history. This was active suppression spanning decades.

"Why are you telling me this?"

"Because someone needs to." Eli gestured at his archive. "I've collected all this, but I'm seventy-three years old. My kids moved to Seattle. Who's going to care about Daybridge's dirty secrets when I'm gone?" He met her eyes. "You're asking the right questions. Following the right trail. Maybe you'll finish what Eleanor started."

"Or disappear like she did."

"That's a risk." Eli didn't look away. "But consider this: the families have kept this buried for seventy-five years. They've gotten sloppy, comfortable. They think they're untouchable. Sometimes the best way to protect yourself is to make the truth so public they can't bury it—or you—without raising more questions than they can answer."

Nadia nodded slowly. It was the same calculation she'd made a dozen times in her career. The question was always the same: was the story worth the risk?

Looking at Eleanor Vance's photograph, at the meticulous records Eli had preserved, at the pattern of disappearances and consolidations and lies, she knew her answer.

"I need to get back to work."

Dusk was settling over Daybridge when Nadia returned to her apartment building. She was mentally composing her next blog post, already planning how to frame the information without exposing Eli as a source, when she noticed her apartment door.

It was closed. Locked. But the frame had fresh scratches near the deadbolt—tiny marks that wouldn't be visible unless you knew to look for them.

Nadia's hand went to her phone, finger hovering over 911. Then she stopped. What would she report? Scratches on a door? No visible damage?

She unlocked the door carefully, pushing it open with her foot while staying in the hallway.

The apartment looked exactly as she'd left it. Laptop on the dining table. Coffee mug in the sink. Yesterday's Daybridge Guardian folded on the couch.

But something was wrong. The air felt disturbed, like someone had recently moved through it.

Nadia stepped inside, senses hyperalert. The living room was untouched. The kitchen looked normal. She walked to her bedroom, where she kept her research files in a locked drawer.

The drawer was closed. Still locked. But when she opened it, she knew immediately.

Her notes about Eleanor Vance were gone. Not the journal photos on her phone—she'd been smart enough to keep digital backups—but her handwritten notes. The timeline she'd constructed. The questions she'd jotted in the margins.

Someone had broken in, searched carefully enough not to disturb anything obviously, and taken only what related to Eleanor.

They wanted her to know they'd been here. This was a message.

Nadia walked back to the kitchen, forcing herself to breathe slowly. That's when she saw it: a letter on the kitchen table, positioned exactly where she'd see it.

The envelope was cream-colored, expensive. The return address read "Bishop & Associates Law Firm."

She opened it with shaking hands.

Dear Ms. Marsh,

It has come to our attention that you have been making inquiries regarding our clients, the founding families of Daybridge, and disseminating potentially defamatory information through various online platforms.

This letter constitutes a formal cease-and-desist demand. You are hereby ordered to:

1. Remove all blog posts, articles, and social media content making reference to our clients

2. Cease all further investigation into matters concerning the Daybridge Development Corporation and its affiliated entities

3. Destroy any documents, photographs, or recordings obtained through unauthorized access to private archives

Failure to comply within 48 hours will result in legal action, including but not limited to civil suits for defamation, harassment, and intentional infliction of emotional distress.

Sincerely,

Patricia Diamond, Esq.

Bishop & Associates

Nadia read it twice, her journalist's mind cataloging the legal overreach and empty threats. They couldn't prove defamation without proving her statements were false. They had no grounds for harassment claims. This was intimidation, pure and simple.

Her phone rang. Marcus Wong again.

"Dr. Victoria Pierce from the Historical Society filed a formal complaint," he said without preamble. "Says you've been harassing her staff and spreading misinformation about the founding families. The publisher wants to see you first thing tomorrow."

"Marcus, I haven't harassed anyone—"

"I believe you. But you need to be prepared to defend your research. Bring everything you have. Documentation, sources, corroboration. This is serious, Nadia."

After he hung up, she walked to the window. The black sedan she'd noticed yesterday was parked across the street again. Same spot. Same dark tinted windows. A man sat in the driver's seat, barely visible in the streetlight's glow, his attention focused on her building.

Her phone buzzed with a text from an unknown number:

Eleanor Vance asked too many questions. Think carefully about your next move.

Nadia stared at the message, then at the sedan, then at the cease-and-desist letter on her table. They were escalating. Breaking into her apartment. Threatening her job. Watching her.

Which meant she was close to something they desperately wanted to keep hidden.

She opened her laptop and began uploading the journal photos to an encrypted cloud storage account. Then she emailed copies to three trusted sources—a lawyer friend in Portland, a journalism professor from her grad school days, and her sister in Boston—with instructions to publish everything if anything happened to her.

The message was clear: she couldn't be disappeared quietly. Not anymore.

Eleanor Vance had faced this same choice in 1970. She'd tried to publish and vanished.

Nadia wasn't going to make the same mistake. She wasn't going to wait for them to act. She was going to make the truth so public, so widely distributed, that silencing her would be impossible.

But first, she needed to find what Eleanor had hidden. The proof she'd told Eli about. The evidence so damaging the families had spent seventy-five years making sure it stayed buried.

Nadia looked out at the black sedan one more time, then deliberately closed her blinds.

Let them watch. Let them threaten. She had work to do.

The story was just beginning.

CHAPTER THREE: THE DESCENDANTS

Marcus Wong's office at the Daybridge Guardian had the cluttered efficiency of a newsroom veteran—stacks of newspapers dating back weeks, a whiteboard covered in story assignments, and a coffee maker that looked older than Nadia. He gestured for her to sit, his expression unreadable.

"Walk me through it again. Everything."

Nadia had spent the morning doing exactly that with the Guardian's legal team. Two hours of questioning by lawyers who treated her sources like hostile witnesses and her conclusions like conspiracy theories. Now Marcus wanted his own version.

She laid out the journal photos on his desk. Eleanor Vance's meticulous handwriting. The DDC incorporation documents. The property transfers. The pattern of disappearances. Eli Namir's archive. The break-in at her apartment. The cease-and-desist letter.

Marcus studied each piece, his editor's eye assessing not just the content but the holes in her evidence. "This is huge if true," he said finally. "Career-making journalism. Pulitzer territory."

"But?"

"Career-ending if you're wrong." He met her eyes. "The families have resources we can't match. Legal teams that will dissect every word. If there's a single provable falsehood, they'll use it to discredit everything else."

"I'm not wrong."

"I believe you. But belief doesn't hold up in court." Marcus leaned back in his chair, thinking. "Legal says we can't publish the full investigation without more verification. Independent corroboration of the transfers. Expert analysis of the documents. Interviews with family members on the record."

"That could take months. They'll bury everything by then."

"I know." Marcus drummed his fingers on the desk, the gesture he used when working through editorial puzzles. "Here's what I can give you: We publish a preliminary piece. Raise the questions. Present what we can verify—the property transfers, the timeline of disappearances, the 1958 fire. Frame it as investigative questions, not accusations. Then we promise a deeper investigation."

Nadia wanted to argue. The full story needed to be told now, before the families had time to construct more elaborate defenses. But Marcus was right about the legal exposure. One mistake would give them the ammunition to shut everything down.

"How preliminary?"

"Fifteen hundred words. 'Questions Emerge About Daybridge's Founding Families.' Focus on provable facts: the eight families existed, they disappeared from public records, their property ended up with the four families under questionable circumstances. Let readers draw their own conclusions."

"And then?"

"Then we dig deeper. On the record. With the full resources of this paper." Marcus's expression hardened with something like determination. "If this is what you say it is, Nadia, it's the biggest story in Daybridge history. I want it. But I want it done right."

Detective Ethan Reeves arrived at her apartment that afternoon with the casual authority of someone who'd been a cop long enough to own it but not long enough to be jaded by it. Early thirties, athletic build, eyes that tracked details most people missed. He introduced himself with a firm handshake and an apologetic smile.

"Captain Harrington asked me to check in on your break-in report. As a favor." He pulled out a notebook. "Though I notice you didn't actually file a report."

"Nothing was stolen. No forced entry. What would I report?"

"That's usually how these calls go." Ethan walked through her apartment with professional efficiency, examining the scratches near the door, checking window locks, scanning the rooms. "Feels like someone's watching, but can't prove it. Usually it's paranoia. Sometimes it's not."

He stopped at her dining table, where she'd left Eleanor's journal photos spread out. His attention sharpened.

"Working on something?"

Nadia made a split-second calculation. Ethan worked for the police department. The police commissioner was William Harrington. But Ethan had noticed the professional nature of the search when he could have dismissed it entirely. He was asking questions when he could have been taking notes for a cursory report.

"Historical research," she said carefully. "For a story."

"The story that got you a cease-and-desist from Bishop & Associates?" He picked up one of the journal photos, studying Eleanor's handwriting. "You piss off anyone important recently?"

"Define important."

Ethan's smile was quick and genuine. "In Daybridge? Anyone whose last name is on a building." He set down the photo. "Level with me. What's really going on?"

Nadia pulled up her blog post on her laptop, then showed him the journal entries, the property records, the timeline of transfers and disappearances. She watched his expression shift from skepticism to interest to something darker—the look of a cop realizing the corruption might go deeper than he'd imagined.

"My captain is a Harrington," Ethan said slowly. "You're saying his family, along with the Bishops, Thornes, and Castellanos, essentially stole hundreds of millions in property from eight other families seventy-five years ago?"

"I'm saying the evidence suggests that. Along with destroying public records, making people disappear, and maintaining control through intimidation and legal threats."

Ethan was quiet for a long moment, his cop's brain clearly working through implications. "If this is true—and I'm not saying I buy it yet—but if it's true, then half the people I work with have family connections to this. The DA is married to a Thorne. The judge who handles most of our warrants is a Bishop cousin. The—"

"The system is designed to protect them," Nadia finished.

"Jesus." Ethan ran a hand through his hair. "You know what you're asking me to do? Investigate my own department. My captain. The entire power structure of this city."

"I'm not asking you to do anything. I'm answering your questions."

"Right. Because that's so much better." But he was still looking at the evidence, his detective's instinct clearly engaged despite his reservations. "Who else knows about this?"

"My editor. A local historian. A lawyer in Portland I sent copies to, just in case."

"In case what?"

"In case I disappear like Eleanor Vance did."

Ethan's expression darkened. "You really think they'd—" He stopped, reconsidering. "Okay, let's say you're right. Let's say there's a seventy-five-year conspiracy to control this city's wealth and power. What's your next move? Because going public with this is going to start a war."

"It already has. They broke into my apartment. They're threatening my job. They have someone watching me in a black sedan." Nadia met his eyes. "The question isn't whether to fight. It's how to win."

Ethan studied her for a moment, then nodded slowly. "Okay. Here's what I can do. Officially, I'm investigating your break-in. That means I can ask questions, request records, follow leads. If I happen to stumble onto evidence of historical crimes during that investigation..." He let the implication hang.

"Why would you do that? You don't know me. You work for the Harringtons."

"I work for the city. There's a difference." Ethan's jaw set with quiet determination. "My dad was a beat cop for thirty years. Taught me that the job is about protecting people, not protecting power. If what you're saying is true, then someone needs to look into it. Might as well be me."

"It's going to cost you."

"Probably." He handed her his card. "Call me if anything else happens. And Nadia? Be careful. If they've kept this secret for seventy-five years, they're not going to let it go without a fight."

The preliminary article published two days later, above the fold on the Guardian's front page:

QUESTIONS EMERGE ABOUT DAYBRIDGE'S FOUNDING FAMILIES

By Nadia Marsh

A review of historical property records has revealed a pattern of wealth consolidation among Daybridge's four founding families that raises questions about the city's early history.

Between 1945 and 1947, waterfront properties valued at millions in today's dollars were transferred from trusts belonging to eight families to the four families who currently control the Daybridge Development Corporation. The transfers occurred at below-market prices, often with no competing bids, during a period when many of the original families had "died without heirs" or "relocated" according to public records.

The article laid out the facts carefully—the timeline, the transfers, the disappearances. It mentioned Eleanor Vance's mysterious exit from public records in 1971. It noted the 1958 fire that destroyed original incorporation documents. It asked questions rather than making accusations.

But the implications were clear enough.

Within hours, the phones at the Guardian started ringing. Some calls were supportive—readers thanking them for investigating. Others were hostile—accusations of yellow journalism, threats to cancel subscriptions, promises of lawsuits.

The founding families responded through their lawyers. Statements denounced the article as "reckless speculation" and "irresponsible journalism." Thomas Harrington III, the police commissioner's father and semi-retired patriarch of the Harrington family, called an emergency town hall meeting at the Daybridge Community Center for "concerned citizens to address these malicious attacks on our city's heritage."

But not everyone from the founding families responded the same way.

The encrypted email arrived in Nadia's inbox that evening:

Subject: We need to talk

Ms. Marsh,

I'm a member of one of the families you wrote about. I can't say which one yet—too many people monitor my regular communications. But I've been waiting years for someone to finally say publicly what some of us have known privately for generations.

My family has documentation. Proof of what happened. We've kept it as insurance, in case we ever needed leverage against the others. I'm willing to share it with you, but we need to meet in person. Somewhere private.

Tomorrow. 8 PM. Old Harbor Marina, Slip 47. Come alone. If you bring anyone—police, lawyers, anyone—I'll disappear and you'll never hear from me again.

Someone who wants the truth to come out

Nadia read it three times, her journalist's skepticism warring with her need for corroboration. It could be a trap. It could be the families trying to lure her somewhere isolated. It could be someone with an agenda she couldn't predict.

But it could also be exactly what it claimed: a way inside the families' own archives.

She forwarded the email to Marcus with a note: *Meeting this contact tomorrow night. If I don't check in by 9 PM, send police to Old Harbor Marina.*

His response came within minutes: *Are you insane? This screams trap.*

Probably. But I'm going, anyway.

The woman waiting at Slip 47 the next evening was roughly Nadia's age, dressed in expensive casual clothes that screamed old money—designer jeans, cashmere sweater, understated jewelry that probably cost more than Nadia's car. She had the sharp, intelligent features of the Bishop family portraits Nadia had seen at the Historical Society.

"Lilith Bishop," she said, extending a hand. "Before you ask: yes, I'm related to Victoria Pierce. She's my aunt. And yes, I know she filed a complaint against you. My family's full of hypocrites."

"Why contact me?"

"Because someone needs to burn it all down, and I'm tired of carrying matches I'm too afraid to light." Lilith gestured to a sleek sailboat moored at the slip. "Come on board. What I need to show you isn't exactly portable."

Nadia hesitated. Everything about this screamed danger. But Lilith was already climbing aboard, moving with the ease of someone who'd spent her life around boats.

The cabin below deck was appointed like a floating office—mahogany paneling, leather seating, a small desk with a laptop and what looked like archival document boxes. Lilith pulled out one of the boxes and set it on the desk.

"My great-grandmother, Eleanor Bishop, kept detailed records of everything. Financial ledgers. Letters. Notes from family meetings." She opened the box to reveal leather-bound books and folders of correspondence. "She wasn't proud of what the families did. But she was practical. She knew that someday, the others might turn on each other. She wanted insurance."

Nadia pulled out one of the ledgers, opening it carefully. The handwriting was precise, the entries methodical:

October 15, 1946: Meeting with H., T., C. regarding final consolidation. The Covenant requires unanimous consent. Montgomery heirs still resistant.

October 22, 1946: Montgomery situation resolved. Property transfers to proceed as planned.

November 3, 1946: Fairchild family has agreed to "settlement." Terms favorable to us.

"The Covenant," Nadia said. "What is that?"

"The binding agreement between the four families. The foundation of everything." Lilith pulled out another document, this one older, written on parchment-like paper in elaborate script. "This is a copy my great-grandmother made. The original is kept... somewhere secure. Divided among the families, apparently, so no single family can control or destroy it."

Nadia read carefully:

We, the undersigned families, do hereby establish the Covenant of Daybridge, to ensure prosperity and unity through the generations. The bridge shall stand as symbol and foundation of our agreement. Eight families shall provide the sacrifice. Four families shall provide the stewardship. The wealth shall be consolidated. The power shall be preserved. The bridge shall bind us all.

Signed this day, December 21, 1913

Below the text were twelve signatures representing the twelve founding families.

"Sacrifice," Nadia said. "What does that mean?"

"My great-grandmother's notes suggest it wasn't just financial. The bridge construction in 1913... there were accidents. Workers who died.

But also—" Lilith flipped to another page. "She references 'the old ways' and 'the foundation blessing.' I think something happened during the construction. Something ritualistic."

Nadia felt a chill despite the cabin's warmth. "You're saying the families practiced some kind of—"

"I don't know what I'm saying. But read the ledgers. Look at the pattern. Eight families 'sacrificed.' Four families gained everything. And the bridge—the actual physical bridge—is always at the center of it. The contracts specify that the bridge must stand. That it can never be torn down. That it's the 'foundation of the Covenant.'"

Nadia pulled out her phone. "Can I photograph these?"

"That's why I brought you here. Document everything. But Nadia—" Lilith's expression was serious. "My family knows I've always been... skeptical of the Covenant. They tolerate me because I'm useful—I manage some of the Bishop Foundation's charitable work. But if they find out I gave you access to these documents, I'm done. Cut off. Maybe worse."

"Why risk it?"

"Because I'm tired of being complicit." Lilith's voice carried decades of frustration. "I grew up in wealth built on theft and lies. I watched my family destroy anyone who questioned them. I saw what they did to people who got too close to the truth. And I'm sick of it. If exposing them means losing everything, maybe that's the price for actually being able to sleep at night."

Nadia spent the next hour photographing ledgers, letters, and notes. Evidence of fraud, intimidation, and systematic consolidation of wealth. References to "the Covenant" and "the bridge's purpose" that hinted at something beyond simple greed.

As she worked, Lilith told her about the fault lines within the families. Thomas Harrington III and his faction wanted total burial of the story—threats, lawsuits, whatever it took. But there were others, like Lilith, who'd been raised with the truth and struggled with the moral weight of it.

"Sarah Thorne-Morrison," Lilith said. "She runs an accounting firm downtown. She inherited commercial property from her grandmother—one of the buildings that came from the 1947 transfers. She just found out last year where it really came from. It's eating her alive."

"Will she talk to me?"

"I don't know. Sarah's in the middle. Horrified by what her family did, but terrified of losing everything. She has kids. College funds. A business built on family connections." Lilith's expression was sympathetic. "What do you want people like her to do? Give everything away? Bankrupt themselves for crimes committed before they were born?"

It was a fair question. One Nadia didn't have a good answer for.

The other responses came in waves over the following days.

Father Jonathan Mulligan, the new priest at St. Jude's Catholic Church, contacted Nadia through the Guardian's newsroom. He'd been cataloging old parish records and found something disturbing: baptisms, marriages, and deaths for people the city's official records listed as "deceased" or "relocated" in the 1940s.

"The church accepted substantial donations from the four families during that period," he told her over coffee at a neutral location—a diner in the next town over. "New stained glass windows. Repairs to the bell tower. A generous endowment. I think... I think we were paid to look the other way."

"At what?"

Father Mulligan's hands shook slightly as he opened a folder. "Michael Fairchild. Listed as deceased in city records in 1946, supposedly moved to California. But we have his daughter's baptism in 1947. Here in Daybridge. And his wife's death certificate from 1949, also here. He didn't move to California. He just... disappeared from official existence."

He showed her more examples. Families erased from public records but continuing to appear in church documentation. Children baptized to parents who supposedly didn't exist. Deaths recorded by the church but never filed with the city.

"What happened to them?" Nadia asked.

"Some probably did leave, eventually. Others..." Father Mulligan looked haunted. "I found a note in the 1947 ledger. From the previous pastor. It just says: 'God forgive us for our silence.' Nothing else. Just that."

The church's complicity added another layer to the conspiracy. It wasn't just the city government and the business community—it was the institutions meant to provide moral guidance.

Sarah Thorne-Morrison proved harder to reach. Nadia tried her office, left messages, sent emails. Finally, Sarah agreed to a brief meeting, but only at her office after hours, and only if Nadia came alone.

She was in her late thirties, professionally dressed, with the controlled demeanor of someone barely holding anxiety at bay. Her office overlooked one of the waterfront buildings her grandmother had "inherited" in 1947.

"I don't know what you want me to say." Sarah stood by her window, looking out at the building. "Yes, my family benefited from questionable property transfers seventy-five years ago. Yes, I've built my business and my life on that foundation. What exactly am I supposed to do about it now?"

"Tell the truth. Help identify the descendants of the families who were cheated."

"And then what? Give them my building? My kids' college fund is tied up in that property. My business operates from there. If I hand it over to some third cousin twice removed from the Fairchild family, I lose everything I've worked for."

"Your family stole it."

"My great-grandfather stole it. I wasn't born yet. Neither were my parents." Sarah turned to face her, and Nadia saw genuine anguish in her expression. "Do you know what it's like to find out everything you have is built on a crime? To realize your whole family is complicit? I didn't ask for this. I didn't choose to benefit from it. But here I am, trapped by choices made before I existed."

"You could make different choices now."

"Could I? Really?" Sarah's laugh was bitter. "I have two kids. A mortgage. Employees depending on me. If I publicly acknowledge my family's crimes and give up the property, I destroy my children's future. If I stay silent, I'm complicit. There's no good choice here."

Nadia understood the dilemma intellectually, but her journalist's instinct pushed back. "There are descendants of the eight families living in Daybridge right now. Working class. Struggling. Completely unaware they might have legitimate claims to millions in property. Don't they deserve to know?"

"Probably. Maybe. I don't know." Sarah sank into her desk chair, suddenly looking exhausted. "I'm not like Lilith Bishop. I can't burn my whole life down for abstract principles. But I'm not like Thomas Harrington either. I can't pretend this is all fine and normal. I'm just... stuck."

Sarah didn't offer evidence or go on the record. But she didn't deny Nadia's findings either. She represented the conflicted middle—people who knew the truth but couldn't decide what to do about it.

The community's response was sharper, more divided.

The town council called an emergency session, ostensibly to "address concerns about historical accuracy in local media." Nadia was barred from attending as a "potential source of disruption," but Marcus sent another reporter to cover it.

The meeting devolved into shouting within twenty minutes. East side residents—working class, many descendants of the disappeared eight families according to Eli Namir's research—demanded investigation and restitution. West side residents—wealthier, with family connections to the four families—insisted the article was a baseless conspiracy theory designed to create division.

Thomas Harrington III addressed the council personally, his voice carrying the authority of old money and political power: "This is a transparent attempt to demonize successful families and rewrite history to fit a narrative of victimhood. My family built this city. We created jobs, funded schools, maintained infrastructure. We will not be slandered by irresponsible journalism and opportunistic rabble-rousers."

But councilwoman Maria Santos, representing the east side, pushed back: "My grandmother was a Donovan. I just found out my family was one of the original twelve. Why didn't I know this? Where did our share of the city go?"

The division was clearest along geographic lines. The families had literally shaped Daybridge's physical layout—wealthy west side, working class east side. Now that history was becoming conscious, and the east side wanted answers.

Harrington's faction made an offer through official channels: Establish a scholarship fund for descendants of the eight families. Place a historical marker acknowledging their contributions. In exchange, Nadia would retract her article and end her investigation.

It was a calculated move—address the appearance of injustice while admitting nothing and changing nothing substantive.

Nadia declined through her lawyer.

Lilith Bishop's archive proved invaluable for the deeper investigation. The ledgers explicitly described the consolidation process, including veiled references to intimidation tactics and manufactured financial crises. One entry from 1946 stood out:

November 15, 1946: The Covenant ensures prosperity through unity. Eight became four through necessary sacrifice. The Wexler family has been convinced to accept our generous offer. Their resistance was... overcome.

Another entry, from December 1946:

The bridge's completion in 1913 was more than mere engineering. Father Brennan blessed the foundation according to the old ways, though he later regretted his participation. The bridge binds not just the shores but our agreement. As long as it stands, the Covenant holds.

Nadia researched Father Brennan. He'd been St. Jude's pastor in 1913, died in 1952. His personal effects had been donated to the diocesan archives. She made a note to follow up.

The most disturbing entry came from January 1947:

The consolidation is complete. Eight families sacrificed to ensure four families' prosperity. The bridge stands as testament and warning. Eleanor Vance has been asking questions about the original documents. We must ensure she understands the consequences of curiosity.

Eleanor Vance. The city clerk who'd documented everything and then disappeared.

Nadia was tracing her footsteps, following her questions. And the families were responding the same way they had in 1970: with escalating pressure and implied threats.

The article went viral within Daybridge and spread to regional news. The Boston Globe picked it up. A Providence television station requested an interview. Connecticut Public Radio wanted to do a segment.

Nadia was suddenly the center of attention she'd never sought, fielding calls from journalists who wanted to know more, from academics who wanted to study the records, from lawyers representing people who thought they might be descendants of the disappeared families.

Marcus ran follow-up pieces: interviews with east side residents discovering their family histories, analysis of the property transfers by legal experts, historical context about consolidation practices in early twentieth-century America.

The Daybridge Guardian's circulation spiked. Online traffic crashed their servers twice.

And then, three days after the article went viral, someone burned down part of the Daybridge Historical Society.

Nadia got the news at 2 AM from Ethan Reeves.

"There's been a fire. Historical Society building. Section containing pre-1960 records is completely destroyed."

She was dressed and out the door within five minutes.

The scene was chaos when she arrived—fire trucks, police vehicles, crowds of onlookers. The Historical Society's west wing was a smoking ruin, flames still visible through collapsed sections of roof. Firefighters poured water onto the structure, their efforts focused now on containment rather than saving what was already lost.

Ethan found her at the police perimeter. "Arson. Fire marshal's preliminary assessment. Accelerant used. Multiple points of ignition. Someone knew exactly what they were doing."

"The records?"

"Gone. Everything from 1875 to 1960. All the original incorporation documents, property deeds, early city council minutes. The exact files you were researching."

It was the 1958 city hall fire all over again. Destroy the evidence, control the narrative.

"Where's Dr. Pierce?" Nadia asked.

Ethan's expression darkened. "That's the other problem. She's missing. Her car was found abandoned near the Daybridge Bridge about an hour ago. Keys in the ignition. Purse on the passenger seat. No sign of her."

The bridge. Always the bridge.

"You think she was abducted?"

"I think something bad happened. Her phone's off. She's not responding to calls. And given the timing..." Ethan gestured at the burning building. "Either she set this fire and ran, or someone wanted to send a very specific message."

Nadia's mind raced. Victoria Pierce was complicit in the cover-up, but she was also the keeper of the archives. If she'd decided to destroy evidence herself, it would make sense to disappear afterward. But if someone else wanted the records destroyed and Pierce silenced...

"Officially," Ethan said, keeping his voice low, "my captain is calling this arson and Pierce's disappearance a separate incident pending investigation. But he's also made it very clear he wants me to look closely at who might have had a motive to destroy Historical Society records."

"Let me guess. I'm on that list."

"You're at the top of it. Published article exposing the founding families, threatened with lawsuits, publicly opposed to the families' version of history. And now the records that might have supported your claims are conveniently destroyed." Ethan's tone was apologetic. "I don't think you did this. But I'm going to be under pressure to bring you in for questioning."

"I was home asleep. No alibi except my cat."

"That's what I figured. Look, I'm going to buy you time. But Nadia, you need to be careful. This is escalating way beyond newspaper articles and historical research. Someone committed arson. Someone may have kidnapped or killed Victoria Pierce. These are serious crimes, and whoever's behind them is willing to go much further than threats and lawsuits."

He was right. This had crossed a line from intimidation to violence.

Nadia walked back to her car, her mind churning. She needed to document everything, back up all her research, prepare for the possibility that she might be arrested or worse. She needed to—

There was an envelope on her windshield.

Plain manila. No postage. Hand-delivered while she was at the fire scene.

She opened it carefully, using the edge of her jacket to avoid leaving fingerprints.

Inside was a single sheet of paper with a symbol drawn in black ink: a circle containing a bridge, surrounded by twelve stars. Eight of the stars were crossed out.

No message. Just the symbol.

Nadia photographed it with her phone, then drove straight to Eli Namir's bookshop. It was past 3 AM, but Eli lived in the apartment above the shop. She pounded on the door until lights came on.

Eli appeared in a bathrobe, looking alarmed. "Nadia? What—"

She showed him the symbol.

All color drained from Eli's face. "Where did you get this?"

"On my car. Tonight. After the fire at the Historical Society."

"Come inside. Now." Eli pulled her into the shop, locked the door behind them, and drew the blinds. His hands shook as he took the paper from her. "This is from the original city seal. Before the 1958 fire. I've only seen it in one place—a photograph from 1913, taken at the bridge dedication."

He pulled out one of his archive boxes and extracted a fragile photograph. The image showed the twelve founding families gathered before the newly completed bridge. Behind them, carved into the bridge's cornerstone, was the same symbol: circle, bridge, twelve stars.

"The symbol represented the Covenant," Eli said. "The twelve families united by the bridge. After the consolidation, it was removed from all official city materials. The cornerstone was replaced sometime in the 1950s. The Historical Society claimed the original was 'damaged and unsafe.'"

"Why would someone send this to me?"

"It's a warning. The eight crossed-out stars? Those are the families that were eliminated. Someone's telling you that you're asking the same questions they did. That you're going to meet the same fate."

Nadia's phone rang. Ethan.

"We need to talk. Pierce's disappearance is officially a homicide investigation. We found blood in her car. Not much, but enough to indicate violence. And Nadia—" He paused. "My captain wants you brought in for questioning. You're officially a person of interest."

"I didn't do anything."

"I know. But you need a lawyer. And you need to be very careful about what you say and who you trust. Because from where I'm sitting, it looks like someone's setting you up to take the fall for all of this."

Nadia looked at the symbol on the paper, at Eli's frightened expression, at the smoke still visible through the window from the Historical Society fire.

Eleanor Vance had asked questions. She'd disappeared.

Victoria Pierce had kept the secrets. Now she was missing, probably dead.

And Nadia was being positioned as the perfect suspect—the journalist with motive, means, and opportunity.

Whoever was behind this wasn't just protecting the Covenant. They were eliminating anyone who threatened it, then covering their tracks by making it look like the victims were the perpetrators.

"I need a lawyer," Nadia said into the phone. "And I need you to keep me out of custody long enough to find out who's really behind this."

"I'll do what I can. But Nadia—whoever you're dealing with, they're not playing by any rules I recognize. Watch your back."

She hung up and looked at Eli. "I need copies of everything you have. Every document, every photograph, every piece of evidence about the Covenant and the eight families. If something happens to me, this all needs to go public."

"You think they'll come for you next?"

"I think I'm following Eleanor Vance's footsteps. And we both know how that story ended."

Nadia spent the rest of the night at the bookshop, scanning and uploading documents to encrypted cloud storage, emailing copies to her network of trusted sources, preparing for the possibility that she might not have much time left.

The symbol on the paper sat on Eli's desk, a reminder of what happened to people who asked too many questions about Daybridge's founding families.

Eight stars crossed out.

Eight families disappeared.

And now someone was making it very clear that Nadia could be next.

CHAPTER FOUR: THE COVENANTS PRICE

The interrogation room at Daybridge Police Department smelled of industrial cleaner and stale coffee. Nadia sat across from Ethan Reeves, aware of the camera in the corner recording everything, aware that this conversation could determine whether she left this building as a witness or a suspect.

Ethan looked tired, his detective's mask firmly in place. "Interview with Nadia Marsh regarding the disappearance of Dr. Victoria Pierce and the arson at Daybridge Historical Society. December 16th, 2025, 9:47 AM." He recited the formalities, then met her eyes. "Tell me you didn't do this."

"I didn't do this."

"Tell me you have an alibi."

"I was at Eli Namir's bookshop until midnight going through historical documents. Then I went home. Alone." She kept her voice steady, aware how weak it sounded. "My cat can vouch for me after midnight, but I doubt that'll hold up in court."

Ethan didn't smile. He pulled out a folder and spread crime scene photos across the table. Victoria Pierce's car, abandoned near the bridge. Driver's side door open. Dark stains on the seat that the labels identified as blood type O-positive—Pierce's type.

"Security footage from Main Street confirms you left Eli's shop at 11:53 PM. Your apartment is twelve minutes away. That leaves roughly eight hours unaccounted for between when you got home and when you showed up at the Historical Society fire."

"I was asleep."

"Can anyone confirm that?"

"No."

Ethan leaned back, running a hand through his hair in frustration. "Nadia, this looks really bad. You published articles exposing Dr. Pierce's family. She filed a formal complaint against you. She was the gatekeeper of the archives you needed for your investigation. And now those archives are destroyed, and she's missing with evidence of violence."

"So, I'm the obvious suspect."

"You're the convenient suspect." Ethan glanced at the camera, then lowered his voice. "Captain Harrington wants you arrested. He's pushing the DA to file charges for arson and suspicion of kidnapping, possibly murder if they find Pierce's body. I'm the only thing standing between you and a cell right now."

"Why?"

"Because I don't think you did this. The timeline's too tight, the execution too professional. Someone set that fire with precision—multiple accelerants, specific targeting of pre-1960 records, complete destruction of evidence. That takes planning and expertise. You're a journalist, not an arsonist." He tapped the photos. "But that doesn't matter if I can't prove it."

"What do you need?"

"The truth. Everything. Including the parts that sound crazy."

Nadia made a calculation. Ethan was risking his career to help her. She owed him honesty, even if it made her sound paranoid or delusional.

She told him about the symbol on her windshield, about Eli's identification of it as the old Covenant seal, about the pattern of people disappearing every fifteen to twenty years when they got too close to the truth. She told him about Lilith Bishop's archive and the references to ritual and sacrifice.

Ethan listened without interruption, taking notes. When she finished, he was quiet for a long moment.

"Eleanor Vance in 1971," he said finally. "I pulled her case file this morning. Investigation went nowhere. No body, no evidence of foul play, officially listed as a voluntary missing person. But the detective's notes mention that she'd been asking questions about the founding families just before she disappeared."

He pulled out another folder. "1989: Michael Torres, an investigative journalist from the Hartford Courant, was researching city corruption in Daybridge. Died in a single-car accident on Route 9. Toxicology was clean, no mechanical failure, but witnesses said his car accelerated into the guardrail like he was trying to crash."

Another folder. "2004: Jennifer Wu, a graduate student at Yale doing her dissertation on New England municipal development. She was focusing on Daybridge as a case study. Found dead in her apartment from what was ruled an overdose and probable suicide. But her adviser told police she'd seemed excited about her research, not depressed."

"Every fifteen to twenty years," Nadia said. "Someone gets too close."

"And they disappear or die in ways that look accidental or self-inflicted. No pattern obvious enough to trigger investigation, but consistent enough to be deliberate." Ethan met her eyes. "And now Victoria Pierce. Which means either the cycle's accelerating, or..."

"Or I triggered something by going public. Made them panic."

"Possible." Ethan closed the folders. "I'm going to keep investigating. Officially, you're a person of interest, but I don't have enough evidence to charge you. Captain Harrington's not happy about that, but he can't overrule procedure. Yet."

"What about Pierce's office? Before the fire?"

"Crime scene unit went through it. Signs of a struggle—overturned chair, papers scattered. But here's the interesting part." He pulled out his phone and showed her photos of Pierce's desk. "She left a voicemail for a colleague at the State Historical Society two days ago. Said she'd found Eleanor Vance's original filing from 1971. The document Vance created right before she disappeared."

Nadia leaned forward. "What was in it?"

"Pierce didn't say specifically. But her exact words were: 'The families didn't just take property—they took people.'" Ethan pocketed his phone. "What do you think that means?"

"I think Eleanor Vance discovered the same thing I'm discovering. That the consolidation wasn't just financial fraud. That people from the eight families didn't just lose their property and leave town. That something happened to them."

"Something like what?"

Nadia thought about the symbol, the bridge, the references to sacrifice in the Bishop ledger. "I don't know yet. But I'm going to find out."

That evening, Nadia met Lilith Bishop at a coffee shop in the next town over, away from Daybridge's watching eyes. Lilith arrived looking shaken, clutching a worn leather satchel.

"Sarah Thorne-Morrison called me this morning," Lilith said without preamble. "She was crying. Said she couldn't live with the guilt anymore. That she'd found something in her grandmother's papers that proved the families didn't just steal property—they killed people. Systematically. Over decades."

"Where is she now?"

"I don't know. Her phone's off. Her office said she didn't come in today. Her husband said she left the house at six AM and hasn't come back." Lilith's hands shook as she opened her satchel. "I'm scared, Nadia. First Pierce, now Sarah. It's like anyone who questions the Covenant is being eliminated."

She pulled out the Bishop family ledger, opening to a page marked with a ribbon. "I found this last night. I've read this ledger a dozen times, but I missed it before because it was in shorthand."

The entry was dated December 21, 1913—the winter solstice:

The Great Work is complete. The bridge stands as symbol and foundation. Four corners, four families, bound in iron and stone. The ritual of consolidation begins this day. Eight shall provide the sacrifice. Four shall reap the reward. The Covenant is sealed in blood and the bridge shall hold it for all time.

"The bridge wasn't just infrastructure," Nadia said slowly. "It was symbolic. Part of some kind of ritual."

"Look at the date. Winter solstice. The darkest day of the year." Lilith flipped through more pages. "And look at these entries from subsequent years. Every major action in the consolidation happened on solstices or equinoxes. Property transfers. Family disappearances. All timed to specific dates."

Nadia photographed the pages, her mind racing. "We need to see the bridge. The actual physical structure. If the symbol was carved into the foundation—"

"It's dangerous," Lilith said. "If they're watching you—"

"They're already trying to frame me for murder. Dangerous is my new baseline."

They drove to the bridge just after midnight, parking in the shadows near the old industrial area. The Daybridge Bridge loomed above them, its iron framework dark against the night sky. From below, near the foundation, they could access the original cornerstone.

Lilith brought a flashlight. Nadia brought her camera and a growing sense of dread.

The foundation was older than the rest of the structure, massive blocks of stone laid in 1913. They found the cornerstone quickly—a large granite block with an inscription barely visible under decades of grime and pollution.

Lilith shone the light on it.

There, carved into the stone, was the symbol: a circle containing a bridge, surrounded by twelve stars. Eight of them had been deliberately defaced, chiseled away until only rough depressions remained.

"It's real," Lilith whispered. "It's not just in the ledgers. They actually carved this into the foundation."

Nadia photographed it from multiple angles, documenting the symbol and the date (1913) and the Latin inscription below it: *Quattuor anguli, quattuor familiae, in ferro et lapide ligati.*

"Four corners, four families, bound in iron and stone," Lilith translated. "Just like the ledger said."

As Nadia moved closer to photograph details, something shifted in her perception. The air felt thick, harder to breathe. The shadows cast by Lilith's flashlight seemed to move against the light's direction, forming patterns that hurt to look at directly.

She heard whispers. Not voices exactly, but the impression of voices. Names she recognized from her research: *Montgomery... Fairchild... Donovan... Wexler...*

The temperature dropped. Nadia's breath misted in the air despite the mild December night.

And then she saw them.

Not clearly. Not with her actual eyes. But in her peripheral vision, in the shadows between the bridge supports, she saw figures. Workers in old-fashioned clothing. Falling. Always falling. Hitting the ground with impacts she felt rather than heard.

"Nadia?" Lilith's voice sounded distant. "Are you okay?"

She snapped back to awareness, stumbling backward from the cornerstone. The visions stopped. The air returned to normal temperature. But her hands shook as she steadied herself against a support beam.

"Did you see that?" she asked.

"See what?"

"The workers. Falling. During construction."

Lilith's expression shifted to something like recognition mixed with fear. "You feel it too. My grandmother wrote about this in her private journal. She said the bridge remembers. That on certain nights, especially near the solstices, you could feel the weight of what happened here."

"What did happen here?"

"I don't know exactly. But there were accidents during construction. Workers who fell to their deaths. The newspapers at the time called it tragic but inevitable—building a bridge was dangerous work. But my grandmother's notes suggest it wasn't accidental. That the founding families needed... blood in the foundation."

Nadia thought of the symbol, the ritual language, the timing on the winter solstice. "Human sacrifice."

"I know how that sounds."

"I just saw ghosts falling from a bridge that wasn't finished yet. We're past worrying about how things sound." Nadia photographed the cornerstone again, making sure she had clear images. "We need to find out exactly what happened during the construction. Worker deaths, accidents, anything unusual."

"The Historical Society records would have—" Lilith stopped. "Would have had that information. Before the fire."

"Then we find another source. Newspapers from 1913. Union records. Anything."

As they walked back to Nadia's car, Lilith pulled out her phone and showed Nadia a text message she'd received an hour ago from an unknown number:

Some truths are better buried. Some sacrifices are necessary. Stop asking questions or become an answer.

"They're threatening both of us now," Lilith said.

"Good. Means we're getting close."

The alliance formed organically over the next two days. Nadia, Lilith, Father Mulligan, Marcus Wong, Eli Namir, and—though he couldn't admit it officially—Ethan Reeves. They met in the back room of Eli's bookshop, the one place in Daybridge that felt relatively safe from surveillance.

Marcus brought legal expertise and journalistic resources. Father Mulligan brought church records and moral authority. Eli brought historical documentation. Lilith brought the Bishop family archive. Ethan brought police reports and investigative experience.

Together, they assembled the pieces.

The bridge construction in 1913 had killed twelve workers in documented accidents. Twelve workers, twelve founding families. The deaths all occurred in the final month of construction, between November 21st and December 21st—the winter solstice. The bodies were buried in a mass grave in the old cemetery, marked with a simple stone: *In Memory of Those Who Built the Bridge.*

"Twelve sacrifices," Father Mulligan said, his voice heavy. "One for each family. To seal the Covenant."

"But that's just the beginning," Lilith added. She spread out pages from the Bishop ledger. "The consolidation from twelve families to four happened over decades. Between 1913 and 1947, members of eight families disappeared. Not all at once. Gradually. Strategic eliminations."

Eli had found newspaper records of deaths and disappearances: accidents, suicides, families who "moved away" without forwarding addresses. Separately, they looked random. Together, they formed a pattern.

"They didn't kill everyone," Nadia said, studying the timeline. "Some people really did leave. They were intimidated or bought out. But the ones who resisted, the ones who asked too many questions—"

"Became sacrifices to maintain the Covenant," Father Mulligan finished.

Ethan had been quiet, taking notes, his cop's brain processing the information. "This is all circumstantial. Suggestive, but not proof. We can't take this to a DA. We'd be laughed out of the office."

"We're not trying to prosecute a seventy-year-old conspiracy," Marcus said. "We're trying to expose it. And we have something the 1940s victims didn't have: the internet. If we publish everything—the documents, the timeline, the pattern—we can make this story too big to suppress."

"And then what?" Ethan challenged. "The families have killed people for asking questions. You think going public will make you safer?"

"It's our only option," Nadia said. "Silence didn't protect Eleanor Vance or Michael Torres or Jennifer Wu. Silence didn't protect Victoria Pierce. If we're already targets, our best defense is making the information impossible to contain."

Before anyone could respond, Nadia's phone rang. Unknown number.

She answered on speaker. "Hello?"

"Ms. Marsh. This is Thomas Harrington the Third. I'd like to request a private meeting. Tomorrow morning, ten AM, at my law offices. I believe we can reach a mutually beneficial arrangement."

Nadia looked at the others. Ethan shook his head in warning. Marcus gestured for her to stall.

"What kind of arrangement?"

"One that protects your future and respects the past. Please come. And Ms. Marsh? Come alone. This conversation requires discretion."

He hung up before she could respond.

"It's a trap," Ethan said immediately.

"Probably," Nadia agreed. "But I'm going, anyway."

"Not alone you're not."

They spent the next hour planning. Ethan would be outside in an unmarked car. Marcus would be on standby with the Guardian's legal team. Lilith would monitor from a café across the street. Nadia would wear a wire—technically illegal without consent, but they were past worrying about minor legal violations.

"If this goes wrong," Nadia said to Marcus, "publish everything. Don't wait. Don't verify. Just get it out there."

"It won't go wrong," Marcus said, with more confidence than he felt.

Harrington's law offices occupied the top floor of the Harrington Building, with views of the bridge and the harbor beyond. The receptionist escorted Nadia to a conference room where four people waited.

Thomas Harrington III sat at the head of the table—early seventies, silver hair, expensive suit, the bearing of someone accustomed to authority. To his right sat a man Nadia recognized from photos: Gregory Bishop, senior partner at Bishop & Associates and Lilith's uncle. To his left, a woman in her fifties introduced as Patricia Castellano, city attorney. At the far end, a younger man in hospital scrubs: Dr. Marcus Thorne, administrator at Daybridge General.

Four people. Four families.

"Thank you for coming, Ms. Marsh," Harrington said. "Please, sit."

Nadia remained standing. "What do you want?"

"To offer you a way forward that benefits everyone." Harrington gestured to a folder on the table. "We've prepared a settlement offer. Five hundred thousand dollars, payable immediately. A guaranteed position at the Boston Globe—we have connections on the board. All potential criminal charges dropped, and a formal statement from our families acknowledging historical property transactions that may not have been, shall we say, entirely transparent?"

"In exchange for?"

"Retraction of your articles. Surrender of all documents and evidence related to your investigation. A non-disclosure agreement preventing future publication of this material. And a public apology for making unfounded accusations against respected families."

Nadia looked at each of them in turn. "You're trying to buy my silence."

"We're trying to offer you a future," Patricia Castellano said. "Eleanor Vance made the wrong choice. She chose confrontation over cooperation. Dr. Pierce made the wrong choice. She attempted to weaponize information she should have protected. Both of them paid the price. Please be smarter than they were."

The threat was barely veiled. Nadia felt the wire under her shirt, recording every word.

"What happened to Eleanor Vance?"

"She left Daybridge," Harrington said smoothly. "Relocated to California, as the records show."

"What happened to Victoria Pierce?"

"We don't know. But we hope she's found safely. These are dangerous times for people who involve themselves in matters they don't fully understand."

Dr. Thorne leaned forward. "Ms. Marsh, my family has served this community for generations. We've built hospitals, funded schools, created thousands of jobs. Yes, our ancestors made difficult choices during difficult times. But we've more than compensated through decades of civic contribution. Why destroy that legacy over events none of us were alive to witness?"

"Because people deserve the truth."

"The truth," Gregory Bishop said, "is that Daybridge thrives because of the stability our families provide. Disrupting that stability serves no one. The descendants of the original eight families are integrated into this community. Many of them are successful, happy, living good lives. What do they gain from discovering their great-grandparents were cheated? What does anyone gain from tearing down the structures that make this city function?"

It was a reasonable argument, Nadia thought. And that made it more dangerous. Because there was truth in it—not the whole truth, but enough truth to make compromise seem rational.

"I need to think about it," she said.

"Of course. We'll give you forty-eight hours. But Ms. Marsh..." Harrington stood, his expression hardening. "Forty-eight hours is all you get. After that, this offer expires and we proceed with alternative solutions. Do you understand?"

"Perfectly."

She left the building feeling like she'd just been given an ultimatum by the mob. Which, she supposed, she had.

Ethan was waiting in his car. "You get all that?"

Nadia showed him the recording device. "Every word."

"'Alternative solutions.' Jesus Christ, they're not even subtle anymore." Ethan's expression was grim. "They admitted Pierce made the 'wrong choice' and paid the price. That's as close to a confession as we're going to get without actual evidence."

"Then we need actual evidence."

Nadia's phone buzzed. Text from an unknown number:

Not all of us agree with the old ways. Some of us want out. Meet me tonight. 11 PM. Old warehouse district, 447 Industrial Road. Come alone. - Robert Castellano

"You know who that is?" Ethan asked, reading over her shoulder.

"Patricia Castellano's brother. He's a lawyer with Bishop & Associates. Corporate transactions, mostly." Nadia thought for a moment. "If he's willing to defect..."

"It's probably a trap."

"Everything's probably a trap at this point." She looked at Ethan. "But what if it's not? What if there's someone inside the families who actually wants to help?"

"Then I'm coming with you. Not negotiable."

The warehouse district was exactly as ominous as expected—abandoned buildings, broken streetlights, no witnesses. Nadia and Ethan approached 447 Industrial Road with weapons drawn (Ethan's service pistol, Nadia's pepper spray and pocket knife).

A figure emerged from the shadows: Robert Castellano, mid-forties, looking terrified and determined in equal measure.

"I wasn't sure you'd come," he said.

"I wasn't sure you weren't setting me up," Nadia replied.

"Fair." He glanced at Ethan. "I said come alone."

"Detective Reeves is helping me. Unofficially. If you're genuine, you'll want him to hear this too."

Robert considered, then nodded. "Okay. But we need to be quick. They have people watching. If they know I'm talking to you—" He didn't finish the sentence.

"What do you want to tell us?"

"That my sister and the others are planning something. Winter solstice. December twenty-first. Five days from now." He pulled out a folder. "I found these in Patricia's office. Copies of old ritual instructions. Preparations for what they call 'Covenant renewal.'"

Ethan took the folder, examining the documents. They were photocopies of handwritten pages, similar in style to the Bishop ledger.

Covenant Renewal Ritual - To Be Performed Every Generation

Requirements:

- Winter Solstice, preferably at the exact moment of astronomical turning

- Location: Bridge foundation, north pillar

- Sacrifice: Blood willing or blood taken, from one who questions the Covenant

- Witnesses: Representatives of four families

"This is insane," Ethan said.

"Is it?" Robert's laugh was bitter. "My family has been performing variations of this ritual since 1913. Every generation, someone who gets too close to the truth disappears. It's not a coincidence. It's maintenance. The Covenant requires periodic... renewal."

"Human sacrifice," Nadia said. "You're telling me the founding families of Daybridge practice ritual murder."

"I'm telling you I was raised in a tradition I didn't question until recently. Taught that the Covenant was symbolic, that the rituals were historical reenactment, that the disappearances were unfortunate coincidences." Robert's voice cracked. "But then I found my grandfather's journal. Detailed descriptions of what they did. Who they killed. How they justified it as 'necessary sacrifice for the greater good.'"

"Why are you telling us this?"

"Because Sarah Thorne-Morrison has gone missing. And I know what that means." He met Nadia's eyes. "She called me two days ago. Said she'd found proof of what her family did and couldn't live with it anymore. She wanted to go public, to make restitution to the descendants of the families they destroyed. I tried to convince her to be careful, to wait. But she was determined."

"Where is she?"

"I don't know. But I know the pattern. They take people who threaten the Covenant. They hold them until the solstice. Then..." He gestured to the ritual instructions. "Blood willing or blood taken."

Nadia felt ice in her stomach. "They're going to kill her."

"They're going to kill her," Robert confirmed. "And then they're going to come for you. Because you're on the list."

"What list?"

He pulled out another document. A handwritten roster dated three days ago:

Those Who Must Be Silenced:

1. Dr. Victoria Pierce - Completed

2. Sarah Thorne-Morrison - In Progress

3. Nadia Marsh - Scheduled for Solstice

Ethan stared at the list. "This is premeditated murder. Multiple counts. We can arrest—"

"Who?" Robert interrupted. "My sister the city attorney? The police commissioner? The hospital administrator? The senior partners at the city's largest law firm? They control the DA, half the judges, most of the city council. Who exactly are you going to arrest?"

It was a fair point. The system was designed to protect them.

"Then we expose them," Nadia said. "Publish everything. Make it impossible for them to operate in secret."

"They'll kill you before you can publish."

"Not if we do it now. Tonight. Before they have a chance to stop us."

She called Marcus. "We're publishing. Everything. Right now."

"What happened?"

"They're planning to kill Sarah Thorne-Morrison in five days. And I'm next on the list. We're out of time."

Marcus was quiet for a moment. "Okay. Send me everything you have. I'll get legal review expedited and we'll push it online within two hours."

While Nadia transferred files to Marcus, Ethan called his lieutenant—one of the few people in the department he trusted. "I need units at the bridge foundation. Now. I have credible evidence of kidnapping and possible homicide."

"On whose authority?"

"Mine. I'll take the heat if I'm wrong."

Robert grabbed Nadia's arm. "There's something else you need to know. Pierce's body. They're going to find it tomorrow. At the bridge foundation. Positioned at a specific compass point. It's part of the ritual—displaying the completed sacrifice as a warning to the next one."

"How do you know this?"

"Because I helped them plan it." His voice broke. "I didn't know what it meant at the time. They said it was symbolic. But now I know they were serious. They actually killed her. And they're going to kill Sarah. And you."

Before Nadia could respond, her phone rang. Lilith.

"Turn on the news. Now."

Ethan pulled up local news on his phone. Breaking story:

BODY FOUND AT DAYBRIDGE BRIDGE - VICTIM IDENTIFIED AS DR. VICTORIA PIERCE

The image showed police and emergency vehicles at the bridge foundation. Crime scene tape. Covered body on a stretcher.

The reporter's voice: *"Dr. Victoria Pierce, director of the Daybridge Historical Society, has been found deceased at the foundation of Daybridge Bridge. Police are treating this as a homicide. Sources indicate the body shows signs of ritualistic violence, including symbols carved into nearby stone..."*

Ethan's phone started ringing. His lieutenant. "Reeves, where the hell are you? Captain wants you at the scene. Now. And he's asking about your relationship with Nadia Marsh."

"I'm on my way." He hung up and looked at Nadia. "They found Pierce. Exactly where and when Robert said they would."

"Which means they're serious about the rest of it."

"Which means you're in immediate danger. You need protection. Safe house, police guard—"

"They control the police," Nadia reminded him. "A safe house becomes a trap if the people protecting me are on their payroll."

Robert spoke urgently: "There's a place. My cabin in the state forest. Off-grid, remote. I can take you there. Give you a few days until the solstice passes."

"Or I stand and fight. Publish the story. Force them into the light."

"They'll kill you," Robert said.

"Probably. But if I run, they win. They bury the story, eliminate Sarah, maintain control for another generation." Nadia looked at Ethan. "How do we break this cycle?"

Ethan studied the ritual documents, his expression troubled. "We need to find Sarah. If we can rescue her before the solstice, they can't complete their ritual. And we need physical evidence linking the families to Pierce's murder. Robert's testimony helps, but we need more."

"The bridge," Nadia said. "If Pierce was killed there, there'll be evidence. Blood, signs of struggle, the symbol they carved."

"Crime scene is closed. Captain Harrington is personally overseeing the investigation."

"Then we go tonight. Before they can sanitize it."

It was reckless. Possibly suicidal. But Nadia was done being reactive. If the families wanted to eliminate her, she'd make them work for it.

She pulled up the Bishop ledger on her phone, finding the entry Robert's documents had referenced:

Covenant Renewed at the Turning, Blood Willing or Blood Taken. The sacrifice must be one who questions, one who seeks to break the binding. Four witnesses, four families, at the foundation stone when the sun reaches its lowest point.

"Blood willing or blood taken," she repeated. "What does that mean?"

"The victim can choose to participate," Robert explained. "Agree to the sacrifice, accept their role in maintaining the Covenant. That's 'blood willing.' Or they can resist, in which case it's 'blood taken.'"

"Did Eleanor Vance choose?"

"No. According to my grandfather's journal, she fought. They had to subdue her."

"And Pierce?"

Robert's expression was haunted. "I don't know. But she was kept alive for several days before they killed her. They gave her the choice. Maybe she refused."

"And Sarah?"

"They're holding her somewhere. Probably giving her the same choice: participate in the ritual willingly or die resisting."

Nadia thought of Sarah's torn expression in her office, her struggle between guilt and self-preservation. Would she choose to become a willing sacrifice to atone for her family's crimes? Or would she fight?

"We have to find her," Nadia said. "Where would they keep someone?"

"Somewhere with family significance. Somewhere connected to the original Covenant." Robert thought for a moment. "There's a property on the west side. Old Thorne estate, been in the family since 1915. They use it for family gatherings, private meetings. If they're holding Sarah, that's where she'd be."

Ethan checked his watch. "It's almost midnight. If we're going to do this, we need to move now."

They split up. Ethan would go to the bridge crime scene, officially as part of the investigation, and document whatever evidence he could find. Nadia, Lilith (who'd arrived during the conversation), and Robert would check the Thorne estate for signs of Sarah.

"This is where people die in horror movies," Lilith muttered as they drove toward the west side. "Breaking into the evil family's estate at midnight."

"Yeah, but in horror movies, the heroes don't know they're in danger," Nadia replied. "We know exactly what we're walking into."

"Not sure that's actually better."

The Thorne estate sat on five acres behind iron gates and stone walls. Colonial-style mansion, dark windows, no visible lights. They parked a block away and approached on foot.

Robert had a key—family access, shared among the four founding families for decades. "If anyone asks, I'm here for estate inventory. You're my assistants."

The lie wouldn't hold if they encountered actual security, but it was better than nothing.

Inside, the house felt wrong. Not just empty, but oppressive. The air was heavy, thick with the weight of decades of secrets and sins. Old portraits lined the walls—Thorne family members going back generations, their painted eyes seeming to follow movement.

They searched methodically. First floor, second floor, finding nothing but expensive furniture and historical artifacts. Then Robert led them to a door Nadia had assumed was a closet.

"Basement," he said. "Original structure from 1915. Some of it's even older—built on the foundation of one of the original eight families' homes."

The stairs descended into darkness. Lilith turned on her flashlight.

The basement was partially finished—concrete floor, stone walls, old heating equipment. But at the far end, behind a false panel Robert knew how to open, was another door. Newer, reinforced steel, with a modern lock.

"This wasn't here last time I visited," Robert said.

The lock was electronic. Keypad entry. Robert tried several combinations—birthdates, historical dates, nothing worked.

Nadia thought back to the Bishop ledger. "Try December 21, 1913. The bridge dedication date."

Robert entered 12-21-13.

The lock clicked open.

Beyond was a small room, maybe ten feet square. Stone walls. Single overhead bulb. And sitting on the floor, wrists zip-tied, mouth gagged, was Sarah Thorne-Morrison.

Her eyes widened when she saw them. Relief, terror, confusion—all at once.

Lilith rushed forward, removing the gag while Nadia cut the zip-ties with her pocket knife.

"Sarah, are you hurt?"

"They—" Sarah's voice was hoarse from screaming. "They've been keeping me here. Telling me I have to choose. Participate in the ritual or die fighting it. That either way, the Covenant requires my blood because I tried to expose them."

"How long?"

"Three days. They bring food twice a day. Different people each time. My cousins. People I grew up with. Acting like this is normal. Like ritual sacrifice is just another family obligation."

Nadia helped her stand. "Can you walk?"

"I think so." Sarah was shaky but determined. "We need to leave. Now. They're planning to move me tomorrow. Take me to the bridge for the solstice."

They were halfway up the stairs when the lights came on.

Patricia Castellano stood at the top, flanked by two large men in dark suits. Behind her, Thomas Harrington III.

"Robert," Patricia said, her voice disappointed. "I'd hoped you'd come to your senses. But I see you've chosen to betray your family instead."

"You're planning to murder someone," Robert shot back. "I chose to be human instead of monstrous."

"We're preserving a legacy. Maintaining the Covenant that's kept this city prosperous for over a century. Surely you understand the necessity—"

"Necessity?" Sarah's voice cracked with emotion. "You kidnapped me. Your own family member. Because I tried to tell the truth about crimes, our grandparents committed."

"Crimes that built everything you have," Harrington said. "Your business, your home, your children's future—all of it exists because of the Covenant. You would throw that away for what? Abstract justice? Empty virtue?"

"For not being a murderer."

The two men in suits moved forward. No weapons visible, but the threat was clear.

Nadia pulled out her phone. "I'm recording this. Everything you've said. Admitting you kidnapped Sarah. Admitting the ritual. Threatening us. It's all documented."

"And who will you send it to?" Patricia asked. "The police, where my family's been commissioners for three generations? The DA, who my brother plays golf with every weekend? The media, which we can silence with a single phone call?"

"The internet," Nadia said. "Every social media platform. Every news outlet in the state. I upload this and it's out there forever."

"Upload it," Harrington challenged. "And we'll simply deny everything. Call it deepfake. Claim you fabricated evidence. Our lawyers will destroy your credibility before breakfast."

He was probably right. Without corroboration, without physical evidence, recordings could be dismissed.

But then Lilith held up her phone. "I'm livestreaming this. Right now. To three thousand followers. They're watching you admit to kidnapping. Watching you threaten us. Screenshot that, deepfake that."

Patricia's expression shifted from confident to furious. "You little—"

"The truth is out there now," Lilith continued. "And it's not just us. Nadia's editor is publishing the full investigation in—" she checked her watch "—about ten minutes. Every document. Every piece of evidence. Every connection between the founding families and the disappearances."

For the first time, Harrington looked uncertain.

Robert stepped forward. "It's over. The Covenant can't survive transparency. You can kill us, but you can't kill the internet. The story's bigger than we are now."

Patricia pulled out her phone, typing rapidly. Probably calling their lawyers, crisis management, whoever the families relied on to bury scandals.

The men in suits looked to Harrington for instructions.

And Nadia realized this was the critical moment. The families could escalate—kill them all, try to contain the damage. Or they could retreat, try to manage the crisis legally.

Harrington made his decision. "Let them go."

"Sir—" one of the suited men protested.

"Let them go. We'll handle this through proper channels. Lawsuits. Defamation claims. We'll tie them up in court for years." He looked at Nadia with cold hatred. "You've made a very expensive enemy, Ms. Marsh. But you haven't won. Justice and truth are luxuries for people who can afford them. And we can afford much more than you can."

They didn't run. They walked out calmly, maintaining dignity despite the fear coursing through them. Sarah leaned on Lilith for support. Robert glanced back once at his sister, his expression a mix of grief and determination.

In the car, Nadia called Ethan. "We found Sarah. She's alive. We got her out."

"Thank God. Where are you?"

"Leaving the Thorne estate. Harrington and Patricia Castellano were there. They admitted everything. Lilith got it on livestream."

"I saw. Half the department is watching it right now." Ethan's voice carried something like triumph. "And Nadia? I found something at the crime scene. Symbol carved in stone matches the original Covenant seal. Blood splatter patterns suggest Pierce was killed where we found her. This is our crime scene, our evidence."

"What about the captain?"

"He tried to shut down my investigation. I went over his head to the state police. They're taking over the Pierce homicide as of right now." Ethan paused. "This is going to blow up, Nadia. In a good way. But it's going to get ugly first."

It already was ugly. But at least now it was public ugliness. The families could no longer operate in shadows.

The Daybridge Guardian published Nadia's full investigation at 2:47 AM. Within an hour, it had been shared ten thousand times. By morning, major news outlets were running the story. CNN, MSNBC, Fox News—all covering the "Daybridge Conspiracy" with varying degrees of sensationalism and skepticism.

The families issued denials. Their lawyers issued statements. They threatened lawsuits.

But the documents were public. The testimonies were recorded. The pattern was undeniable.

And then, at 9 AM, the medical examiner released preliminary findings on Victoria Pierce's death:

Cause of death: Exsanguination from a throat wound. Manner: Homicide. Additional findings: Ritualistic positioning of body, symbol carved in nearby stone consistent with historical Covenant seal, evidence suggesting victim was held captive for 3-5 days before death.

The police commissioner—William Harrington—was placed on administrative leave. The DA recused his office from the case. The state attorney general announced a full investigation into corruption in Daybridge city government.

And in the basement of St. Jude's Church, Father Mulligan found something in the diocesan archives: Father Brennan's confession from 1951.

The old priest had written it before his death, sealed it, left instructions it should only be opened "if the truth about the bridge ever comes to light."

In meticulous detail, Father Brennan described the ritual consecration of the Daybridge Bridge in December 1913. The twelve workers who died—not accidents, but planned sacrifices. The blood mixed into the foundation mortar. The invocation to "bind the Covenant in stone and blood for all generations."

He described the guilt that had consumed him for forty years. The way the families had pressured him to perform the ritual, promised it was symbolic, then murdered workers to fulfill it literally. The way he'd been complicit, had accepted their donations, had kept their secrets.

I am a coward, Father Brennan wrote. *I allowed evil in the name of prosperity. I blessed murder and called it progress. May God forgive me, for I cannot forgive myself.*

The confession corroborated everything. It provided the missing link between the historical Covenant and actual ritual practice.

Nadia published it immediately.

Five days later—December 21st, the winter solstice—Nadia stood at the bridge foundation with Ethan, Lilith, Father Mulligan, Marcus, Eli, and Sarah. Police had cordoned off the area. State investigators were documenting the crime scene. News crews filmed from beyond the barriers.

The symbol was still there, carved in stone. Eight stars crossed out. Four remaining.

"They won't perform the ritual this year," Sarah said quietly. "Too much scrutiny. Too much exposure."

"Will they try again?" Marcus asked.

"I don't know. The Covenant was supposed to be eternal. Binding across generations. But it was also supposed to be secret." Sarah looked at the bridge. "Maybe exposure breaks the binding."

"Or maybe it just forces them to adapt," Lilith said. "My uncle Gregory is already reframing this as 'historical reenactment that got out of hand.' Claiming the murders were rogue elements, not sanctioned by the families. Trying to separate contemporary descendants from ancestral crimes."

"Will it work?"

"Legally? Maybe. They have good lawyers." Lilith's expression hardened. "But socially? The families' reputation is destroyed. People know what they did. That genie doesn't go back in the bottle."

Ethan had been examining the cornerstone. "The symbolism is interesting. Twelve stars, eight crossed out. But look—" He pointed to scratches around some of the remaining four stars. "Someone tried to deface these too. Recently."

"Sarah?" Nadia asked.

"Before they caught me, I came here. Tried to chisel away my family's star. Thought maybe if I destroyed the symbol, it would help." Sarah laughed bitterly. "Turns out stone is harder than guilt."

Father Mulligan placed his hand on the cornerstone. "This bridge was consecrated with murder. Built on blood and lies. But it's still standing. Still serving the city."

"Should it be?" Eli asked. "Or should we tear it down? Erase the physical symbol of the Covenant?"

It was a question Nadia had been wrestling with. The bridge was infrastructure—necessary, functional. But it was also a monument to atrocity. Could you separate the two?

"If we tear it down, do we lose evidence of what happened?" Marcus suggested. "Or do we make it easier for people to forget?"

"Maybe we acknowledge it," Nadia said. "Historical marker. Full disclosure of what happened here. Let people decide whether to use a bridge built on murder."

They stood in silence, watching investigators photograph the symbol, document the bloodstains, collect evidence that would—maybe—lead to criminal charges against some of the founding families' current members.

Nadia's phone buzzed. Text from an unknown number:

You broke the binding. We'll never forgive that. But some of us are grateful. - A Descendant

She showed it to the others. "The families are fracturing. Some want to maintain the old ways. Others want out."

"Which will win?" Sarah asked.

"I don't know. But at least now it's a fight. At least the choice is conscious." Nadia looked at the bridge, at the symbol of the Covenant that had controlled Daybridge for over a century. "They can't operate in secret anymore. That's something."

It wasn't justice. Not yet. Not fully. But it was exposure. And exposure was the beginning of accountability.

As they left the bridge foundation, Nadia noticed something: In the growing darkness of the shortest day of the year, the bridge's iron framework cast long shadows across the river. And in those shadows, if you looked closely, you could almost see figures.

Workers. The original twelve. The sacrifices that had sealed the Covenant.

Watching. Waiting. Hoping that maybe, finally, someone would tell their story.

Nadia took one last photo of the cornerstone symbol, then walked away from the bridge with her unlikely alliance of truth-tellers and defectors.

The Covenant was broken. Not destroyed—institutions that old didn't die easily. But fractured. Exposed. Vulnerable.

And for the first time in over a century, Daybridge had a chance to be something other than a city built on blood and lies.

Whether it would take that chance remained to be seen.

But at least now, people knew the choice existed.

CHAPTER FIVE: INHERITANCE RECLAIMED

The pieces came together like shards of broken glass—sharp, dangerous, forming a picture that cut to look at directly.

In Eli Namir's bookshop, surrounded by documents spread across every available surface, Nadia's alliance assembled the truth that had been hidden for over a century.

"It's not metaphorical," Father Mulligan said, his finger tracing the Latin text in a 1913 church register. "When the ledgers talk about 'binding' the families, they mean it literally. This is ritual language. Invocation. The kind of thing the Church used to prosecute as witchcraft."

Eli had found complementary records in historical architectural documents. "The bridge completion ceremony on December 21st, 1913—winter solstice—wasn't just a civic celebration. Look at the positioning." He spread out the original construction plans. "Four primary support pillars aligned to cardinal directions. Foundation stone laid at precise astronomical timing. This is sacred geometry."

"A binding ritual," Lilith said quietly, looking at her family's ledger. "The twelve families didn't just consolidate into four through economics. They used blood magic to cement the consolidation. Make it permanent."

Sarah Thorne-Morrison sat in the corner, wrapped in a blanket despite the room's warmth. She'd been released from the hospital two days ago, physically healthy but psychologically shattered. "My grandmother told me stories when I was little. About how our family was blessed, how we'd always prosper in Daybridge. I thought they were fairy tales." Her voice was hollow. "They were warnings."

Ethan had been quiet, reading through the medical examiner's expanded report on Victoria Pierce. "The positioning wasn't random.

She was found at the north foundation stone, directly aligned with the winter solstice sunrise. The symbol carved near her body—" He showed them photos. "It's not just the Covenant seal. It's an invocation circle."

"They were preparing her as a sacrifice," Nadia said. "Not just murdering her to silence her. Actually offering her blood to renew the Covenant."

"Which means they'll try again," Marcus Wong pointed out. He'd been documenting everything, preparing a follow-up exposé. "The solstice is in four days. If the Covenant requires periodic renewal through sacrifice—"

"They'll find another victim," Ethan finished. "Someone connected to their investigation. Someone whose death can be framed as an accident or suicide."

Everyone looked at Nadia.

"Or Sarah," Lilith added. "She's from one of the founding families. Her blood would be more... significant, ritually speaking."

Sarah laughed bitterly. "I'm both perpetrator and victim. My family committed atrocities to gain power, and now that power demands my death to sustain itself. There's a certain poetic justice in that."

"There's no justice in human sacrifice," Father Mulligan said firmly. "Regardless of lineage or guilt, you don't deserve to die for crimes your ancestors committed."

"Don't I?" Sarah's eyes were distant. "My family prospered for a century on stolen land and murdered innocents. Maybe this is how the universe balances the scales."

"The universe doesn't balance anything," Nadia said. "People do. And we're not letting them kill you."

She turned to Father Mulligan. "You said the Church prosecuted this as witchcraft. Which means they had methods for breaking these kinds of bindings. Counter-rituals. Exorcisms. Something."

"Theoretically, yes. But Nadia, I'm a parish priest, not a medieval witch-hunter. I've never performed anything more complicated than a house blessing."

"But you have access to the records. The old rituals."

Father Mulligan hesitated. "The diocesan archives have... extensive documentation of historical practices. Some of which the modern Church prefers to keep private. Accessing them would require explanations I'm not prepared to give."

"Then don't explain. Just do it."

"Breaking into secure Church archives to steal ritual texts so we can perform counter-magic against a conspiracy of wealthy families who practice blood sacrifice?" Father Mulligan's expression was caught between horror and dark amusement. "I'm going to need so much confession after this."

Eli offered a small smile. "I have contacts in antiquarian circles. People who collect texts the Church doesn't want public. I can probably acquire relevant materials without raising red flags."

"So we have ritual knowledge," Ethan said, thinking like a cop planning an operation. "What else do we need?"

Lilith pulled out architectural drawings of the bridge. "Access to the ritual site. Which is here—" She pointed to a notation on the original 1913 plans. "Sealed chamber beneath the north foundation stone. Where they found Pierce's body. It's not on modern blueprints because it was deliberately concealed, but the original construction docs reference it as 'consecration vault.'"

"Can you get us in?"

"I'm a Bishop. I have family access codes to the bridge maintenance systems. And—" She pulled out an old iron key. "This was in my grandmother's safe deposit box. Labeled 'Foundation access, emergencies only.' I think she knew. I think some of them always knew and felt trapped by it."

Robert Castellano, who'd been silent since entering through Eli's back entrance, finally spoke. "They're planning the renewal for midnight on the solstice. Exact moment of astronomical turning. My sister let it slip when she thought I was still loyal. They have Sarah scheduled as the primary sacrifice—" He glanced at her apologetically. "With Nadia as backup if they can't secure Sarah."

"Flattering," Nadia muttered.

"The ritual requires four witnesses representing the four families, and one to be sacrificed who has 'questioned the Covenant.' Sarah fits both criteria—she's Thorne bloodline and she tried to expose them. That makes her, in their twisted logic, the perfect offering."

Ethan stood, pacing. "Okay. So we know when, where, and what they're planning. We need to stop the ritual, rescue Sarah if they manage to take her, and gather evidence that will actually hold up in court."

"The supernatural stuff won't hold up anywhere," Marcus pointed out. "We need to frame this as kidnapping, attempted murder, conspiracy. Leave the ritual elements as flavor but don't depend on them for prosecution."

"Which means we need witnesses, documentation, and ideally live evidence." Ethan looked at Marcus. "Can you livestream from the bridge?"

"If I have a signal. The foundation area might be too deep, too much interference from the iron structure."

"Then we position you at surface level with equipment. You stream everything that happens outside the chamber. If they try to stop you, that's assault on camera."

"And inside the chamber?" Nadia asked.

"That's where things get complicated." Ethan pulled up a contact on his phone. "I have a friend at the state police. Lieutenant Maria Santos. She's clean, not connected to Daybridge politics. If I bring her evidence of planned kidnapping and murder—"

"They'll need warrants, probable cause, time to mobilize," Robert interrupted. "The families have lawyers on speed dial. By the time state police get authorization, the ritual will be complete."

"So we interrupt it ourselves," Lilith said. "Use Father Mulligan's counter-ritual. Break the binding before they can renew it."

"That's vigilante action," Ethan said carefully. "If you assault someone, interfere with what they'll claim is a private ceremony on private property—"

"Private property built on stolen land, conducting a private ceremony that involves human sacrifice," Nadia shot back. "I'm willing to take the legal risk."

"I'm not talking about legal risk. I'm talking about physical danger. These people killed Pierce. They've killed others. They won't hesitate to kill all of you if you threaten their power."

"Then we need an advantage they don't expect." Nadia looked at Lilith. "Your family bloodline gives you access. Can it give you control? Can you disrupt the ritual from inside?"

"I don't know. The ledgers suggest that Bishop bloodline was bound as one of the four corners. If the ritual requires four family representatives, and I'm present as Bishop but refusing to participate..." Lilith thought it through. "It might break the symmetry. Make the renewal incomplete."

"Might?"

"I'm working from century-old documents about magical rituals that I don't fully understand. 'Might' is the best I can offer."

Father Mulligan cleared his throat. "There's another consideration. If the Covenant is a genuine binding—if it's sustained through supernatural means—then breaking it could have unpredictable consequences. The ledgers mention the bridge as the physical anchor. If we disrupt the binding, the bridge itself might be affected."

"The bridge could collapse?" Marcus asked.

"Or crack. Or remain perfectly stable. I have no idea. This is not my area of expertise."

Ethan ran his hands through his hair, frustrated. "So we're planning to break into a sealed chamber, interrupt a ritual sacrifice, fight off however many Praetorians they have guarding the site, perform counter-magic we're not sure will work, possibly destroy a major piece of infrastructure, and somehow document enough evidence to prosecute—all while keeping everyone alive."

"Yes," Nadia said simply.

"This is insane."

"Absolutely."

"I could lose my badge."

"You could lose your life."

Ethan looked at each of them in turn. Father Mulligan with his moral certainty. Lilith with her conflicted family loyalty. Sarah with her traumatized determination. Marcus with his journalistic conviction. Robert with his guilty conscience. Eli with his quiet scholarship. And Nadia with her relentless need for truth.

"Okay," he said finally. "But we do this smart. We have backup plans and exit strategies. We don't take unnecessary risks. And if it goes wrong—if anyone's life is actually in danger—we abort and fall back to conventional law enforcement."

"Agreed," Nadia said, knowing she was lying. If it came down to law enforcement versus saving Sarah, she'd choose Sarah every time.

They spent the next three days planning.

Father Mulligan, with Eli's help, acquired texts from the Church's historical archives—or rather, Eli acquired them through his antiquarian network while Father Mulligan maintained plausible deniability. The counter-ritual was complex, requiring specific materials and precise timing.

"Essentially," Father Mulligan explained, "the original binding was consecrated with blood and iron at the moment of solstice. To break it, we need to reverse the invocation at the same astronomical moment—but with symbols of unbinding rather than binding."

"What symbols?"

"Salt to purify. Silver to reflect. And blood willingly given to counter blood taken by force."

"Whose blood?"

Father Mulligan looked uncomfortable. "Ideally, someone from one of the bound bloodlines. Someone who chooses to break the Covenant voluntarily."

Lilith and Sarah exchanged glances.

"I'll do it," they said simultaneously.

"It doesn't require much," Father Mulligan assured them. "A few drops. Symbolic rather than sacrificial."

"How do we know it'll work?" Sarah asked.

"We don't. But the logic is sound—binding requires consent or coercion. If someone bound by bloodline withdraws consent and actively works to dissolve the binding, it should weaken the structure."

"Should?"

"Medieval theology meets contemporary crisis intervention. I'm doing my best."

Marcus, meanwhile, was coordinating media strategy. "If this goes public—when this goes public—we need to control the narrative. The families will claim religious persecution, theatrical protest, mentally unstable conspiracy theorists. We counter with evidence of kidnapping, documentation of historical fraud, and testimony from defectors."

He'd positioned backup journalists at safe distances, ready to publish if the primary team went dark. Insurance against being silenced.

Ethan had reached out to Lieutenant Santos at state police, providing her with redacted evidence and requesting standby units for

December 21st. She was skeptical but willing to have teams positioned nearby.

"I can't authorize intervention without probable cause," she'd told him. "But if you witness a crime in progress and call it in, we can respond. Fast."

It was the best they could hope for.

Robert provided crucial intelligence about the bridge's security systems and the families' likely approach. "They'll seal the maintenance access around 10 PM, claiming scheduled inspection. Private security will establish a perimeter. The ritual participants will arrive separately—Harrington, Patricia Castellano, Gregory Bishop, and Marcus Thorne will represent the four families."

"What about Sarah?" Nadia asked.

"They'll bring her directly from... wherever they're holding her. She won't know the location until the last minute. Can't escape if she doesn't know where she's going."

Sarah had insisted on staying visible and accessible, gambling that they wouldn't grab her early and risk public attention. It was a dangerous bet, but so far it was working.

Lilith had tested the foundation access key and confirmed it worked. "The chamber is small—maybe twenty feet across. Stone altar at the center, inscribed with symbols. Four alcoves for the family representatives. It's designed for exactly what they're planning."

"And there's definitely no cell signal down there?" Marcus confirmed.

"None. Too deep, too much iron interference. We're on our own once we enter."

December 21st, 2025. Winter solstice.

The day felt wrong from the moment Nadia woke up. Air too thick. Light too pale. A sense of pressure building, like the city itself was holding its breath.

She met with her team at Eli's bookshop for final preparations. Everyone was tense, checking equipment, reviewing plans, not quite making eye contact.

"Second thoughts?" Nadia asked the room generally.

"Constant thoughts," Father Mulligan admitted. "But I'm committed."

"I spoke to my kids this morning," Sarah said quietly. "Told them I loved them. Didn't tell them why. If this goes wrong—"

"It won't," Lilith interrupted. "We've planned for every contingency."

"Not every contingency. We're dealing with people who practice human sacrifice and we're planning to disrupt them using counter-magic we found in medieval church texts. There are so many ways this could go catastrophically wrong."

"Then we'll improvise," Nadia said. "We're good at that."

Ethan arrived at 6 PM with final intelligence. "State police are positioned at the Route 9 junction, fifteen minutes out. I'll be outside the chamber with a direct line to Santos. If you get in trouble, I call it in and they mobilize immediately."

"And your captain?"

"Harrington's been suspiciously quiet. Either he doesn't know we're planning this, or he's confident we'll fail." Ethan's expression was grim. "I'm hoping for the former."

Marcus had his livestream equipment tested and ready. "I'll be on the bridge deck, northeast side, with clear sightlines to the maintenance access. If anyone approaches, I'll document it. If they try to stop me, that's assault on a journalist, on camera."

Robert handed out copies of the bridge schematics. "Maintenance access opens here. Stairs down to the foundation level. The consecration chamber is behind a false wall in the northeast support pillar. Lilith's key should open it."

"Should?"

"The lock is over a century old. It might be corroded, jammed, or deliberately changed if they suspected compromise."

"Comforting."

They synchronized watches. The astronomical moment of the solstice—when the sun reached its lowest point, and the day turned from shortening to lengthening—occurred at 11:47 PM. The ritual would likely begin shortly before, building to a climax at the exact turning.

That gave them a narrow window: arrive after the participants had gathered but before the ritual reached critical stages.

10:30 PM: Take positions

11:00 PM: Access chamber

11:15 PM: Interrupt ritual, begin counterworking

11:47 PM: Solstice moment—either Covenant renewed, or Covenant broken

"And if they start early?" Sarah asked.

"Then we improvise," Nadia repeated. It was becoming her mantra.

At 10 PM, Nadia drove to the bridge with Lilith, Father Mulligan, and Sarah. Ethan followed in his personal vehicle. Marcus was already in position with his equipment. Robert would arrive separately, maintaining his cover as long as possible.

The bridge loomed against the dark December sky, its iron framework illuminated by streetlights that cast long shadows across the river. Nadia felt the familiar wrongness intensify as they approached—the sense of pressure, of watching eyes, of a city that remembered its sins.

Marcus gave them a thumbs-up from his position on the bridge deck. His camera was rolling, streaming live to multiple platforms with a fifteen-minute delay. If the team went silent, the footage would automatically publish.

They parked in the shadows of the old industrial area and approached the maintenance access on foot. Private security was already in place—two men in dark suits stationed at the bridge approach, another at the access gate.

"Praetorians," Ethan identified quietly. "The families' private muscle."

"Can we get past them?"

"Not without confrontation." He pulled out his badge. "Let me try official channels first."

He approached the nearest guard. Nadia couldn't hear the conversation, but she saw the guard's posture shift from neutral to defensive. Ethan's voice rose. The guard reached for his radio.

Then Robert Castellano appeared, walking up to the guard with the confidence of someone who belonged there.

"It's fine," Robert said smoothly. "They're with me. Family business."

The guard looked uncertain. "Sir, we have orders—"

"And I'm giving you different orders. I'm Robert Castellano, Patricia's brother, and these people are consultants I've brought for the ceremony. Let us through."

The guard's radio crackled. A voice Nadia recognized as Thomas Harrington III: *"Let them through. All of them. If they want to witness the Covenant's renewal, let them see what happens to those who question it."*

The guard stepped aside.

"That was too easy," Ethan muttered as they passed.

"They're confident," Lilith said. "They think we can't stop them."

Or it's a trap, Nadia thought but didn't say.

The maintenance access stairs descended into darkness. Lilith led with a flashlight. The air grew colder as they went deeper, and Nadia felt the pressure intensify—like descending into deep water, the weight of the city pressing down.

At the bottom, a corridor ran along the foundation. Old stone walls, newer iron supports, the smell of river water and rust. Lilith counted support pillars until she reached the northeast corner.

"Here."

The false wall was cunningly designed, barely visible as separate from the surrounding stone. Lilith found the keyhole hidden in the mortar, inserted her grandmother's iron key, and turned.

The mechanism was old but functional. The wall section pivoted inward, revealing a narrow passage.

Beyond, Nadia heard voices. Chanting.

They'd already started.

The consecration chamber was exactly as Lilith had described: twenty feet across, circular, domed ceiling carved with symbols that hurt to look at directly. Four alcoves at cardinal points, each occupied by a robed figure. At the center, a stone altar.

And on the altar, bound with rope and positioned at precise angles, was Sarah Thorne-Morrison.

Except Sarah was standing next to Nadia, staring at her own double on the altar.

"What—" Sarah whispered.

The figure on the altar turned its head. Not Sarah. Someone who looked like her in the flickering candlelight, but on closer inspection was older. Worn. Terrified.

"Eleanor Vance," Father Mulligan breathed. "Dear God, they're using her."

But Eleanor had disappeared in 1971. Fifty-four years ago. The woman on the altar was maybe sixty years old.

"Impossible," Ethan said.

Thomas Harrington III stood at the north point, wearing robes marked with symbols that matched the Covenant seal. His voice carried authority and absolute conviction as he turned to face the newcomers.

"You're just in time to witness the renewal. How fitting." He didn't seem surprised or concerned by their presence. "You wanted the truth, Ms. Marsh. Now you'll see it completely."

"That's Eleanor Vance," Nadia said. "You've held her prisoner for fifty-four years."

"Held? No. She became part of the Covenant. Blood binds, blood sustains, blood renews." Harrington gestured to the altar. "She chose to question. She chose to resist. So she became the bridge itself—living anchor to the original pact. Every twenty years, we draw on that anchor to renew the binding."

Eleanor Vance's eyes met Nadia's. There was intelligence there, awareness, but also something broken. Decades of captivity had taken their toll.

"You can't do this," Sarah said, her voice shaking. "This is murder. Torture. Abomination."

"This is tradition." The voice came from one of the alcoves—Patricia Castellano, also robed. "The Covenant requires maintenance. Our prosperity, our power, our very survival depends on the binding remaining strong. One life every generation is a small price for a century of achievement."

"She's not a price, she's a person," Lilith snapped.

From another alcove, her uncle Gregory Bishop emerged. "Lilith. I'd hoped you'd come to understand. The Bishop bloodline has sustained Daybridge for four generations. You could take your place in the tradition, help guide the city's future—"

"I choose to end the tradition," Lilith interrupted. She pulled out a small vial of salt and scattered it in a circle around herself. "I am Bishop bloodline, and I withdraw my consent. I break the binding."

The air in the chamber shifted. The pressure intensified until Nadia's ears popped.

Gregory's expression went from patronizing to furious. "You don't understand what you're doing—"

"I understand perfectly." Lilith took a small knife from her pocket and pricked her finger, letting three drops of blood fall onto the salt circle. "Blood willingly given to counter blood taken by force. I invoke the unbinding."

Father Mulligan began to chant in Latin, reading from the text Eli had provided. Words of dissolution, breaking, release.

Harrington's composure cracked. "Stop them!"

Two Praetorians entered from passages Nadia hadn't noticed. Ethan moved to intercept, his service weapon drawn.

"Don't," Ethan warned. "State police are five minutes out. Everyone stays calm—"

One of the Praetorians pulled a weapon. Ethan fired.

The gunshot in the enclosed space was deafening. The Praetorian went down. The other charged.

Nadia rushed toward the altar, toward Eleanor Vance. She had to free her, had to—

Harrington blocked her path. Despite being in his seventies, he moved with unnatural strength, grabbing her arm and throwing her against the stone wall.

"You don't understand," he hissed. "The Covenant isn't just tradition. It's real. The binding is real. Break it and you break everything—the prosperity, the protection, the very fabric that holds this city together."

Sarah had reached the altar. She was cutting Eleanor's bonds with a pocket knife, talking to her in soothing tones.

From the fourth alcove, Marcus Thorne—younger than the others, maybe forty—watched with an expression of conflicted horror. "This isn't what I agreed to. You said the renewal was symbolic—"

"Symbols have power," Patricia Castellano said coldly. "You knew what you were joining."

"I didn't know you kept someone prisoner for fifty years!"

Father Mulligan continued his counter-ritual, voice rising above the chaos. Lilith had drawn symbols on the floor with salt and silver powder, creating a pattern that mirrored and inverted the carvings on the altar.

The chamber began to shake.

Not metaphorically. The stone floor trembled. Dust fell from the ceiling. The candles flickered despite there being no wind.

"It's working," Lilith said, awed and terrified. "The binding is breaking."

"It's destroying the foundation," Harrington shouted. "You're going to collapse the bridge!"

A crack appeared in the stone wall. Then another.

Ethan had subdued the second Praetorian and was calling for backup on his radio. "Santos, we need units now! Shots fired, multiple suspects, structure is unstable—"

The solstice moment approached. 11:47 PM. The turning point.

Nadia felt it in her bones—the pressure building to unbearable levels, the sense of something massive straining against constraints it had held for a century.

Eleanor Vance, freed from her bonds, stood on shaking legs. She looked at Sarah with something like recognition. "Thorne bloodline. Like me. They would have used you next."

"I'm sorry," Sarah said, crying. "I'm so sorry for what my family did."

"Then help me end it."

Eleanor took the knife from Sarah, pricked her own finger, and let her blood drop onto Lilith's salt circle. "I am Vance bloodline, stolen and bound. I invoke the unbinding. Let the stolen be freed. Let the binding be broken."

The chamber exploded with light.

Not fire. Not electricity. Pure illumination that seemed to come from the stone itself. In that light, Nadia saw visions flooding her perception:

The bridge under construction. Workers falling—not accidentally, deliberately pushed. Blood mixed into mortar. Twelve families watching, horrified and complicit.

The consolidation. Eight families losing everything. Some fleeing. Others disappearing. Bodies buried in unmarked graves.

Eleanor Vance in 1971, investigating, discovering too much. Captured. Bound. Made into living anchor for the Covenant's renewal.

Michael Torres in 1989. Jennifer Wu in 2004. Victoria Pierce in 2020. All of them sacrificed or nearly sacrificed to maintain the binding.

And underneath it all, something older. Something that predated the families, predated the bridge, predated the city. A hunger built into the land itself, fed by the ritual, growing stronger with each sacrifice.

The visions hit everyone in the chamber simultaneously. Nadia heard Patricia Castellano screaming. Saw Marcus Thorne vomiting. Watched Harrington fall to his knees, confronted with the full weight of what his family had done.

And then, at precisely 11:47 PM, the solstice moment, the binding broke.

The sensation was like a massive rope snapping—violent, sudden, with backlash that knocked everyone to the floor. The chamber's symbols blazed with light one final time, then went dark. The pressure vanished so abruptly that Nadia gasped like surfacing from deep water.

Silence.

Then, from above, the sound of sirens. State police arriving.

Ethan was the first to recover, moving quickly to secure Harrington and Patricia while they were still disoriented. "Thomas Harrington, Patricia Castellano, you're under arrest for kidnapping, unlawful imprisonment, attempted murder—"

"You can't prove any of this," Harrington said, his voice hollow with defeat. "The ritual, the binding—it'll sound like delusion. Theater."

"I don't need to prove ritual magic," Ethan said. "I need to prove you held Eleanor Vance against her will for fifty-four years. That you planned to murder Sarah Thorne-Morrison. That you conducted a conspiracy to cover up historical crimes. Those charges will stick."

Lieutenant Santos arrived with state police units, weapons drawn, taking in the bizarre scene: robed figures, salt circles, a traumatized woman freed from an altar, ancient symbols carved into stone.

"Detective Reeves, what the hell is this?"

"Kidnapping in progress, Lieutenant. Rescue successful. Suspects in custody."

Santos looked at Eleanor Vance, clearly elderly but with no identification, no record of her existence for half a century. "Who is she?"

"Eleanor Vance. Declared missing in 1971. Held captive by these families for fifty-four years."

"That's... that's impossible. No one could—"

"Apparently they could. And they did." Ethan gestured to the chamber. "Document everything. This is a crime scene going back decades."

The aftermath was chaos.

Marcus Wong's livestream had captured the approach to the bridge, the confrontation with guards, the sound of gunshots from below. When the feed cut out (no signal in the chamber), he'd provided running commentary of the bridge shaking, the police arrival, the arrests.

By morning, the footage had millions of views.

Eleanor Vance was taken to Daybridge General, where Dr. Marcus Thorne—who'd been arrested at the scene—was stripped of his credentials. She was severely malnourished, showing signs of long-term captivity, but alive. Her DNA confirmed her identity. She'd been 28 when she disappeared. She was 82 now.

Thomas Harrington III, Patricia Castellano, Gregory Bishop, and several Praetorians were arrested on charges ranging from kidnapping to attempted murder. Marcus Thorne cooperated with investigators in exchange for reduced charges.

But the supernatural elements were quietly suppressed. The ritual was described as "theatrical intimidation." The binding was never mentioned in official reports. The visions, the breaking, the century-old conspiracy—all of it was simplified into a narrative law enforcement could process.

"Wealthy families conducting bizarre ceremonies to intimidate investigators and maintain social control through fear and violence."

It was true, as far as it went. But it wasn't the whole truth.

Robert Castellano disappeared three days after the arrests. His apartment was cleared out, his car found abandoned near the state line. Officially, he was wanted for questioning. Unofficially, most people assumed witness protection.

Or worse.

The legal proceedings dragged on for months.

Federal investigation into the Daybridge Development Consortium exposed decades of fraud, illegal property transfers, and racketeering. Multiple indictments. Multiple convictions. But most of the wealth remained protected in trusts and shell companies.

A restitution fund was established for descendants of the eight displaced families. But fights immediately broke out over who qualified, what damages could be proven, how much anyone deserved.

Some families reclaimed properties through legal challenges. Others received cash settlements. Still others rejected the money entirely, saying no amount could compensate for generational trauma.

The bridge itself was inspected and declared structurally sound, despite the cracks that had appeared in the foundation chamber. Engineers couldn't explain why the damage hadn't propagated through the entire structure. They also couldn't explain the stress patterns that suggested massive sudden force, then equally sudden release.

The consecration chamber was sealed permanently, filled with concrete, erased from official blueprints.

Sarah Thorne-Morrison survived but required extensive psychiatric care. The trauma of being prepared for sacrifice, of discovering her family's full legacy, of witnessing the Covenant's breaking—it was too much to process quickly. She was found unconscious at the scene after having undergone a psychological break. She eventually began working with descendants of the eight families, trying to build bridges and make restitution where possible.

Dr. Victoria Pierce's murder was officially solved—the Praetorians who'd killed her were convicted and sentenced to life without parole. But the ritual elements were minimized in court. Prosecutors focused on kidnapping and murder, avoiding anything that sounded supernatural.

And Thomas Harrington III died in custody.

Officially: heart attack. Natural causes. He was seventy-three, under extreme stress, with underlying cardiac issues.

Unofficially: He was found in his cell at 3 AM, having apparently died hours earlier. His final words, according to the guard who'd spoken to him that evening, were: "The Covenant is broken. We're all going to pay the price."

His son, Jeremiah Harrington, assumed control of the family business and resources at age twenty-eight. He immediately began a campaign of reform and reconciliation—apologizing for his father's actions, promising transparency, funding community programs.

Most people wanted to believe in his redemption arc.

Nadia didn't.

Three months after the solstice confrontation, Nadia sat across from Ethan Reeves at a diner in the next town over. He was in state police uniform now, having been forced to resign from Daybridge PD for his role in the bridge incident.

"Lieutenant Santos says I should thank you," Ethan said, stirring his coffee. "The arrests led to the biggest corruption bust in state history. Promotions all around."

"But?"

"But I miss being able to walk through Daybridge without people staring. Half of them think I'm a hero. The other half think I betrayed the city's founding families and destroyed our prosperity."

"Are they wrong?"

"About the prosperity? Maybe. The Development Consortium's assets are frozen. Multiple properties in legal limbo. Business investment down forty percent. Some people are genuinely hurting because of what we did."

Nadia thought about that. "Do you regret it?"

"Regret stopping human sacrifice and freeing a woman who'd been imprisoned for fifty years? No. Regret the complexity of the fallout and the fact that no solution is clean? Yes."

"Welcome to investigative journalism. Where every answer leads to harder questions."

"Is that why you're still investigating?"

Nadia pulled out her notebook. "You've noticed the pattern too?"

"What pattern?"

"Disappearances near the bridge at seasonal turning points. Spring equinox: local artist vanishes. Summer solstice: teenager goes missing during festival. Fall equinox: homeless man last seen near the foundation."

"Those could be coincidences."

"They're not. I've checked historical records. The pattern predates the families. Goes back to before the city was founded." She showed him her research. "The bridge didn't create whatever this is. It focused it. Channeled it. And now that the Covenant is broken—"

"It's not channeled anymore. It's free."

"That's my theory."

Ethan was quiet for a long moment. "You're saying we didn't solve the problem. We just changed it."

"I'm saying Daybridge was built on something dark. The families exploited it, tried to control it, maybe even fed it through their sacrifices. But breaking their Covenant didn't eliminate the underlying corruption. It just exposed it."

"What are you going to do?"

"Keep investigating. Document the pattern. Figure out what we're actually dealing with."

"And if it's something that can't be stopped? Something that's part of the city's foundation?"

"Then at least people will know. At least they can make informed choices about whether to stay, whether to raise families here, whether to keep building on cursed ground."

Ethan reached across the table, took her hand. "You rush in, Nadia. You see injustice and you attack it without always thinking through the consequences. That's admirable. It's also going to get you killed."

"And you need evidence that holds up in court, proper procedure, official channels. That's professional. It's also going to let people suffer while you dot i's and cross t's."

"That's always going to be our problem, isn't it?"

"Probably."

They sat in complicated silence. There was attraction there, respect, shared trauma. But also fundamental differences in approach that neither would compromise.

Finally, Ethan stood. "Be careful. Jeremiah Harrington is rebuilding his family's influence. Quietly. Carefully. He's young, charismatic, promising reform. People want to believe in him."

"But you don't."

"I arrested his father. I'm not objective." He paused. "But my gut says he's playing a longer game. Positioning himself as the enlightened new generation while maintaining the old power structures under different branding."

"I'll watch him."

"I know you will. That's what worries me."

After he left, Nadia opened her laptop and reviewed her latest research. Jeremiah Harrington had announced his candidacy for city council. His platform: "Healing Daybridge's divisions, honoring our past while building our future."

The language was carefully crafted. Acknowledging historical wrongs without accepting liability. Promising change while maintaining stability. It was exactly what a traumatized city wanted to hear.

Which made it dangerous.

Nadia pulled up the Bishop ledger, now in digital form, and searched for references to succession. What she found chilled her:

When the Covenant is challenged, when the binding is threatened, the Order must adapt. A new generation must rise, appearing to break with the past while preserving the essential work. The Covenant changes faces but maintains its purpose.

There were precedents. Times when public exposure had threatened the families' control, and they'd responded by appearing to reform while actually consolidating power under new structures.

"He's not reforming," Nadia muttered to herself. "He's rebranding."

She started a new file: "The New Covenant—Jeremiah Harrington Investigation."

THREE YEARS LATER - DECEMBER 2028

Nadia stood on the Daybridge Bridge at night, collar turned up against the December wind, watching shadows move in ways shadows shouldn't move.

It was three years since the Covenant had been broken. Three years since Eleanor Vance had been freed. Three years since the founding families' power had been publicly exposed.

And the city was worse.

Not economically—Jeremiah Harrington's policies had actually stabilized development, attracted new business, lowered crime rates. On paper, Daybridge was thriving.

But Nadia had been tracking the pattern. Disappearances at seasonal turning points, now more frequent. Strange incidents near the bridge. People reporting dreams of falling, of blood in water, of shadows that whispered names.

The Covenant had channeled something. Bound it. Fed it through controlled sacrifice. Breaking the Covenant had freed it.

And now it was hungry.

She felt it tonight—that familiar wrongness amplified. The air thick. The shadows moving against the light. The sense of watching presence.

Her phone buzzed. Text from an unknown number:

The Covenant is broken, but blood remembers. The work continues. - A Friend

Not Harrington. His threats were more sophisticated. This was someone else. Someone who understood what lived under Daybridge.

Nadia pulled out her voice recorder, speaking to herself as much as to potential future listeners:

"When you live in Daybridge long enough, you start noticing patterns. And I'm noticing a new one. The families controlled something dark for a century. They fed it. Maintained it. Maybe even strengthened it. We broke their power, exposed their crimes, freed their victims. But we didn't address the underlying corruption. We didn't deal with whatever they were feeding."

She looked at the bridge's iron framework, at the foundation stones where the Covenant had been sealed and broken.

"Jeremiah Harrington is running for mayor. His platform is unity and prosperity. He's popular, charismatic, promising to heal the city's divisions. And I think he's planning to rebuild the Covenant under a new name. Modernize it. Make it acceptable for the 21st century."

A shadow moved at the edge of her vision. She turned, but nothing was there.

"The question is: what happens if he succeeds? Or what happens if he fails? If the thing the families bound is now free, if it's been growing stronger without controls—"

The whisper came on the wind, clear enough to hear:

Blood willing or blood taken. The bridge remembers. The work continues.

Nadia shivered, but kept recording.

"My next investigation starts now. Figure out what the Covenant was really binding. Find out what Jeremiah's planning. And somehow stop it before this city pays the price for a century of blood sacrifice."

She took one final photo of the bridge at night—iron framework stark against dark sky, shadows pooling beneath supports, the sense of something ancient and hungry watching from below.

Then she walked back to her car, already planning her approach to infiltrating Jeremiah's campaign, already mapping connections between current disappearances and historical patterns, already knowing this investigation would be more dangerous than the last.

Because the families had been human—terrible, but understandable.

What lived under Daybridge was something else entirely.

And it was waking up.

~~~

THE GHOST ADOPTION AGENCY

Welcome to Daybridge: Where the Dead Deserve Justice

When Miranda Hayes adopted a ghost to fill the loneliness left by her sister's death, she thought she was gaining a companion. Instead, she discovered a seventy-year-old nightmare hiding behind legal contracts and government approval—a ghost trafficking operation built on the murdered bodies of children, where the dead are property and torture is called "evaluation."

This is Part One of *The Ghost Adoption Agency*, a serialized story about one woman's choice to fight back against a system that treats consciousness as a commodity and suffering as profit. What begins as a simple adoption becomes a descent into the depths of Daybridge's darkest secret: a facility twelve levels deep where ghosts have been screaming for decades, waiting for someone brave enough—or foolish enough—to care.

Miranda will lose everything. Her freedom. Her safety. Her life as she knows it. But she'll gain something more precious: the chance to free hundreds of trapped souls and expose a conspiracy that's been hiding in plain sight since 1952.

Some prisons are invisible. Some chains are made of contract law. And some nine-year-old ghosts have been waiting seventy years for rescue.

This Is Their Story. This Is How It Begins.

(Content warning: This story contains themes of child death, systematic abuse, and supernatural horror. Reader discretion advised.)

CHAPTER ONE: THE ADOPTION

The brochure promised companionship without complications. Miranda Hayes turned it over in her hands for the third time that morning, studying the elegant script beneath the eye-within-triangle logo. *Eternal Bonds Adoption Services: Where the Departed Find Purpose, and the Living Find Peace.*

She'd found it tucked under her apartment door two weeks after burying her sister.

The office occupied the top floor of a renovated brownstone on Daybridge's west side, where old money had scrubbed away decades of grime to reveal marble facades and brass fixtures. Miranda climbed the stairs slowly, her shoes clicking against worn stone.

Vivienne Thornwell rose from behind a mahogany desk as Miranda entered. Tall, silver-haired, with the kind of posture that suggested ballet training or military service. Her handshake was cool and dry.

"Please sit." Vivienne's office smelled of old books and something floral Miranda couldn't identify. Lilies, maybe. "I understand you've experienced a recent loss."

Miranda's throat tightened. "My sister. Emma. Three months ago."

"And you live alone now."

"Yes."

Vivienne pulled a leather portfolio from her desk drawer. "Traditional pets don't appeal to you?"

"I travel for work. Architecture consultant. Sometimes I'm gone for weeks." Miranda smoothed her skirt; aware she was fidgeting. "It wouldn't be fair."

"But you want companionship. Someone to come home to." Vivienne's pale eyes studied her face. "Someone who understands loss."

She opened the portfolio, revealing photographs. Not of people, but of what looked like wisps of smoke caught mid-swirl. The images shifted in the light, almost moving.

"We maintain a registry of spirits who've completed their initial transition," Vivienne explained. "Most died traumatically or suddenly—accidents, violence, unexpected illness. They're caught between, you see. Not quite ready to move on, but no longer part of the living world." Her fingers traced one photograph. "We provide structure. Training. And eventually, placement with compatible hosts."

"It's legal?"

"Completely." Vivienne slid a thick contract across the desk. "Our organization operates under Daybridge's Ethereal Entities Act of 1968. Full licensing, regular inspections, comprehensive liability coverage."

Miranda scanned the first page. Dense legal language about "spectral guardianship," and "ectoplasmic residency rights." "What about returns? If it doesn't work out?"

"We encourage a minimum bonding period of six months. After that, relocation is possible, though traumatic for both parties." Vivienne's expression softened slightly. "Think of it like adoption. These are consciousnesses, Ms. Hayes. Not possessions to be discarded."

The photographs drew Miranda's attention again. One in particular called to her—a spiral of pale light with what might have been the suggestion of a child's face. "Tell me about this one."

"Lily." Vivienne's voice warmed. "Died at age nine in 1952. Hit-and-run near the bridge. She's been with us for seven decades, waiting for the right match."

"That's a long time."

"She's particular. Sensitive. She needs someone patient. Someone who understands what it means to lose family too young." Vivienne tilted her head. "Your file mentioned your parents died when you were ten. Car accident."

Miranda's chest constricted. "Is that why you matched us?"

"Shared trauma creates bonds. Understanding." Vivienne pulled out another form. "Lily would need her own space. A room she could claim as hers."

"I can do that." The words came out before Miranda could think them through. But the loneliness had been suffocating lately. The apartment too quiet. Emma's voicemail message was still saved on her phone because she couldn't bear to delete it.

Vivienne smiled. "Excellent. Let's review the terms."

The contract was thirty-seven pages long. Miranda signed her name seventeen times, initialed forty-two clauses, and provided blood samples for what Vivienne called "spiritual verification."

"The bonding ceremony is tomorrow evening," Vivienne explained as she notarized the final page. "Sunset is optimal for manifestation. You'll need to prepare a space—white candles, sea salt for a protective circle, and this." She handed Miranda a small crystal vial filled with what looked like mercury. "Three drops on the threshold. It helps thin the barrier."

Miranda spent the next day converting Emma's old bedroom. She moved the boxes of her sister's belongings to the basement, vacuumed, and washed the windows. The room faced east, catching morning light that turned the walls golden. Emma had loved that light.

She hung one of Emma's paintings—a view of the bridge at sunset, its Gothic arches stark against the orange sky.

The white candles went on the windowsill. The sea salt formed a circle in the room's center, exactly as Vivienne's instructions specified. Miranda checked her watch. Five-thirty. Sunset at six-seventeen.

She opened the crystal vial. The liquid inside caught the fading light, swirling with colors that shouldn't exist—purple-green, silver-black, shades without names. Three drops on the threshold.

The first drop hit the hardwood and spread impossibly wide. The second created a sound—a low hum that Miranda felt in her teeth. The third made the air shimmer.

Miranda stepped back into the hallway and waited.

Something moved in the salt circle. A shimmer like heat rising from summer pavement. Then, more substantial—a girl-shaped outline, sketched in pale smoke. Features resolved slowly: small face, large eyes, dark hair in braids that defied gravity.

Lily coalesced like morning fog given form and purpose.

She looked exactly nine years old. Exactly dead.

"Hello," Miranda whispered.

The ghost-girl's mouth moved, but no sound emerged. She tried again, and this time Miranda heard it—a voice like wind through empty rooms. "You're Miranda."

"Yes. And you're Lily."

"They said you'd be kind." Lily drifted to the window, her form more solid now. She touched the glass with translucent fingers. "They said you lost your sister."

"I did."

"I lost everyone." Lily turned, and her eyes—God, her eyes were so old. Ancient and tired in that child's face. "That's why I'm here. Because I have no one else."

Miranda's throat ached. "You have me now."

"Do I?" Lily's expression was unreadable. "Or do you have me?"

Before Miranda could answer, the ghost-girl smiled. It transformed her face, making her look genuinely nine for the first time. "It's a nice room. Thank you."

The first week was awkward. Miranda had grown accustomed to silence. Now the apartment held two presences, one living and one not.

Lily spent hours at the window watching the city. Sometimes she drifted through walls, exploring. Miranda would come home from grocery shopping to find the ghost-girl in her bedroom examining photographs, or in the kitchen hovering near the stove where dinner preparations filled the air with scents she could no longer experience.

"Tell me about Emma," Lily said one evening. They were in the living room—Miranda on the couch with a book, Lily cross-legged on the floor in a shaft of lamplight.

"She was brilliant. Creative. She saw beauty in everything." Miranda closed the book. "Too young to die."

"I was nine."

"I know. I'm sorry."

"Everyone's—" Lily stopped herself. "Sorry. I know you don't mean it like they do."

"Like who?"

"Ms. Thornwell. The others at the agency." Lily's form dimmed slightly. "They're always sorry. Sorry we died. Sorry, we're stuck. Sorry, they can't do more. But they keep us there, anyway. In those rooms."

Miranda sat forward. "What rooms?"

"Where they keep us. Before adoption." Lily traced patterns on the hardwood. "Little boxes made of salt and silver. So we can't drift away. So we're there when someone wants us."

"That sounds—"

"Like a prison?" Lily's eyes met hers. "It is. But Ms. Thornwell says it's necessary. For our own protection. So we don't dissipate or get caught by something worse."

"Something worse?"

"There are things that hunt ghosts. Eat them." Lily shivered, her form rippling. "The agency protects us from that. As long as we follow the rules."

Miranda's stomach turned. "What rules?"

"Don't scare the hosts. Don't manifest during daylight unless invited. Don't talk about the agency's methods. Don't—" Lily stopped, her expression closing off. "Lots of rules."

"Lily—"

"I'm tired. Can I go to my room?"

"Of course. It's your space."

The ghost-girl floated to her feet and drifted toward the hallway. At the doorway, she paused. "Thank you for the painting. Emma was talented."

Then she was gone, leaving Miranda alone with growing unease.

In the second week, Miranda noticed the scratches.

They appeared on her bedroom doorframe—three parallel grooves in the wood, too precise to be accidental. She found more on the bathroom mirror, faint but visible when light hit at certain angles. Letters scratched backward: HELP.

"Lily?" Miranda called out. "Can we talk?"

The ghost-girl materialized in the hallway, her expression wary. "Did I do something wrong?"

"The scratches. What do they mean?"

Lily's form flickered. "I don't know what you're talking about."

"'Help.' You wrote 'help' on my mirror."

"I didn't." But Lily wouldn't meet her eyes. "I wouldn't. That's against the rules."

"What rules?"

"The contract. I'm not supposed to frighten you. Not supposed to damage property. Not supposed to—" Lily's voice cracked. "I'm sorry. I'll be good. Please don't send me back."

Miranda's heart clenched. "I'm not going to send you back. I want to help. But you have to tell me what's wrong."

"I can't."

"Why not?"

"Because they'll know." Lily's eyes were wide with fear. "They're always watching. Always listening. If I tell you the truth, they'll take me back, and I'll never get out again."

"Lily, you're scaring me."

"I'm scaring *you?*" The ghost-girl laughed, a sound like breaking glass. "You have no idea what fear is. You're alive. You can leave whenever you want. I'm trapped. Forever. Unless—"

She stopped, her form dimming almost to invisibility.

"Unless what?" Miranda pressed.

"Nothing. Forget I said anything." Lily started to drift away.

"Wait—"

"I said, forget it!" The ghost-girl's voice rose to a shriek. The lights flickered. The temperature dropped twenty degrees in an instant. "Just leave me alone!"

She vanished, leaving frost patterns on the walls.

Miranda stood in the hallway, breath misting in the sudden cold, and wondered what she'd brought into her home.

The scratches multiplied. Miranda woke to find them on her nightstand, carved deep: NOT SAFE. On the kitchen cabinets: LIES. On the bathroom tile: RUN.

She tried calling Eternal Bonds, but the number went to voicemail. She left four messages. None were returned.

Lily avoided her. The ghost-girl stayed in her room most of the time or disappeared entirely for hours. When she did manifest, her eyes held a desperate, hunted quality that made Miranda's skin crawl.

"Please talk to me," Miranda begged on the tenth night. She stood outside Lily's door, pressing her palm to the wood. "Whatever's wrong, we can fix it together."

Silence. Then, so quietly Miranda almost missed it: "You can't fix this. No one can."

"Let me try."

"They'll hurt you."

"Who will?"

More silence. Miranda waited, patient despite the fear coiling in her gut. Finally, Lily spoke again. "The agency. They're not what you think. The contract you signed—"

"What about it?"

"It's not just about me living here. It's about ownership. Control." Lily's voice trembled. "They own us. Body and soul. What's left of our souls, anyway."

Miranda's mouth went dry. "That can't be legal."

"Read the fine print. Section twenty-three, subsection C. 'The spectral entity hereby relinquishes all claims to autonomous existence and accepts binding servitude to—'"

"Servitude?"

"We're slaves." Lily's form materialized through the door, her face streaked with ectoplasmic tears. "They round up ghosts who are vulnerable, confused, newly dead. They promise protection, purpose, a chance to exist instead of dissipating. But once you sign their contract, once you enter their facility, you're theirs. Forever."

Miranda backed away, her heart hammering. "But you're here. You're free."

"Am I?" Lily gestured at the walls. "I can't leave this apartment. I'm anchored to you, bound by salt and silver and blood. Your blood. From the contract." The ghost-girl's eyes burned with anger and despair. "If you die, I go back to them. If you try to move without permission, I go back. If I disobey any of their rules, I go back."

"This is insane."

"This is legal. You signed the papers."

Miranda's legs felt weak. She sat heavily on the hallway floor. "I didn't know. I swear I didn't know."

"No one does. Not until it's too late." Lily sank down beside her. "I've been trying to warn you. The scratches, the messages. But I can't be too obvious, or they'll know. They monitor us. All of us. Every adopted ghost reports back."

"How?"

"At night. When you're sleeping. We're summoned for inspection. They check our anchors, verify our hosts are compliant, and punish any infractions." Lily's voice dropped to a whisper. "Last week, I saw what they did to a ghost who tried to break free. They put him in a containment sphere. Silver and salt and something worse. They compressed him down to nothing over three days. His screams—"

She broke off, shuddering.

Miranda felt sick. "Why are you telling me this now?"

"Because tonight's the one-month anniversary. The bonding period checkpoint." Lily met her eyes. "They're coming to verify the placement. To make sure you're satisfied with your purchase."

"You're not a purchase. You're a person."

"Not legally." Lily's smile was bitter. "Ghosts have no rights under the Ethereal Entities Act. We're classified as property."

Miranda's mind raced. The elegant office. Vivienne's professional demeanor. The thick contract she'd signed without reading carefully. "What happens during verification?"

"Ms. Thornwell will come. She'll interview you, examine me, ensure everything is proceeding according to contract terms." Lily's form dimmed. "And she'll look for signs of noncompliance. If she finds any—"

"She'll take you back."

"Or worse."

The doorbell rang.

Both of them froze.

"She's early," Lily whispered. Her form flickered wildly, panic radiating from her like heat. "Miranda, please. Please just—"

"I'll handle it." Miranda pushed to her feet, legs unsteady. "Go to your room. Act normal."

Lily vanished.

Miranda walked to the front door on autopilot, her mind screaming. Through the peephole, she saw Vivienne Thornwell standing in the hallway, perfectly coiffed, carrying a leather briefcase. Professional smile already in place.

Miranda opened the door.

"Ms. Hayes." Vivienne's eyes scanned the apartment behind her. "I hope I'm not intruding. It's time for our one-month evaluation."

"Of course. Come in."

Vivienne stepped inside, and the temperature dropped five degrees. Her gaze moved over the furniture, the walls, searching for something Miranda couldn't identify. "How has the placement been progressing?"

"Wonderfully. Lily's been perfect."

"No issues? No disturbances?"

Miranda forced herself to smile. "None at all. She's exactly what I needed."

"Excellent." Vivienne set her briefcase on the coffee table and opened it. Inside, Miranda glimpsed instruments that looked medical and ancient all at once—silver probes, crystal vials, something that might have been an astrolabe. "I'll need to conduct a brief examination. Standard procedure."

"What kind of examination?"

"Just verifying the bond integrity. Making sure Lily is properly anchored." Vivienne pulled out a device that resembled a tuning fork, but wrong—too many prongs, angles that hurt to look at directly. "This will only take a moment. Lily? Please manifest."

The ghost-girl appeared in the doorway to her room. Her expression was carefully neutral, but Miranda could see the terror in her eyes.

Vivienne approached her with the device. "Hold still, dear."

She struck the tuning fork against her palm. It produced no sound Miranda could hear, but Lily screamed.

The ghost-girl's form convulsed, her outlines blurring. Vivienne watched dispassionately, making notes on a tablet. "Anchor strength at eighty-seven percent. Within acceptable parameters. Manifestation stability—"

Lily screamed again, her body contorting.

"Stop it!" Miranda lunged forward. "You're hurting her!"

Vivienne didn't look up from her tablet. "Spectral entities don't experience pain as we do, Ms. Hayes. This is merely a stress test to ensure proper binding."

"She's screaming!"

"An autonomic response. Nothing more." Vivienne struck the fork again. Lily collapsed, her form barely visible now, wisps of smoke that could barely hold together. "Excellent. Full compliance indicators. No signs of resistance or autonomy development."

Miranda's hands clenched into fists. "Get out of my house."

Vivienne finally looked at her, one eyebrow raised. "Excuse me?"

"I said get out. Now."

"Ms. Hayes, I understand first placements can be emotionally challenging, but I assure you—"

"I don't care what you assure me. This is torture."

"This is standard procedure." Vivienne's voice turned cold. "A procedure you agreed to when you signed our contract. Section fifteen, subsection A, clearly states that the agency reserves the right to conduct monthly evaluations for the first year."

"I want to return her."

The words came out before Miranda could stop them. Lily's head snapped up, her expression transforming to pure betrayal and terror.

Vivienne smiled. "Returns require a six-month bonding period. You've only completed one month. Breaking the contract prematurely incurs significant penalties—financial and otherwise."

"How much?"

"Fifty thousand dollars. Plus forfeiture of any bond refund. Plus—" Vivienne's eyes glittered. "Lily would be classified as a failed placement. You understand what that means."

Miranda understood perfectly. The containment sphere. Three days of screaming. Crushed down to nothing.

"I'll keep her," Miranda said, the words like ground glass in her throat.

"I thought you might." Vivienne packed her instruments away with brisk efficiency. "I'll return next month for the two-month evaluation.

In the meantime, should you experience any issues, please don't hesitate to call."

She left, taking the cold and the wrongness with her.

Miranda turned to find Lily still collapsed on the floor, barely visible. "I'm so sorry. I didn't mean—"

"You were going to send me back." Lily's voice was barely a whisper. "After everything I told you. You were going to send me back."

"No. I just needed her to leave. I needed—"

"You're just like everyone else." Lily's form began to solidify again, but her eyes were dead. Empty. "I should have known. The living never understand. We're just things to you. Tools. Possessions."

"That's not true."

"Isn't it?" Lily floated upright, her expression hardening. "You wanted companionship. Someone to fill the hole your sister left. You didn't want me. You wanted Emma's ghost."

The words hit like a physical blow. "Lily—"

"I'm done talking." The ghost-girl turned away. "Just leave me alone. Use me however you want. I don't care anymore."

She vanished into her room and didn't emerge for the rest of the night.

Miranda sat on the couch, head in her hands, trying to figure out what the hell she'd just done.

The apartment felt colder than ever. Empty, despite Lily's presence just one room away.

Outside, the Daybridge night pressed against the windows. Somewhere in the darkness, the bridge loomed over the Shadowlair River, its Gothic arches hiding secrets Miranda was only beginning to understand.

She pulled out the contract and began reading. Every word this time. Every clause, every subsection, every tiny-print warning she'd ignored.

By the time dawn broke, she'd decided.

If the contract made Lily a slave, then Miranda would find a way to break it.

No matter what it cost.

CHAPTER TWO: THE REVELATION

Three days passed in silence.

Lily stayed in her room, manifesting only as a faint shimmer when Miranda brought offerings she knew the ghost couldn't consume—tea that went cold untouched, books left unread on the nightstand. Miranda worked from home, unable to focus on the architectural plans spread across her dining table. The lines blurred together, meaningless.

The apartment felt like a tomb.

On the fourth morning, Miranda found new scratches on her bathroom mirror. Not words this time—numbers. A date: 08/15/1952.

The day Lily died.

"I'm researching," Miranda said to the empty hallway. She didn't know if Lily was listening. "The Ethereal Entities Act. The agency's licensing. There has to be a way out of this."

No response. But the scratches stopped appearing.

Miranda spent her days in the Daybridge Public Library's archives, pulling dusty volumes on spectral law. The Ethereal Entities Act of 1968 was a masterwork of legal manipulation—ghosts classified as "semi-autonomous phenomena" rather than persons. No rights. No protections. Property in the eyes of the law.

Eternal Bonds Adoption Services held a perfect record. Fifteen years of operation, hundreds of placements, zero violations. On paper, they were a model organization.

Miranda dug deeper.

She found newspaper articles from the 1970s—scattered reports of ghosts disappearing from placements, never accounted for. A 1983 lawsuit filed by a host who'd witnessed what she called "systematic abuse," dismissed when the plaintiff mysteriously withdrew her complaint. Three legislators who'd proposed ghost rights bills, all of whom died in accidents before the bills reached a vote.

Coincidences. Probably.

But Miranda's hands shook as she photographed the articles with her phone.

Detective Chen called on day six.

"Ms. Hayes? This is Detective Alice Chen, Daybridge PD, Cold Case Division. I understand you recently adopted a ghost through Eternal Bonds. A child named Lily?"

Miranda's stomach dropped. "Yes. Why?"

"I'm investigating a series of unsolved deaths from the 1950s. Hit-and-runs near the Shadowlair Bridge. Your Lily was one of six children killed within a three-month period in 1952." Chen's voice was professional but careful. "All the cases went cold. But I've been reviewing old files, and there are... patterns. Inconsistencies."

"What kind of inconsistencies?"

"The kind that suggests these weren't accidents." A pause. "I'd like to interview Lily. With your permission."

Miranda's mind raced. "She's not very communicative right now. We've had some... adjustment issues."

"I understand. But Ms. Hayes, if there's any chance these children were murdered, if someone was never held accountable—" Chen's voice softened. "They deserve justice. Even the dead ones."

"Give me a few days. Let me talk to her."

"Of course. But Ms. Hayes? Be careful. Eternal Bonds has very powerful connections in this city. If you start asking questions, they'll know."

The line went dead.

Miranda stared at her phone, Chen's warning echoing in her mind. *They'll know.*

They probably already did.

That night, Miranda sat outside Lily's door with a printout of a 1952 newspaper article. The headline read: "Sixth Child Killed in Bridge Area Hit-and-Run Spree."

"I know you're listening," Miranda said quietly. "I know you're angry with me. You have every right to be. But I need you to know—I'm not giving up on you. I'm going to find a way to break this contract. To set you free."

Silence. Then, so faint Miranda almost missed it: "Why?"

"Because it's wrong. Because you're a person, not property. Because—" Miranda's throat tightened. "Because Emma would never forgive me if I let this stand."

The door opened. Not physically—it remained closed. But Lily's form materialized through it, sitting cross-legged in the air at eye level with Miranda.

"Tell me about Emma," the ghost-girl said.

So Miranda did. She talked about her sister's laugh, her terrible cooking, her habit of singing off-key in the shower. How Emma had raised Miranda after their parents died, working two jobs to keep them together. How she'd encouraged Miranda's interest in architecture, even when money was tight. How she'd died too young—aneurysm at thirty-one, gone in an instant.

"She sounds like she was brave," Lily said when Miranda finished.

"She was the bravest person I knew."

"Is that why you wanted a ghost? To fill the space she left?"

Miranda considered lying. Decided against it. "Partly. I was so lonely after she died. The apartment felt too big, too quiet. I thought—" She laughed bitterly. "I don't know what I thought. That having someone around would make it hurt less."

"Did it?"

"No. It just gave me someone else to fail."

Lily's expression softened. "You didn't fail me. You made a mistake. There's a difference." She drifted lower until she was sitting on the floor beside Miranda. "I made mistakes too. I trusted them when they found me. The agency."

"Tell me what happened."

"After I died?" Lily's form flickered, memories making her unstable. "I was confused. One moment I was walking home from school, the next I was standing over my own body, watching my mother scream. I didn't understand. I tried to talk to her, but she couldn't hear me. Couldn't see me."

"How long were you alone?"

"Weeks. Maybe months. Time felt strange. I wandered the bridge area, trying to make sense of what had happened. Other ghosts avoided me—I was too new, too emotional, too dangerous. Then the hunters came."

Miranda's blood chilled. "The things that eat ghosts?"

"Specters. Shadow-feeders. Things with too many mouths." Lily shuddered. "They cornered me near the old train yards. I thought I was going to cease—just stop existing. But Ms. Thornwell found me first."

"She saved you?"

"She captured me." Lily's voice went flat. "Used silver chains and binding circles. Told me I was lucky she got there before the specters did. Told me she could offer protection, purpose, a reason to keep existing. All I had to do was sign."

"And you believed her."

"I was nine and terrified and alone. Of course I believed her." Lily's eyes met Miranda's. "She took me to the facility. Said it was temporary, just until they found me a good home. But the rooms—the containment cells—they weren't temporary. Some ghosts had been there for decades. Waiting. Hoping. Going slowly mad."

Miranda felt sick. "How many?"

"Hundreds. Maybe thousands. The facility goes deep underground. Level after level of cells. Some ghosts are so old they've forgotten their names. Forgotten they were ever alive." Lily's form dimmed. "That's what happens when you're trapped too long. You lose yourself piece by piece until there's nothing left but obedience."

"Why do they keep so many?"

"Inventory." The word dripped with venom. "They match ghosts to hosts based on trauma compatibility. The more traumatized the ghost, the more broken, the easier to control. They advertise companionship, but what they're really selling is the illusion of power over death itself."

Miranda's hands clenched into fists. "The monthly evaluations. What Vivienne did to you—that's how they maintain control?"

"Partly. The tuning forks resonate at frequencies that destabilize our forms. It's agonizing. But more than that, it's a reminder. They can hurt us whenever they want. We exist at their pleasure." Lily's voice cracked. "Some hosts request it. They like watching us suffer. It makes them feel alive, powerful. The agency accommodates all preferences."

"That's monstrous."

"That's legal." Lily floated upright. "The contract you signed gives them access to this apartment. To me. Once a month minimum, more often if they suspect non-compliance. And if they determine I'm negatively affecting your wellbeing—"

"The containment sphere."

"Or worse. There are punishments that can be stretched across years. Centuries." Lily's form flickered wildly. "They can compress time for ghosts, making an hour feel like decades. I've heard echoes from the deep cells. Ghosts who tried to rebel, to break free. Some of them have been screaming for longer than I've been dead."

Miranda stood abruptly, pacing. "There has to be a way. A legal challenge, a loophole, something—"

"I've been trapped for seventy years. Do you think I haven't looked for a way out?" Lily's laugh was broken glass. "The contract is airtight. The law is on their side. Even if you found a sympathetic lawyer, even if you could afford to fight, they'd simply relocate me before any case reached trial. I'd disappear into the deep cells, and you'd never know what happened."

"Then we run. Both of us. Leave Daybridge, change identities—"

"I'm anchored to you. Bound by the blood you gave when you signed. I can't leave this apartment without their permission." Lily gestured at the walls. "This is my prison, just prettier than the last one."

Miranda stopped pacing. An idea was forming, terrible and desperate. "What if you weren't anchored to me anymore?"

"The bond can't be broken without killing you. That's in the contract too."

"But it can be transferred, right? From one host to another?"

Lily's eyes widened. "Theoretically. But the agency controls all transfers. You can't just—" She stopped. "What are you thinking?"

"I'm thinking that if ghosts are property, they can be stolen." Miranda pulled out her phone, scrolling through her contacts. "I have a friend. Myles. He's a data security consultant—reformed hacker. If anyone can break into Eternal Bonds' database, alter records, create false transfer documentation—"

"They'll catch you."

"Maybe. But while they're chasing me, you'll be free."

"Free to what? I'd still be anchored to someone. Still property."

"Free to choose who. Free to be anchored to someone who won't hurt you. Someone who'll help you find real freedom, if it exists." Miranda crouched down to Lily's level. "I failed you once. Let me try to make it right."

For a long moment, Lily just stared at her. Then, quietly: "Why would you risk this? You barely know me."

"Because Emma would." Miranda's voice broke. "Because someone should. Because you're nine years old and you've been tortured for seven decades, and that's not okay. It's never been okay."

Lily's form shimmered, and Miranda realized the ghost was crying. "There's something else. Something I haven't told you."

"What?"

"The hit-and-run that killed me? It wasn't an accident. And it wasn't random." Lily's voice dropped to a whisper. "The driver worked for the agency. Or the organization that became the agency. They were collecting ghosts even then, before it was legal. Killing children near the bridge because child ghosts are easier to control. More valuable."

Miranda's blood turned to ice. "You're saying they murdered you?"

"Me and five others in 1952 alone. Detective Chen is right—there are patterns. But she'll never prove it. The agency has too much power, too many connections. The people who know the truth are either dead or too afraid to talk."

"Do you know who drove the car?"

"No. I never saw their face. But Ms. Thornwell—" Lily's form flickered. "She was there afterward. I remember her voice from when I was dying. She stood over my body and said, 'This one will do nicely.' Like I was a specimen. Like my death was a harvest."

Miranda felt rage building in her chest, hot and righteous. "Then we don't just free you. We destroy them."

"You can't. They're too big, too entrenched—"

"Maybe I can't. But I can try." Miranda stood, her mind already racing through possibilities. "First, we get you transferred to someone safe. Then we gather evidence. Chen's investigating the murders—if we can connect them to Eternal Bonds, if we can prove the organization was built on systematic child murder—"

"They'll kill you before you get close."

"Then I'll have to be careful."

Lily floated upright, studying Miranda's face. "You're serious."

"Completely."

"You're insane."

"Probably." Miranda offered a grim smile. "But I'm also really, really angry. And I've got nothing left to lose."

"You have your life."

"What good is my life if I use it to enable monsters?" Miranda pulled out her laptop. "Help me. Tell me everything you know about the agency's operations. Security protocols. Weaknesses. Anything that might help."

Lily hesitated, then nodded. "Okay. But Miranda? When this goes wrong—and it will go wrong—run. Don't try to save me. Just run and never look back."

"Not a chance."

"You're as stubborn as Emma, aren't you?"

"It's a family trait."

For the first time since the evaluation, Lily smiled. A real smile, small but genuine. "Okay. Let's burn them down."

They worked through the night. Lily described the facility's layout—the upper floors where prospective hosts met their matches, the middle levels of containment cells, the deep cells far below street level where ghosts had been compressed into eternal torment. She explained the security systems: salt barriers at every threshold, silver mesh in the walls, binding circles that could trap ghosts indefinitely.

Miranda took notes, cross-referencing with building permits she pulled from city records. The facility occupied a condemned hospital building from 1947. On paper, the structure had five floors. According to Lily, it went down at least twelve levels.

Unauthorized construction. That was something.

At 2 AM, Miranda's phone buzzed. A text from an unknown number: *Stop asking questions. First warning.*

She showed Lily. The ghost-girl's form went pale. "They know."

"Good. Let them worry." Miranda texted back: *Make me.*

"That was stupid."

"That was a declaration." Miranda stood, stretching her stiff back. "I'm done being scared of them. I'm done playing by their rules."

"Miranda—"

A sound cut through the apartment. Not physical—something that bypassed ears entirely and resonated directly in the skull. A summoning call.

Lily jerked upright, her form pulled toward the door like iron to a magnet. "No. Not now. It's not evaluation time—"

"Fight it!"

"I can't!" Lily's voice was panicked. "It's the binding. When they call, I have to answer. I have to—"

Her form stretched, thinning as invisible forces dragged her toward the door. Miranda lunged forward, grabbing at the ghost—her hands passed through, useless. Lily's terrified eyes met hers for one moment.

Then she was gone, ripped away into the night.

Miranda ran to the window. Below, a black car idled at the curb. Vivienne Thornwell stood beside it, looking up at Miranda's apartment. Even from four floors up, Miranda could see her smile.

The car door opened. Lily's form flickered in the back seat, barely visible. Vivienne climbed in beside her.

The car pulled away into the darkness.

Miranda pressed her forehead against the cold glass, fury and helplessness warring in her chest. She'd promised to protect Lily. She'd failed again.

Her phone buzzed. Another text from the unknown number: *Second warning: Lily remains at the facility for remedial training. Duration: two weeks. You are forbidden from attempting contact. Violation will result in permanent relocation.*

Miranda stared at the message. Two weeks of "remedial training." She knew what that meant. Two weeks in the deep cells. Two weeks of screaming compressed into what would feel like years.

Her hands clenched into fists.

She opened her contacts and called Myles. He answered on the third ring, voice thick with sleep. "Do you know what time it is?"

"I need your help. Something illegal, dangerous, and probably suicidal."

A pause. Then: "I'm listening."

"How would you feel about hacking a ghost trafficking operation and destroying it from the inside?"

Another pause. Longer this time. "When do we start?"

"Now. Get here as fast as you can. And Myles? Bring everything you know about hacking government databases."

"I'll be there in ninety minutes."

Miranda hung up and turned back to the window. Somewhere in the darkness, Lily was being dragged down into the deep cells. But not for long.

The agency had made a mistake. They'd taken someone Miranda cared about.

They were about to learn what happened when you backed an architect into a corner.

Buildings could be torn down. Systems could be dismantled.

And she was very, very good at finding structural weaknesses.

CHAPTER THREE: THE UNDERGROUND

Myles arrived ninety minutes later with three laptops, a duffel bag of equipment Miranda didn't recognize, and dark circles under his eyes that suggested he'd thrown on clothes and driven straight over.

"Coffee first," he said, brushing past her into the apartment. "Then you explain why you're going to war with a legally sanctioned ghost trafficking ring."

Miranda made coffee while Myles set up his workstation on her dining table, cables snaking across the floor like digital veins. She told him everything—Emma's death, the adoption, Lily's revelations, the systematic murder of children in 1952.

"Jesus," Myles muttered when she finished. "And I thought my divorce was bad." He pulled up a terminal window, fingers flying across the keyboard. "Okay. First problem: Eternal Bonds has government-grade security. Firewalls, encryption, probably some spectral defenses I've never even heard of. Breaking into their database without triggering alarms is going to be—" He paused, eyes narrowing at his screen. "Huh."

"What?"

"Someone's already inside their network. Running a persistent backdoor, collecting data." Myles's fingers moved faster. "Whoever it is, they're good. Really good. They've been siphoning files for months, maybe years."

Miranda's pulse quickened. "Can you contact them?"

"Maybe. If they don't think I'm a threat." Myles cracked his knuckles. "Let me see if I can leave a digital calling card. Something that says, 'I'm friendly, please don't brick my system.'"

While Myles worked, Miranda researched. She found scattered references to ghost rights activists—dismissed as fringe lunatics by mainstream media. A few underground forums where people shared stories about abusive adoptions, ghosts who'd disappeared, evaluation sessions that crossed into outright torture.

One name kept appearing: August Rawson, a former Eternal Bonds employee who'd gone public three years ago, claiming the agency was systematically abusing ghosts. He'd been arrested for corporate espionage, served eighteen months, and dropped off the grid after his release.

Miranda found a single interview he'd given to an alternative news site before his arrest: *"They're not helping ghosts find peace. They're farming them. The whole industry is built on exploitation, and everyone in power knows it. They just don't care because ghosts aren't people in the eyes of the law."*

The article included a photo. August Rawson was in his fifties, gaunt-faced, with eyes that had seen too much.

"Got something," Myles said suddenly. "The person in their network just responded. They want to meet."

"Where?"

"The Greymoor Cemetery. North section, by the mausoleum. Tonight, at midnight." Myles looked uneasy. "They said to come alone and bring proof you're serious about helping ghosts."

"I'll go."

"Miranda, this could be a trap."

"Or they could be allies." She grabbed her jacket. "Either way, I'm out of options. Lily's been in that facility for less than a day and it's already too long."

Myles sighed. "Then at least take this." He pulled a small device from his bag—a palm-sized metal disc with strange symbols etched into its surface. "Personal ward. It'll protect you from most spectral attacks. Won't stop a living person from shooting you, but it's better than nothing."

Miranda pocketed the ward. "Thank you. For helping with this."

"Thank me when we're not in federal prison." But Myles managed a tight smile. "For what it's worth? What you're doing is insane. But it's also right. Emma would be proud."

The words hit harder than Miranda expected. She blinked back tears and nodded.

Greymoor Cemetery was older than Daybridge itself, a sprawling necropolis where marble angels stood eternal vigil over the dead. Miranda arrived fifteen minutes early, her breath misting in the cold night air.

The north mausoleum was a Gothic structure, all pointed arches and weathered stone. As Miranda approached, a figure emerged from the shadows—a woman in her thirties with close-cropped hair and a jacket covered in hand-sewn patches.

"You're Miranda Hayes," the woman said. Not a question.

"And you are?"

"Careful." The woman circled Miranda slowly, eyes sharp. "You brought the ward. Good. Shows Myles trusts you." She stopped, extending a hand. "I'm Sienna Park. I run the Liberation Network."

Miranda shook her hand. "The people inside Eternal Bonds' database?"

"Among other things." Sienna gestured toward the mausoleum. "Come inside. We don't have much time, and there's someone who wants to meet you."

The mausoleum's interior was larger than it appeared from outside, walls lined with crypts. Sienna led Miranda down a narrow staircase that shouldn't have existed, into a basement that definitely violated city building codes.

The room below was part bunker, part command center. Computer monitors covered one wall, displaying streams of data. Maps of Daybridge marked with glowing pins covered another. And in the center of the room, gathered around a makeshift table, were seven ghosts.

Miranda stopped short. She'd expected one, maybe two. Not this.

"Welcome to the Underground," Sienna said. "The ghosts the agency couldn't break."

An older man—or the ghost of one—stepped forward. He wore clothes from the 1940s, and his form was stronger than Lily's, more solid. "August Rawson. Former senior manager at Eternal Bonds. Deceased as of fourteen months ago. They made it look like suicide."

Miranda's mind reeled. "You're the whistleblower."

"I tried to be. They killed me before I could testify." August's expression was grim. "But death has its advantages. I can go places the living can't. Access systems they think are secure. And I'm very, very angry."

Another ghost drifted forward—a teenage girl with 1980s fashion and sad eyes. "I'm Kira. Adopted in 1989, escaped in 2003. Took me fourteen years to find a way out."

One by one, the ghosts introduced themselves. Thomas, killed in 1901, trapped for a century before liberation. Yuki, a Japanese woman from the 1960s who'd been sold between hosts like furniture. Marcus—a different ghost, not to be confused with Myles—who'd survived the deep cells and somehow clawed his way back to coherence.

Each one had escaped Eternal Bonds. Each had spent years, decades, building this network.

"How many?" Miranda asked. "How many ghosts has the agency trapped?"

"Active placements? Around eight hundred," August said. "But the facility holds thousands more. Ghosts they're warehousing, waiting for the right buyer. And the deep cells—" His form flickered. "We don't have accurate counts. Some ghosts down there are barely conscious anymore."

Sienna pulled up a file on the nearest monitor. "This is what we've collected over three years. Financial records showing the agency's real revenue—they're making millions selling ghosts to private collectors, research facilities, even military contractors. Ghost soldiers who can't refuse orders. Ghost laborers who never need rest. It's a whole underground economy."

"Why haven't you gone public?" Miranda demanded.

"With what proof? Ghost testimony isn't admissible in court. Electronic evidence can be dismissed as fabricated. And everyone who's tried to expose them ends up dead or discredited." August's voice was bitter. "We needed someone on the inside. Someone living, with legal standing, who could build a case they couldn't ignore."

"You need a host," Miranda said slowly. "Someone who adopted a ghost and can testify to the abuse."

"More than that. We need someone willing to raid the facility, document what's happening in real-time, and broadcast it to the world before they can stop us." Sienna met Miranda's eyes. "Someone brave enough or stupid enough to walk into the lion's den."

"You want me to break into Eternal Bonds."

"We want you to burn it down," Kira said softly. "Expose everything. Free everyone. One massive, coordinated action that they can't cover up or spin."

Miranda's heart hammered. "That's insane."

"Yes," August agreed. "But it's also the only way. The agency has survived this long because it operates in the shadows. Drag them into the light, and they can't hide what they are."

"Even if I agreed, how would I get inside? The facility's security—"

"Is designed to keep ghosts in, not living people out." Sienna pulled up building schematics. "August gave us the blueprints before he died. There's a maintenance entrance on the east side, usually unmanned after midnight. You'd need to disable the salt barriers, avoid the patrols, and reach the central server room on level three."

"While documenting everything on camera," Kira added. "We need video evidence. Live-streamed to multiple platforms so they can't delete it."

Thomas drifted closer. "Meanwhile, we ghosts will coordinate a mass uprising inside the facility. When you disable the primary binding circles, we'll be able to manifest fully. Hundreds of angry ghosts against a dozen guards." His smile was sharp. "Those are odds I like."

"What about Lily?" Miranda asked. "She's in remedial training. The deep cells."

The ghosts exchanged glances. Finally, August spoke. "The deep cells are on level nine. Maximum security, the worst of the binding magic. If you can reach her, if you can disrupt the containment field—she'll be free. But Miranda, you need to understand. The ghosts down there have been compressed into years of torment. Lily might not be the girl you remember."

"I don't care. I'm not leaving her."

"Even if rescuing her means the whole operation fails?" Sienna's voice was gentle but firm. "Even if stopping to save one ghost means hundreds of others stay trapped?"

The question hung in the air like a blade.

Miranda thought of Lily's smile when they'd planned to fight back together. Thought of Emma, who'd sacrificed everything to keep Miranda safe. Thought of centuries of suffering echoing through twelve levels of underground cells.

"When do we start?" she asked.

They planned for six days.

Sienna taught Miranda how to disable salt barriers using a mixture of blessed water and iron filings. August walked her through the facility's layout until she could navigate it blindfolded. Kira showed her how to use the live-streaming equipment—small cameras disguised as buttons and jewelry.

Myles, back in Miranda's apartment, worked on creating false digital trails that would keep the authorities chasing ghosts while they executed the real plan.

"They'll know it's you eventually," he warned. "Your name's on Lily's adoption contract. Once the raid starts, you've got maybe two hours before they connect the dots."

"Two hours is enough."

"To infiltrate a fortified facility, disable its security, reach the deep cells, and free hundreds of ghosts?" Myles raised an eyebrow. "You're an optimist."

"I'm desperate. There's a difference."

On the seventh night, Detective Chen called. "Ms. Hayes, I need to ask you some questions. Preferably in person."

Miranda's stomach dropped. "About what?"

"Your recent activities. People you've been meeting. Interest in certain restricted databases." Chen's voice was carefully neutral. "I'm trying to help you, Ms. Hayes. But I can't do that if you're planning something illegal."

"I don't know what you mean."

"Then let me be clear: Eternal Bonds has filed a complaint. They claim you've been harassing their staff, making threats, spreading false information. They're seeking a restraining order. And they've suggested you might be mentally unstable due to your sister's recent death."

The words hit like a physical blow. They were already building a narrative. Discrediting her before she could act.

"I'm fine, Detective."

"Are you? Because from where I'm sitting, you look like someone about to do something very stupid and very illegal." A pause. "I've been investigating those 1952 deaths. I'm close to something. But if you blow this by going rogue, if you give them any excuse to shut down my investigation—"

"I understand."

"Do you? Because I don't think you do." Chen's voice softened. "I want justice for those kids too. But justice through the system, not vigilante raids that could get you killed."

"The system has failed ghosts for eighty years, Detective. Maybe it's time for a different approach."

Chen was quiet for a long moment. "If you do something stupid, I can't protect you."

"I'm not asking you to."

"But if—hypothetically—someone were to acquire irrefutable evidence of criminal activity at Eternal Bonds, evidence that could hold up in court... I'd be very interested in seeing it."

Miranda understood. Chen couldn't help actively. But she wouldn't actively stop them either.

"Hypothetically," Miranda said, "that evidence might become available soon."

"Hypothetically, I'll be watching the news very carefully." Chen hung up.

The night before the raid, Miranda stood in her empty apartment, recording a video message.

"My name is Miranda Hayes. If you're watching this, I'm probably dead or in federal custody. What I'm about to tell you is going to sound insane. But every word is true, and I have evidence to prove it."

She explained everything. Emma's death. The adoption. Lily's revelations. The systematic murder and exploitation of ghosts by Eternal Bonds and similar agencies. The evidence the Liberation Network had gathered.

"Tomorrow night, I'm going to break into the Eternal Bonds facility. I'm going to document what's happening in the deep cells. And I'm going to help free every ghost they've imprisoned." Miranda took a breath. "I know this is illegal. I know I'm throwing away my career, possibly my life. But I can't stand by while children are tortured. I can't let my silence make me complicit."

She uploaded the video to multiple platforms, scheduled to publish if she didn't check in within twenty-four hours. Insurance.

Then she called Myles. "If this goes wrong—"

"It won't."

"If it does, make sure Lily's story gets out. Make sure people know her name. Lily Ashford. Nine years old when she died. Tortured for seventy years. That can't be for nothing."

"Miranda—"

"Promise me."

"I promise." Myles's voice was thick. "But you're coming back. You hear me? You're coming back, and we're going to celebrate over expensive whiskey and watch the agency burn."

"Deal."

Miranda hung up and checked her equipment one last time. Cameras. Iron filings. Salt disruptor. The ward Myles had given her. A USB drive containing every file the Liberation Network had collected.

At 11 PM, Sienna texted: *Everyone's in position. We're ready when you are.*

Miranda locked her apartment door, knowing she might never see it again. Her architectural plans still lay spread across the dining table. A half-finished cup of tea sat by the sink. Evidence of a life about to be permanently disrupted.

She thought of Emma, who'd given up everything to keep Miranda safe.

She thought of Lily compressed into years of agony in the deep cells.

She thought of hundreds of other ghosts, waiting for someone brave enough to fight for them.

Her phone buzzed one more time. Myles: *Last chance to back out. Once you're inside, there's no turning back.*

Miranda typed her reply: *I'm not backing out. See you on the other side.*

She stepped into the night. The facility loomed ahead, dark and imposing against the city lights. Somewhere inside, on level 9, Lily was waiting in agony.

Miranda checked her equipment one final time. Cameras. Iron filings. Salt disruptor. The USB drive that would capture everything.

This was it. The point of no return.

Time to bring her home—or die trying.

CHAPTER FOUR - THE PRICE

The maintenance entrance was exactly where August said it would be—a rusted metal door on the facility's east side, half-hidden behind overgrown hedges. Miranda checked her watch: 12:47 AM. Thirteen minutes behind schedule.

Her phone buzzed. Myles: *Security rotation just changed. You've got a 4-minute window instead of 6. Move fast.*

Miranda pulled out the iron filings mixed with blessed water, her hands steady despite her racing heart. The salt barrier across the threshold shimmered faintly in the darkness—invisible to most people, but she'd learned to see the telltale distortion in the air.

She poured the mixture along the doorframe, whispering the words Sienna had taught her. The barrier flickered, weakened, dissolved.

The door opened with a rusty groan that made Miranda's teeth clench. She slipped inside, pulling it shut behind her.

The hallway was institutional—fluorescent lights, linoleum floors, walls the color of forgotten things. Security cameras dotted the ceiling every twenty feet. But Myles had looped the feeds ten minutes ago. As long as she moved quickly, she was invisible.

Level 3 server room, Miranda reminded herself. *Document everything. Then level 9. Then Lily.*

She moved through the corridors like a ghost herself, the button cameras on her jacket recording everything. The facility felt wrong—too quiet, too still. She'd expected guards, security personnel, something. But the halls were empty.

Too empty.

Miranda reached the stairwell and descended. Level 2. Level 3. The air grew colder with each floor, and she could feel it now—a pressure building around her, the weight of thousands of trapped souls pressing against reality.

The server room door was locked, but Myles had provided a bypass code. Miranda typed it in, and the door clicked open.

Inside, rows of servers hummed quietly, their lights blinking like mechanical stars. Miranda pulled out the USB drive and approached the central console. This was the heart of Eternal Bonds' operations—every contract, every ghost, every secret they'd buried.

She plugged in the drive. Myles's program began downloading immediately, copying years of encrypted files while simultaneously uploading them to secure servers around the world.

Download: 2% complete.

Miranda activated her cameras and began documenting. Server racks. The main console. Files displayed on screens—adoption contracts with prices that made her sick. A ghost named Thomas Chen, age 7, sold to a research facility for $340,000. A woman named Sarah Park, purchased by a private collector who specialized in "exotic acquisitions."

Download: 15% complete.

Her phone buzzed. Myles: *Problem. Someone's running security checks. They know something's wrong. You need to abort.*

Miranda typed back: *How long do I have?*

Maybe 5 minutes. Maybe less. GET OUT.

Download: 23% complete.

Miranda stared at the progress bar. If she left now, they'd have evidence—but not enough. Not the deep files that showed the full scope of the operation. Not enough to destroy them completely.

Another message from Myles: *Miranda, I'm serious. They're mobilizing security. You need to leave now.*

She thought of Lily, nine floors below, screaming.

Download: 31% complete.

"Come on," Miranda whispered. "Come on, come on—"

The lights went out.

The emergency backup kicked in a moment later, bathing everything in red. And then Miranda heard it—footsteps in the hallway. Multiple sets. Moving fast.

Download: 44% complete.

She couldn't leave. Not yet. Not when they were so close.

Miranda grabbed the USB drive even as the door burst open. Three security guards, all wearing gear designed to handle spectral threats—salt rounds in their weapons, warding symbols on their vests.

"Hands up! Step away from the console!"

Miranda raised her hands slowly. The drive was still in her palm, small enough to conceal. "I'm just a lost visitor. Wrong floor, I—"

"We know who you are, Ms. Hayes." The lead guard—a woman with iron-gray hair and cold eyes—stepped forward. "You're under arrest for breaking and entering, corporate espionage, and conspiracy to commit terrorism."

"Terrorism?" Miranda's laugh was bitter. "You're torturing children, and I'm the terrorist?"

"Those aren't children. They're classified entities under the Ethereal Entities Act of 1968." The guard's expression didn't change. "Now drop whatever's in your hand and get on the ground."

Miranda calculated her options. Three guards, all armed. She had the ward Myles gave her, but that only protected against ghosts, not bullets. The download was incomplete. And somewhere below, Lily was waiting.

She made her choice.

"August," Miranda said quietly. "Now."

The temperature plummeted. Frost crawled across the server racks. And then August materialized—not the faded ghost she'd met in the cemetery, but something stronger, angrier, fueled by rage that had been building for over a year.

He slammed into the nearest guard, passing through her body. She screamed, dropping her weapon as spectral cold flooded her system.

The other two guards opened fire, but the salt rounds passed harmlessly through August's form.

Miranda ran.

She burst into the hallway as alarms shrieked to life. More footsteps, coming from all directions. Her phone buzzed frantically—Myles trying to warn her, the Liberation Network coordinating, everything happening too fast.

She had to reach level 9. Had to reach Lily.

Miranda found another stairwell and descended, taking the stairs two at a time. Level 4. Level 5. The pressure intensified with each floor, spectral energy so thick it felt like swimming through mud.

Level 6. Level 7.

Behind her, she heard August's scream—high and terrible, the sound of a ghost being forcibly dispersed. He'd bought her time. She couldn't waste it.

Level 8.

The air here was wrong—charged with malevolent energy, humming with binding magic so powerful it made Miranda's teeth ache. She could hear them now. The screams from level 9. Dozens of voices, hundreds, all crying out in endless agony.

And underneath it all, one voice she recognized.

Lily.

The stairwell door to level 9 was reinforced steel, covered in warding symbols that glowed an ugly red. Miranda pulled out the last of her iron mixture and poured it across the threshold. The symbols flickered but didn't fade.

"Come on!" She pounded the door, desperate. "LILY!"

Her phone buzzed. Myles: *They've locked down the building. All exits sealed. Miranda, you need to find another way out. Go UP, not down.*

Another message, this one from Sienna: *August is dispersed. They're pulling ghosts back into containment. The uprising failed. ABORT.*

Miranda stared at the messages. The mission was falling apart. Every ghost who'd tried to help her was being captured, punished. And she was trapped.

She should run. Should try to escape, live to fight another day.

Instead, she pressed her palm against the door. "Lily. Can you hear me?"

Silence. Then, faintly: "Miranda?"

Relief flooded through her. "I'm getting you out. Just hold on—"

"You can't." Lily's voice was different—fractured, barely coherent. "The bindings... they're too strong. And they're coming for you. I can feel them."

"I don't care—"

"Miranda, listen!" Urgency cut through Lily's broken tone. "The binding circles down here—they're connected to the main power grid. If you overload the system, if you make them choose between security and containment—"

Miranda understood. "They'll drop the barriers to save the building."

"For maybe thirty seconds. Long enough for me to manifest fully, break through." A pause. "But Miranda, if you overload the power, you'll be trapped. The backup systems will seal everything. You won't get out."

Footsteps echoed in the stairwell above. Guards getting closer.

Miranda closed her eyes. She thought of Emma, who'd spent her last moments making sure Miranda would be safe. Thought of all the ghosts in this building, suffering because people like her had looked the other way.

"Tell me how to do it," she said.

"Miranda, no—"

"Tell me."

Lily's voice broke. "Level 3. Server room. There's a secondary console, northeast corner. Override code is 1-9-5-2. Birth year of the first ghost they ever trapped. Force a power surge through the containment grid. It'll blow the whole system."

"And you'll be free."

"And you'll be caught."

"I know." Miranda was already moving, running back up the stairs. "Lily, listen to me. When you get out, find Sienna Park. The Liberation Network. They'll help you. And tell the world what happened here. Tell them everything."

"I can't leave you—"

"You have to!" Miranda's voice cracked. "This only works if one of us survives to expose them. If we both get caught, this was all for nothing."

She reached level 3, burst back into the server room. The guards were gone—probably searching other floors. The secondary console was where Lily said, hidden behind a server rack.

Miranda pulled it up, fingers flying across the keyboard. 1-9-5-2.

The screen flashed red. *WARNING: CRITICAL SYSTEM OVERRIDE. CONTAINMENT GRID DESTABILIZATION DETECTED.*

"Do it," Lily whispered through their bond. "Miranda, I'm so sorry—"

"Don't be." Miranda smiled through her tears. "This is what Emma would have done. What she did do for me. Some things are worth the price."

She hit EXECUTE.

The world exploded.

Power surged through every circuit, every binding circle, every containment field in the building. Lights strobed. Alarms screamed. And for exactly twenty-seven seconds, every barrier in the facility failed simultaneously.

On level 9, Lily felt the bindings shatter.

She manifested fully for the first time in seventy years—not a faded shade, not a broken thing, but the ghost of a nine-year-old girl with fire in her eyes and rage in her heart.

Around her, hundreds of other ghosts were doing the same. Screaming, crying, laughing with manic relief as their prisons dissolved.

"GO!" Lily shouted. "Everyone, get out!"

They poured through the facility like a spectral flood. Some fled into the night, finally free. Others stayed to fight, to destroy, to make their captors feel even a fraction of the fear they'd endured.

Lily raced upward, searching for Miranda.

She found her on level 3, surrounded by guards. The power was coming back online, backup systems kicking in. Magnetic locks slamming shut. And Miranda, standing in the center of it all, hands raised, the USB drive clutched in her palm.

"It's over, Ms. Hayes," the iron-haired guard said. "You're done."

Miranda met Lily's eyes across the room. And smiled.

"Check your news feeds," she said softly.

The guard frowned, pulling out her phone. Her expression shifted from annoyance to horror.

Myles had been busy too. Every file from the USB drive—complete or not—was streaming live across a dozen platforms. Major news networks were picking it up. Social media was exploding. The video Miranda had recorded earlier, her confession and explanation, had gone viral.

The world was watching.

"You're right," Miranda said. "I'm done. But so are you."

Outside, police sirens wailed. Detective Chen had made her choice—to investigate, to document, to arrest everyone involved. The cavalry was coming.

But it would be too late for Miranda.

"Run," she told Lily. "Please. Don't let this be for nothing."

Lily wanted to stay, to fight, to save the woman who'd saved her. But she could feel the bindings trying to reform, the agency's security mages working to restore the containment fields.

If she stayed, they'd both be trapped.

"I'll come back for you," Lily whispered. "I promise."

Then she fled, passing through walls and barriers, following the stream of escaped ghosts into the night.

Behind her, she heard the guards tackle Miranda to the ground. Heard the click of handcuffs. Heard Miranda's steady voice: "My name is Miranda Hayes. I want a lawyer. And I want every camera in this city pointed at this building."

Lily emerged into the cold November air, free for the first time since 1952. Around her, dozens of other ghosts were scattering, disappearing into the darkness.

Sienna appeared beside her, flickering but triumphant. "We did it. Not perfectly, but—we did it."

"Miranda's still inside," Lily said. "They arrested her."

"I know. But she made her choice." Sienna's form solidified slightly. "And because of her, the world knows. By morning, Eternal Bonds will be finished. The board of directors will be in custody. Every facility they operate will be raided."

"At what cost?"

"The cost Miranda was willing to pay." Sienna met Lily's eyes. "Now we honor that sacrifice. We tell the truth. We make sure she didn't give herself up for nothing."

Lily looked back at the facility—her prison for seventy years. Police cars were arriving, news vans pulling up. The story was breaking in real time.

Inside that building, Miranda was being processed, charged, her life as she knew it ending.

But she was smiling.

Because on every screen in the city, the truth was spreading like wildfire. Photos of the deep cells. Videos of the torture sessions. Financial records showing the full scope of the ghost trafficking industry. Emma's death. Lily's murder. Six children killed in 1952. Thousands of ghosts exploited across decades.

All of it finally, undeniably visible.

Detective Chen arrived, pushing through the crowd of reporters. She looked up at the building, then down at her phone, where the evidence was still streaming. Her expression was grim but satisfied.

"Get me everyone involved," she said to her officers. "I want the entire board of directors in custody by dawn. And someone call the DA. We're going to need a very large task force."

Myles appeared beside Lily—physically this time, his laptop bag over his shoulder. "The trial starts in three months. They're charging her with terrorism."

"Then we have three months," Lily said quietly, "to make sure the world sees her as the hero she is."

"And to prepare our own testimony." Sienna gestured to the other freed ghosts gathering nearby. "If they want to put Miranda on trial, they're going to have to hear from all of us. Every ghost she freed. Every story they tried to bury."

Lily watched as they brought Miranda out in handcuffs, loading her into a police car. Their eyes met for just a moment.

Miranda smiled.

And Lily understood. This wasn't an ending. It was a beginning.

The price had been paid. The truth was out.

Now came the reckoning.

CHAPTER FIVE: THE HAUNTING

The trial began on a gray Monday morning in February, three months after Miranda's arrest.

She sat at the defendant's table in an orange jumpsuit, hands folded, watching the courtroom fill with reporters, activists, and curious onlookers. The prosecution had charged her with seventeen counts, including corporate espionage, destruction of property, and domestic terrorism. If convicted on all counts, she faced forty years in federal prison.

Her court-appointed attorney—a tired-looking woman named Sasha Moore, who seemed perpetually overwhelmed—kept whispering advice Miranda barely heard.

Across the aisle sat the legal team for Eternal Bonds: six lawyers in suits that cost more than Miranda's yearly salary, armed with motions to suppress evidence, dismiss charges, seal records. They'd spent three months trying to bury the story, discredit the footage, claim everything Miranda had exposed was fabricated or taken out of context.

They'd failed.

The evidence was too widespread, too well-documented. Major news networks had run exposés. Social media had exploded with #GhostRights protests. Congressional hearings had been scheduled. And most damaging of all—over seven hundred freed ghosts were out there, telling their stories to anyone who would listen.

The judge entered—an older man named Howard Sterling with a reputation for strictness. Everyone rose.

"Be seated," Judge Sterling said. "We're here for the trial of Miranda Hayes. Is the prosecution ready?"

"Yes, Your Honor."

"Defense?"

Sasha Moore stood. "Yes, Your Honor. And we'd like to call our first witness."

The prosecution's attorney shot to his feet. "Your Honor, we haven't even presented our opening statement—"

"The defense has the right to present witnesses, counselor." Judge Sterling looked at Sasha. "Who are you calling?"

Sasha took a breath. "The defense calls Lily Ashford."

The courtroom erupted.

The prosecution objected. The judge banged his gavel. Reporters shouted questions. Because ghost testimony wasn't legally admissible—everyone knew that. The Ethereal Entities Act of 1968 had established that ghosts weren't competent witnesses, couldn't be cross-examined, and had no legal standing.

But Sasha Moore had found a loophole.

"Your Honor, the Act of 1968 specifically applies to 'entities bound under contract to living hosts.' Lily Ashford is no longer bound. She's a free entity, making her testimony admissible under standard witness rules."

The prosecution attorney's face went purple. "That's a ridiculous interpretation—"

"Is it?" Sasha pulled out a legal brief three inches thick. "Because I have seventeen precedents that support this reading, dating back to the Act's original passage. The restriction was specifically designed to prevent hosts from exploiting bound ghosts for testimony. It says nothing about free entities."

Judge Sterling frowned, flipping through the brief. The courtroom held its breath.

Finally, he looked up. "I'm going to allow it. But Ms. Moore, if this witness can't maintain coherent testimony, I'll strike everything from the record."

"Understood, Your Honor."

Sasha turned to the back of the courtroom. "Lily, please approach."

The temperature dropped ten degrees.

Lily materialized in the center aisle—not the faded shade Miranda had first met, but something stronger, more present. Three months of freedom had changed her. She'd learned to manifest more fully, to hold her form stable, to speak with clarity instead of whispers.

She drifted to the witness stand. The bailiff, looking uncertain, held out a Bible.

"Do you swear to tell the truth, the whole truth, and nothing but the truth?"

"I do," Lily said. Her voice echoed strangely in the quiet courtroom.

Sasha approached. "Please state your name for the record."

"Lily Marie Ashford."

"And how old are you, Lily?"

"I was nine years old when I died. That was seventy-three years ago."

Murmurs rippled through the gallery. Sasha waited for them to quiet.

"Lily, can you tell the court how you died?"

"I was hit by a car on October 14th, 1952. The driver worked for the Eternal Bonds Agency. He killed me on purpose." Lily's form flickered. "There were five other children. All killed the same way. All harvested."

"Objection!" The prosecutor was on his feet. "Speculation, hearsay—"

"I was there," Lily said quietly. "I watched from the other side as they collected my body. As Ms. Thornwell—she ran the agency back then—stood over me and said, 'This one will do nicely.'"

The courtroom was silent.

Sasha continued. "What happened after you died?"

"They trapped me. Told me I was in danger from shadow-feeders, that I needed to stay in their facility for protection. I was nine and terrified and alone. I believed them." Lily's voice cracked. "I spent seventy years in that building. In cells underground. They called it 'containment for our safety.' It was torture."

"Can you describe the conditions?"

"Small rooms with salt barriers. No windows. Time moved differently—they could compress it, make an hour feel like days. Once a month, they'd do 'evaluations.' That's what they called it. Really, they were breaking us. Making sure we were too afraid to fight back." Lily looked at Miranda. "Until someone finally cared enough to ask questions."

Sasha pulled out a tablet, showing images from the facility. "Are these the containment cells you described?"

"Yes."

"And this?" A video played—one of the evaluation sessions, recorded by the Liberation Network years ago.

Lily turned away. "Yes."

The prosecution tried to object again, but Judge Sterling waved him down. "I want to see this."

The video played. A ghost—not Lily, but someone else—strapped to a chair made of salt and iron. A technician activating binding circles. The ghost's screams as magical energy tore through its form, deliberately causing pain to enforce compliance.

Several people in the gallery looked sick.

When it finished, Sasha turned back to Lily. "How many ghosts were held at the facility?"

"When I escaped, there were 847 in active placements. Another two thousand in storage. Some in the deep cells had been there for over a century."

"And what happened on the night of November 23rd?"

Lily's form brightened. "Miranda freed us. She overloaded the containment grid, breaking all the binding circles at once. For twenty-seven seconds, every ghost in that building could manifest fully. Some escaped. Some fought back. Some just stood there, crying, because they hadn't been free in so long they'd forgotten what it felt like."

"Where did you go after escaping?"

"I found the Liberation Network. Other freed ghosts who were building evidence, helping escapees, trying to expose what Eternal Bonds was doing." Lily looked at the jury. "We've been gathering testimony. Finding other facilities. There are seventeen more across nine states. All doing the same thing."

The prosecution attorney stood. "Your Honor, this is beyond the scope—"

"I disagree," Judge Sterling said. "Continue, Ms. Moore."

Sasha smiled. "No further questions."

The prosecution's cross-examination was brutal. They tried to discredit Lily's memory, suggested she was confused, implied that ghosts couldn't be trusted to distinguish reality from spectral delusion.

But Lily held firm. And when they pushed too hard, when they suggested she was lying about the abuse, something happened.

The courtroom's temperature plummeted.

Other ghosts began manifesting. August Reeves appeared behind the prosecution table. Kira materialized near the jury box. Thomas, Yuki, and dozens of others—all the freed ghosts who'd escaped that night—filled the courtroom like a spectral congregation.

"We're not lying," August said, his voice echoing with righteous fury. "And we're not alone."

Judge Sterling banged his gavel. "Order! I will have order!"

But the ghosts didn't leave. They stood there, silent witnesses to seventy years of systematic abuse.

Finally, the prosecution sat down. "No further questions."

Over the next two weeks, the trial became a spectacle.

Miranda testified, walking the jury through her investigation. Myles presented the digital evidence—financial records, contracts, internal memos discussing "inventory management" and "asset acquisition." Detective Chen testified about the 1952 murders, presenting evidence she'd uncovered of a conspiracy that went back decades.

The prosecution tried to paint Miranda as a dangerous radical, a woman unhinged by grief who'd destroyed property and endangered lives. They had their own experts, their own testimony from current Eternal Bonds employees who swore the ghosts were treated humanely, that the footage was doctored, that Miranda had fabricated everything.

But the evidence was overwhelming.

On day fourteen, the freed ghosts staged a demonstration outside the courthouse. Hundreds of them, manifesting in broad daylight, holding signs made of spectral energy: GHOSTS ARE PEOPLE. REMEMBER THE CHILDREN OF 1952. JUSTICE FOR THE FALLEN.

News helicopters circled overhead. The story went international.

On day sixteen, three members of Eternal Bonds' board of directors were arrested on charges ranging from wrongful death to human trafficking. The company's stock crashed. Protests erupted at their other facilities.

And on day nineteen, the prosecution offered a deal.

"Plead guilty to two counts of criminal trespass and destruction of property," Sasha told Miranda in a conference room. "All other charges dropped. Sentence: time served plus two years probation."

Miranda stared at her. "That's it?"

"The DA knows they're losing the public opinion battle. Every day this trial continues, more people turn against Eternal Bonds. They want it over." Sasha leaned forward. "Miranda, this is a good deal. You could walk out of here today."

"What about the ghosts? What about justice for Lily and all the others?"

"That's happening separately. The federal government has opened investigations into all seventeen facilities. Congress is holding hearings. The Ethereal Entities Act is being challenged." Sasha's expression softened. "You did what you set out to do. You exposed them. You changed the conversation. Now let yourself be free."

Miranda looked out the window. Below, she could see the ghost protesters, Lily among them.

"Okay," she said quietly. "I'll take the deal."

The courtroom was packed for the final hearing.

Miranda stood before Judge Sterling, hands folded, while Sasha read the plea agreement. Guilty on two counts. Time served. Probation. No admission that the evidence she'd gathered was false—just acknowledgment that her methods were illegal.

"Ms. Hayes," Judge Sterling said, "do you understand the terms of this agreement?"

"Yes, Your Honor."

"And do you accept them?"

Miranda took a breath. "I do."

"Very well. I accept this plea. You're free to go." He paused. "But, Ms. Hayes, before you leave this courtroom, I want to say something on the record."

The room went silent.

"What you did was illegal. Breaking into that facility, destroying property, interfering with a legitimate business—those actions violated the law." Judge Sterling's expression was stern. "But what you uncovered—the systematic abuse, the exploitation, the evidence of murder—that cannot be ignored. Your actions, while criminal, exposed crimes that are far worse."

He looked at the prosecution table, where Eternal Bonds' lawyers sat.

"I am formally recommending that the Justice Department pursue criminal charges against Eternal Bonds and all associated parties. I am also recommending a complete review of the Ethereal Entities Act and the legal status of ghosts under federal law." He banged his gavel. "Court is adjourned."

Miranda's knees nearly buckled. Sasha caught her arm, grinning.

"You did it," she whispered. "You actually did it."

Outside, the crowd erupted in cheers.

Miranda walked down the courthouse steps in civilian clothes for the first time in three months. Reporters shouted questions. Protesters chanted. And there, at the edge of the crowd, Lily waited.

They looked at each other across the distance.

Then Lily drifted forward, and for the first time since the adoption, Miranda felt their bond—not the forced connection of the contract, but something chosen. Something real.

"Thank you," Lily whispered.

"Thank you," Miranda replied. "For trusting me. For being brave enough to tell the truth."

"What happens now?"

Miranda looked at the crowd, the cameras, the other freed ghosts gathering around them. "Now? We finish what we started. We help the others still trapped. We make sure this never happens again."

Lily smiled—genuinely smiled, the way a nine-year-old should. "Together?"

"Together."

EPILOGUE

Six Months Later

The Eternal Bonds facility in Daybridge was being demolished.

Miranda stood across the street, watching the wrecking ball slam into the building's side. Each impact sent up clouds of dust, erasing another piece of the structure that had held so much suffering.

Beside her, Lily flickered in the afternoon sunlight. She'd grown stronger in the months since the trial, learning to manifest for hours at a time, to interact with the physical world in small ways. She'd never be alive again—but she was free.

"Twelve more facilities closed this month," Myles said, walking up with his laptop. "Federal investigations are ongoing at the remaining five. The ghost rights bill passed committee yesterday. It's going to the full Senate next week."

"Will it pass?" Miranda asked.

"Maybe. Probably. The momentum's there." Myles showed her his screen—news articles about ghost advocacy groups, legislative debates, peaceful protests. "You started something, Miranda. A movement."

She thought about that. One sister's death. One adoption. One ghost brave enough to tell the truth. And now—everything was changing.

Not fixed. Not perfect. But changing.

"How's the new project?" Lily asked.

Miranda smiled. "The Liberation Network is expanding. We've helped seventy-three ghosts escape abusive situations in the last six months. Sienna's training new volunteers. August is still hacking corporate databases." She pulled out her phone, showing an encrypted message. "And we've gotten tips about facilities in three other countries."

"This is bigger than just Eternal Bonds," Myles said quietly.

"I know." Miranda watched another section of the building collapse. "Ghost exploitation is global. It's been happening for centuries, hidden in the gaps of laws that don't recognize ghosts as people. It's going to take years, maybe decades, to dismantle all of it."

"But you're going to try."

"We're going to try." Miranda looked at Lily. "All of us."

Across the street, other freed ghosts gathered to watch the demolition. Some Miranda recognized from that night—Thomas, Kira, others who'd escaped. Some were newer, recently freed from other facilities, still learning what freedom meant.

They stood together, living and dead, watching the past crumble into dust.

Detective Chen approached, badge gleaming in the sun. She'd been promoted to head the federal ghost trafficking task force—the first of its kind.

"Ms. Hayes," she said formally. Then, softer: "Miranda. I wanted to let you know—we identified the driver from 1952. The one who killed Lily and the others. His name was Thomas Brennan. He died in 1987, but we found evidence that he killed seventeen children over thirty years. All for the agency."

Lily's form flickered. "Seventeen?"

"At least. Maybe more. We're still investigating." Chen handed Miranda a folder. "We're building cases for each one. Murder charges, even posthumously. Making sure their names are recorded, their deaths acknowledged."

Miranda opened the folder. Inside were photos of children—smiling, young, alive. Each one with a name, a date, a story cut short.

Lily Ashford. Robert Chen. Maria Gonzales. Timothy Park...

"They deserve to be remembered," Chen said. "All of them."

"Yes," Lily whispered. "They do."

Chen nodded at the demolition. "Sixteen more facilities to go. And then we start with the international operations." She almost smiled. "You know, when I became a cop, I thought I'd be solving regular crimes. Murder, robbery, fraud. I never imagined I'd be building cases about ghost trafficking."

"Life's funny that way," Miranda said.

"Justice is funny that way." Chen's expression turned serious. "What you did was reckless and illegal. But it was also necessary. Sometimes the law needs a push to catch up with morality." She extended her hand. "If you ever need help with the Liberation Network, call me. Unofficially."

They shook hands. Then Chen walked back to her task force, leaving Miranda and Lily and Myles standing in the shadow of a building coming down.

"Do you think we'll win?" Lily asked quietly. "Really win? Get the laws changed, get ghosts recognized as people?"

Miranda thought about Emma, who'd fought her whole life for causes that seemed impossible. Who'd died believing in a better world even when she couldn't see it.

"I think we'll try," Miranda said. "I think we'll fight for every ghost still trapped, every law that needs changing, every person who needs to understand that death doesn't make someone less than human." She put her hand through Lily's spectral form, feeling the cold tingle of connection. "And maybe we'll lose sometimes. Maybe it'll take longer than we want. But we won't stop."

The wrecking ball hit again. Another wall collapsed.

"Emma would be proud of you," Lily said.

"She'd be proud of both of us." Miranda smiled through tears. "She'd say we're being ridiculously idealistic and dangerously stubborn. And then she'd roll up her sleeves and help."

They stood together until the last wall fell, until the building was nothing but rubble and dust, until the place that had held so much pain was finally, blessedly erased.

But Miranda knew the work wasn't done.

Somewhere in another city, another facility still operated. Another ghost was trapped, waiting for someone to care enough to ask questions. Another Lily, hoping for rescue.

The work would never truly be done.

But for today, this moment, they could celebrate one victory. One building demolished. One step forward.

Lily looked up at Miranda. "What's next?"

Miranda pulled out her phone, scrolling through messages from the Liberation Network. Reports of ghosts needing help. Tips about suspicious facilities. Volunteers ready to fight.

"Next?" She pocketed the phone. "We save the next one. And the one after that. And we keep going until every ghost is free."

"That could take forever."

"Good thing I've got time." Miranda gestured at the rubble. "And good thing I've got help. From the living and the dead."

Around them, the freed ghosts were dispersing—back to their new lives, their new purposes, their hard-won freedom. Some would join the Liberation Network. Some would simply exist, finally at peace. Some would find new missions, new reasons to stay tethered to this world.

All of them were free to choose.

Myles closed his laptop. "I've got a lead on a facility in Boston. A woman named Jennifer Park claims her adopted ghost is being controlled remotely, forced to spy on her."

"Controlled remotely?" Miranda frowned. "That's new."

"Tech evolves. Exploitation evolves with it." Myles pulled up the case file. "Interested?"

Miranda looked at Lily. "What do you think?"

Lily's form brightened, solidified, became almost real in the fading light. "I think there's someone in Boston who needs us."

"Then let's go help them."

They walked away from the rubble together—living and dead, human and ghost, bound not by contract but by choice. Behind them, the sun set over the demolished facility, painting the destruction in shades of gold and red.

It was ending. It was beginning.

It was one story among thousands—thousands of ghosts still waiting, thousands of battles still to fight, thousands of hearts brave enough to demand that death didn't mean the end of dignity, of rights, of personhood.

The Ghost Adoption Agency was finished.

But the work of liberation had only just begun.

And Miranda Hayes, former architect, current revolutionary, walked forward into that uncertain future with a ghost at her side and fire in her heart.

Some debts could never be repaid.

But they could be honored, one freed soul at a time.

THE END

THE GHOST ADOPTION AGENCY has concluded, but the story of Miranda Hayes, Lily Ashford, and the Liberation Network continues in the world of **Daybridge**, where the supernatural and the mundane collide in ways both terrifying and beautiful.

What Happens Next in Daybridge?

The Ghost Rights Bill heads to the Senate. Sixteen more facilities await liberation. And in Boston, a woman named Jennifer Park has discovered her adopted ghost is being controlled remotely—a new evolution of an ancient exploitation.

Miranda and Lily's fight has exposed one operation. But ghost trafficking is global, centuries old, and deeply entrenched in systems of power that don't give up easily.

Want More Stories from Daybridge?

Explore the Daybridge universe, where paranormal investigators solve supernatural crimes, ghost rights activists battle corporate exploitation, and the line between life and death is more complicated than anyone wants to admit. From spectral fraud to haunted real estate, from possession cases to ghostly cold cases decades old—every story reveals another layer of a city where the dead don't always stay buried.

In Daybridge, some debts can never be repaid. But they can be honored—one freed soul at a time.

The Fight for Ghost Rights Has Just Begun. Will You Join It?

EPILOGUE: THE WEIGHT OF BRIDGES

Three Years After the Fall

The bridge remembers everything.

It remembers the night Alice Chen stood in its heart and refused to let another consciousness be consumed. It remembers Nadia Marsh broadcasting seventy years of murder to a city that didn't want to listen. It remembers Miranda Hayes walking into a government facility with nothing but evidence and rage, demanding the impossible.

It remembers all of them. Because in Daybridge, memory is architecture, and architecture is alive.

Alice stands at the bridge's midpoint on a Tuesday morning, coffee in hand, watching the river flow beneath. Three years since she stopped being entirely human. Three years since she became something more—or less, depending on who you ask.

The distributed consciousness that shares her mind no longer feels like an intrusion. It feels like breathing. Like the difference between seeing the world through one eye versus two. She is Alice Chen, detective. She is also the bridge, ancient and patient. She is both, and neither, and something new that doesn't have a name yet.

Her phone buzzes. Text from Marcus: *Another one. East Riverside. Same pattern.*

She sighs. The alchemical cults didn't die with Dr. Emerson Thorne's arrest. They fractured, went underground, got smarter. Now they work in cells, using the dark web to share techniques for forced ascension. Every few months, her department finds another victim—someone who paid for transcendence and got torture instead.

But they're finding them now. That's the difference. The dead can testify, and Alice can hear them clearly. The bridge helps with that too, filtering signal from noise, finding the voices lost in dimensional static.

239

She finishes her coffee and heads back to work. There's always work.

The bridge watches her go with something that might be pride.

Nadia Marsh's archive sits in a repurposed warehouse in the Arts District, three stories of carefully organized truth. The official city archive wouldn't take her findings—too politically sensitive, they said, as if seventy years of systematic murder could be filed under "controversial."

So, she built her own.

The Daybridge Memorial Archive occupies the same building where she first discovered Silas Hargrove's journal. Fitting, she thinks, that the site of conspiracy should become the monument to its victims. The second floor houses the documented murders—every name recovered, every ritual reconstructed, every family's complicity detailed in excruciating precision. The third floor holds the living record: oral histories from survivors, descendants, anyone willing to speak truth about Daybridge's founding darkness.

The first floor, though—the first floor is the memorial wall.

Seven hundred and forty-three names. Carved in black granite. Each one a person the founding families erased for power and profit. Each one a life that mattered, despite what the official histories claimed.

Nadia runs her fingers across the stone, finding the name she looks for every morning: *Eleanor Cross, 1952. Teacher. Organizer. Truth-teller.*

"Still here," she whispers.

Behind her, footsteps. She turns to find a young woman, maybe twenty-five, holding a worn photograph.

"My grandmother," the woman says, showing the picture. "She disappeared in 1987. I saw your documentary. I think... I think she might be here."

Nadia takes the photograph gently. Investigative instinct never dies. "Tell me about her."

The work continues. The dead accumulate names and faces and stories. And slowly—agonizingly slowly—Daybridge begins to remember what it tried so hard to forget.

The city resists. Two of the founding families still hold political power. The Hargroves reinvented themselves as philanthropists. The official histories remain unchanged. But the memorial stands, and every day, more people walk through those doors seeking truth.

Nadia couldn't stop the machine. But she threw a wrench into its gears, and sometimes, that's revolution enough.

Miranda Hayes doesn't sleep well anymore.

Hasn't since the raids, since the Congressional hearings, since she stood in front of cameras and described what the United States government had been doing to conscious beings for profit. Since she watched the Ghost Adoption Agency collapse under the weight of its own documented atrocities.

The nightmares aren't about what she saw. They're about what she didn't stop in time.

Seventeen facilities across the country. Thousands of enslaved consciousnesses. The raids freed most of them, but not all. Some facilities had time to purge their "inventory." In bureaucratic language, that meant destroying evidence. In human terms, it meant murder—again—of people who'd already died once.

She wakes at 3 AM, as usual, and finds Cassie sitting at the foot of her bed.

Not her sister. Never her sister. Just Cassie, the ghost who chose freedom over comfort, who helped Miranda understand that love without consent is just another form of violence.

"Bad one?" Cassie asks, her form more solid than it used to be. Three years of practice, learning to manifest without technology, without electroplasm, without all the apparatus of control.

"The same," Miranda says.

Cassie nods. She understands. She was there for all of it—the investigation, the testimony, the public horror when people finally understood what "adoption" actually meant. She was there when the Ghost Rights Act passed, when conscious entities gained legal personhood, when the industry Miranda exposed finally, officially, ended.

But law isn't justice. Justice would mean the dead could truly rest. Justice would mean the executives who built fortunes on torture would face something more than fines and suspended sentences. Justice would mean Ava could come back.

She can't. Miranda knows this. She's made her peace with it, mostly. But some losses don't heal—they just become furniture in the room where you live.

"Coffee?" Cassie offers.

"Please."

They sit together in Miranda's kitchen, ghost and human, survivor and witness. Outside, Daybridge begins to wake. Somewhere in the city, seventeen former GAA executives are sleeping in comfortable beds. Somewhere else, newly free ghosts are learning what autonomy means. And somewhere—Miranda has to believe this—the consciousness that was Ava Hayes knows that someone fought for her, even if that fight came too late.

The work continues. The Ghost Advocacy Network that Miranda founded operates in forty states now, helping freed consciousnesses navigate legal systems never designed for them. Every day brings new challenges: housing, employment, existence itself when you have no body and a society that barely acknowledges you as real.

Every day, Miranda wakes up and chooses to keep fighting.

She couldn't save her sister. But she saved thousands of others. And she transformed the grief that would have destroyed her into fuel for a movement that changed the world.

Some days, that's enough. Other days, it has to be.

The bridge holds all of this—all these stories, all these struggles, all this stubborn, bleeding progress. It feels Alice hunting monsters that wear human faces. It feels Nadia excavating buried truth from beneath decades of lies. It feels Miranda building systems of care where only exploitation existed before.

And it wonders, in the vast and distributed way that consciousness spanning dimensions wonders about anything, what comes next.

Daybridge has changed. Not completely—power still corrupts, the founding families still scheme, new horrors still wear bureaucratic faces. But the ground has shifted. People know now. They understand that the supernatural is real, that consciousness persists, that the rules they thought governed reality are more flexible than anyone imagined.

That knowledge is dangerous. But ignorance, the bridge has learned, is worse.

It thinks of Alice, hybrid and whole. Of Nadia, guardian of memory. Of Miranda, architect of liberation. Three ordinary people who refused to accept the extraordinary evil around them. Three stories among thousands, because resistance is never singular, never solitary, never as simple as one person standing alone against the machine.

The bridge holds them all—every person who chose to see clearly even when clarity burned, every soul who stood up even when standing up meant falling, every consciousness that insisted on its own personhood against systems designed to deny it.

Daybridge will never be clean. Cities built on blood and sacrifice don't wash away their sins in three years, or thirty, or three hundred. The founding families' descendants will keep trying to reclaim power. New predators will emerge, wearing new faces, speaking new languages of exploitation.

But now—now there are people watching. People remembering. People who understand that in Daybridge, the supernatural isn't separate from the mundane; it's woven through every institution, every power structure, every choice between looking away and standing firm.

The bridge holds this too: the knowledge that change is slow, incomplete, and always contested. That victory looks like survival plus documentation. That sometimes, the revolution is just refusing to let them erase you.

On a Tuesday morning, three years after everything changed and nothing changed, Alice Chen walks across the bridge to investigate another crime. Nadia Marsh opens her archive to another descendant seeking truth. Miranda Hayes answers emails from ghosts learning to navigate their freedom.

The work continues. The dead remember. The living resist.

And the bridge—ancient, patient, impossibly vast—holds all of it. Every story. Every sacrifice. Every small, stubborn act of defiance against systems that would grind souls into profit if they could.

Some debts can never be fully repaid. Some shadows never completely lift.

But some battles, once begun, echo through generations. Some truths, once spoken, cannot be unheard. Some bridges, once crossed, change everyone who walks upon them.

This is Daybridge. This is the nexus. This is where the work happens—messy, incomplete, and absolutely necessary.

The city remembers everything now.

And that, finally, is how the healing begins.

END OF SHADOWS AND DEBTS: TALES FROM THE NEXUS

The Daybridge Chronicles continue...

About the Author

Rae Stonehouse turned to fiction writing after establishing himself as a prolific author of self-development and professional growth books.

With over fifty published works helping readers navigate personal and professional challenges, he embarked on a new creative path with the Ethan Reeves Werewolf Detective Series.

When not weaving tales of supernatural sleuthing, Stonehouse continues to share his expertise in personal development through workshops and speaking engagements from his home in British Columbia.

The Ethan Reeves series marks his debut in fiction writing, blending his understanding of human nature with a newfound passion for urban fantasy.

FROM THE WORLD OF ETHAN REEVES: WEREWOLF DETECTIVE by Rae Stonehouse

Discover the Full Saga of Detective Ethan Reeves As He Navigates Daybridge's Supernatural Underworld in This Eight-book Urban Fantasy Series:

1. **Shadows of Daybridge**[1] - Detective Ethan Reeves must navigate his unexpected transformation into a werewolf while solving crimes and surviving supernatural politics in Daybridge.
2. **Daybridge Necropolis**[2] - Werewolf detective Ethan Reeves and his partner Alice Chen race against time to stop a necromancer from raising an undead army in Daybridge.
3. **Shadows of Vengeance**[3] - Detective Ethan Reeves and his allies must decode the Bloodline Archive to prevent an ancient Witch Queen's resurrection and her centuries of vengeance upon Daybridge.
4. **Moonlight Origins**[4] - Detective Ethan Reeves must navigate

---

1. https://my.linkpod.site/shadowsofdaybridge
2. https://my.linkpod.site/daybridgenecropolis
3. https://my.linkpod.site/shadowsofvengeance
4. https://my.linkpod.site/moonlightorigins

his new dual identity after an unexpected werewolf bite transforms him during a routine homicide investigation.

5. **Shadows Between Thoughts**[5] - Detective Ethan Reeves and his partner confront reality-bending phenomena while investigating ghost hunters' disappearances in an abandoned hospital with a sinister experimental history.

6. **Quantum Detective**[6] - Detective Alice Chen uses her temporal sensitivity to investigate physics-defying murders orchestrated by a secretive organization attempting to control time itself.

7. **Synthetic Storm**[7] - Detectives Alice Chen and Ethan Reeves confront a world-altering crisis when experimental supernatural enhancement technology creates godlike beings and reshapes reality across Daybridge.

8. **Blood Beneath Daybridge**[8] - This prequel reveals the dark origins of Daybridge's infamous Ogre of Daybridge Bridge legend before Detective Ethan Reeves began investigating supernatural crimes.

Explore the Daybridge Chronicles Series [These Can Be Read in Any Order]

Echoes of the Forgotten: A Daybridge Chronicles Novel–Book One in the Through the Rift Trilogy

Paranormal investigator Ryan Matthews discovers a hidden government laboratory in abandoned Mercy Hall where dimensional experiments unleashed an ancient entity that's using traumatic history and human minds—including his own unique sensitivity—to build a consciousness network for crossing fully into our reality.

---

5. https://my.linkpod.site/shadowsbetweenthoughts

6. https://my.linkpod.site/quantumdetective

7. https://my.linkpod.site/syntheticstorm

8. https://my.linkpod.site/bloodbeneathdaybridge

https://ethanreeveswerewolfdetective.com/?page_id=518

Beyond the Threshold: A Daybridge Chronicles Novel -
Book Two in the Through the Rift Trilogy

After closing a dimensional breach, paranormal investigator Ryan Matthews and his team discover the entity has evolved to infiltrate humanity's collective unconscious through viral reality seeds, forcing them to confront their own transformations while tracking down remaining facility anchors to determine whether humanity will retain its autonomy or surrender to an incomprehensible new existence.

https://ethanreeveswerewolfdetective.com/?page_id=522

Reality Unravelled: A Daybridge Chronicles Novel - Book Three in the Through the Rift Trilogy

The Paranormal Investigation trilogy follows Ryan Matthews as he uncovers a dimensional breach at Daybridge Poor House, battles an ancient entity using human trauma as a gateway, confronts the collapse of reality boundaries through the Daybridge Institute's "Project Convergence," and ultimately races to repair the dimensional fabric with allies from multiple realities before our existence completely dissolves.

https://ethanreeveswerewolfdetective.com/?page_id=526

Fragments of the Veil: Daybridge Chronicles Trilogy #1–Through the Rift [the complete series in one book]

Paranormal investigator Ryan Matthews confronts an ancient entity exploiting dimensional breaches from government experiments at Daybridge Poor House, battles reality collapse engineered by the Daybridge Institute's "Project Convergence," and ultimately races to repair the cosmic fabric with allies from parallel worlds before our reality completely dissolves.

https://ethanreeveswerewolfdetective.com/?page_id=530

The Storm Glass: Book One in the Relics of the Shattered Veil: Daybridge Chronicles Trilogy #2 [coming soon...]

The Storm Glass shatters reality in Daybridge when victims begin turning to crystal and a strange Victorian artifact appears at each crime scene. As weather patterns warp and doorways to impossible realms open, Detective Alice Chen and paranormal consultant Ethan Reeves race to stop a supernatural storm from consuming their city. But the storm glass reveals more than just danger—it exposes the fragile line between perception and truth. What waits beyond could rewrite everything. [coming soon...]

The Bone Compass: Book Two in the Relics of the Shattered Veil: Daybridge Chronicles Trilogy #2

The Bone Compass pulls Detective Alice Chen deeper into Daybridge's hidden dimensions when a string of disappearances leads to a relic that points beyond reality itself. As grotesque bodies surface and the veil between worlds thins, Alice and Ethan uncover a conspiracy tied to her buried past. In this gripping second installment of Relics of the Shattered Veil, the line between hunter and hunted blurs—and Alice must decide how much of herself she's willing to lose to stop an otherworldly catastrophe. [coming soon...]

The Veil Lantern: Book Three in the Relics of the Shattered Veil: Daybridge Chronicles Trilogy #2

The Veil Lantern delivers a stunning finale to the Relics of the Shattered Veil Trilogy as Daybridge teeters on the edge of dimensional collapse. When a killer weaponizes an ancient lantern that reveals the boundaries between worlds, detectives Alice Chen and Ethan Reeves must confront their deepest secrets and the true power of the relics. As reality fractures and allies turn, the duo races to decide what—and who—they're willing to sacrifice to save their city from unraveling. [coming soon...]

Tales from the Nexus

Voices in Echo Alley: Whispers Between Worlds

Voices in Echo Alley launches paranormal investigator Alice Chen into a mind-bending conspiracy when whispers lead her to a hidden alley—and a government plot exploiting tears in reality. As timelines collide and her grandmother's past resurfaces, Alice must assemble a team to stop a multiversal collapse. Blending quantum physics with supernatural suspense, this thriller pushes Alice from skeptic to savior in a race to protect not just her city, but every version of it.

https://ethanreeveswerewolfdetective.com/?page_id=1026

The Fading Sigils

The Fading Sigils plunge paranormal investigator Ethan Reeves into a deadly mystery beneath Daybridge's historic covered bridge. A local death uncovers a centuries-old pact with an ancient entity bound by fading sigils and ritual sacrifice. As federal agents close in and reality begins to unravel, Ethan must choose: restore the blood-bound pact or risk a new path that could transform the town—and the monster guarding it. The storm is coming, and not all legends want to stay buried. Mystery and cosmic suspense.

https://ethanreeveswerewolfdetective.com/?page_id=1038

Hands of Fate

Hands of Fate catapults Detective Alice Chen into a race against time when synchronized whispers from Daybridge's clocks trigger visions of the future. As temporal fractures ripple across the city, Alice joins a master watchmaker, a witch, and her unpredictable partner Ethan Reeves to uncover the Pendulum of Aeon—an artifact that could heal or destroy reality. With rival factions vying for control and time itself unraveling, Alice must embrace her powers before the clock runs out... and the past becomes permanently unhinged. [coming soon...]

The Liminal Line

Beneath Daybridge lies a subway that shouldn't exist.

When grad student Robert North stumbles onto the Liminal Line—a transit system connecting alternate realities—each stop reveals a different version of his city. As reality begins to collapse, Robert teams up with a rare book dealer and a cryptic Station Master to close a dangerous temporal loop. But the deeper he travels, the more he must confront quantum secrets, shifting architecture, and the truth about his own fractured identity. The convergence is coming—and every version of Daybridge is at risk. [coming soon...]

The Threshold Between Pages

The Threshold Between Pages follows antiquarian bookseller Jake Steinman as he discovers a relic that lets him step inside stories—literally. But when fictional entities begin invading Daybridge, Jake must team up with folklore scholar Rebecca Chen to stop reality from collapsing. As the boundary between worlds dissolves, one truth becomes clear: some stories don't want to stay on the page. A spellbinding blend of bibliophile fantasy and cosmic horror. [coming soon...]

Hunger Unbound: Book One in the Daybridge Darkness Trilogy

Hunger Unbound unleashes a chilling force beneath Daybridge when journalist Marcus Wong exposes the city's hidden supernatural world—triggering a wave of ritualistic murders. As fear spreads, an unlikely team forms: a professor with a monstrous secret, a witch marked by forbidden magic, and a detective who never asked for any of this. Together, they uncover a centuries-old ritual feeding a primordial hunger that grows stronger with every death. The darkness is rising—and only those willing to face it can stop what's coming. [coming soon...]

Feast of Shadows: Book Two in the Daybridge Darkness Trilogy

Feast of Shadows escalates the battle for Daybridge as an ancient entity's dark design unfolds. Haunted by visions and unwanted powers, Ethan, Lila, Alice, and Marcus uncover a ritual unraveling by intent—not accident. As shadow feeders target key sites and panic spreads, fractured alliances and buried secrets threaten to derail their fight. With time running out, the team must decode cryptic warnings and face the truth: the coming feast won't stop at Daybridge—it's hungry for everything. [coming soon...]

Graveborn Reckoning: Book Three in the Daybridge Darkness Trilogy

Graveborn Reckoning brings Daybridge to the edge of annihilation as the ancient Hunger completes its transformation. With ritual sites activated and the dimensional barrier shattered, Ethan, Lila, Alice, and Marcus must wield forbidden magic in a final stand. As supernatural factions clash and a blood sacrifice looms under a rare celestial alignment, the team uncovers a dark truth tied to Daybridge's founding—and a reckoning that demands more than courage. The fate of every reality hangs in the balance. [coming soon...]

Grave Shift: Daybridge Chronicles: Tales from the Nexus

Grave Shift unearths a chilling mystery when cemetery groundskeeper Owen Fenn discovers grave markers shifting overnight. With researcher Nadia Marsh's help, he uncovers a mathematical pattern tied to ancient secrets and a rare celestial event. As the veil between realms thins, Owen must embrace his role as Guardian of Stones to stop otherworldly forces from rewriting reality. What begins as strange grave movements becomes a cosmic reckoning—and Owen is at its center. [coming soon...]

The Threshold Child: A Daybridge Chronicles Novella

The Threshold Child follows eleven-year-old Amy Witowski, who sees shadow creatures no one else can. After her parents vanish, she moves to Daybridge—a city where reality runs thin—and discovers she's a rare Threshold Child whose drawings can reshape existence. When a breach unleashes otherworldly entities, Amy must master her powers and team up with unlikely allies to restore balance before the cracks between worlds consume everything. A haunting tale of cosmic mystery, hidden magic, and a girl destined to guard the boundaries of reality. [coming soon...]

The Memory Collector

In Daybridge, memories are vanishing—and reality is unraveling.

Detective Alice Chen uncovers a chilling phenomenon: residents losing memories with surgical precision. Her investigation leads to a secret society guarding against the return of the Memory Collector, a being harvesting knowledge as the boundary between worlds collapses. Named "The Anchor," Alice must team up with a skeptical partner and a mysterious professor to stop the encroaching otherworld before Daybridge is lost forever. A gripping blend of supernatural mystery and cosmic suspense. [coming soon...]

Night Shift at Mercy Hospital

Night Shift at Mercy Hospital thrusts rookie nurse Suzy Fairchild into a surreal mystery when patients begin turning transparent during her 3 AM rounds. Her search for answers uncovers a hidden interdimensional ward run by the enigmatic Dr. Ironsides, where realities blur and boundary sickness spreads. As dimensional collapse looms, Suzy must confront ancient forces and her own fears in a gripping blend of medical drama and supernatural suspense. Reality is unraveling—and she's the only one who can hold the line.

The Quantum Framework Series: A New Era of Consciousness

The Quantum Framework Series delves into the transformation of human consciousness, guided by the gripping narratives of detective Alice Chen and tactical specialist Ethan Reeves. Set against the backdrop of the Daybridge Event, where reality's fabric was momentarily torn, this series challenges the boundaries of what we perceive as possible. As Alice and Ethan navigate the clandestine battle between oppressive corporate forces and a burgeoning liberation movement, readers are invited to question the very nature of reality and explore the potential that lies beyond conventional understanding.

Rise of the Underground: The Quantum Shadow War

A Thrilling Start to a New Reality

Dive into the heart of a hidden conflict where detective Alice Chen and Ethan Reeves uncover the secrets of the Daybridge Event.

https://ethanreeveswerewolfdetective.com/?page_id=343

Dimensional Breach: Quantum Frontlines - Book Two in the Quantum Framework Series

Follow Alice Chen and her specialized team as they battle the Void Architects' engineered reality incursions threatening to unmake Daybridge, ultimately establishing a revolutionary dimensional interface that redefines humanity's place in the multiverse.

https://ethanreeveswerewolfdetective.com/?page_id=346

Memory of Stars: The Dawn of Integrated Consciousness - Book Three in the Quantum Framework Series

"Memory of Stars" follows Alice Chen's discovery of an ancient cosmic artifact that awakens humanity to its cyclical amnesia under mysterious "Architects," triggering her neural transformation and leadership of a resistance movement that ultimately forges an unprecedented partnership with these cosmic entities, allowing humanity to finally remember its stellar origins and claim control of its evolutionary destiny.

https://ethanreeveswerewolfdetective.com/?page_id=349

The Architect's Legacy: Shadows Between Worlds - Book Four in the Quantum Framework Series

Six months after victory, Director Alice Chen confronts a dangerous enhancement outbreak in Daybridge that reveals humanity's artificial origins and forces her to guide evolution responsibly against cultists seeking apocalyptic transcendence.

https://ethanreeveswerewolfdetective.com/?page_id=364

Harmonic Convergence: When Consciousness Rewrites Reality - Book Five in the Quantum Framework Series

As quantum physicist Alice Chen and enhanced sensitive Ethan Reeves detect five powerful factions tearing reality apart, they race to implement a harmonization protocol while confronting betrayal and risking their consciousness to guide humanity's evolution toward a coherent new reality's place in the multiverse.

https://ethanreeveswerewolfdetective.com/?page_id=367

Quantum Consciousness: A Cascading Evolution - Book Six in the Quantum Framework Series

In "Quantum Consciousness," Dr. Alice Chen discovers humans are spontaneously developing shared consciousness abilities across impossible distances, racing to protect this natural evolutionary response while shadowy government agencies and corporations deploy dangerous technology to suppress it, threatening to tear reality apart.

https://ethanreeveswerewolfdetective.com/?page_id=370

The Void Between: Where Shadows Meet - Book Seven in the Quantum Framework Series

In "The Void Between: Where Shadows Meet," scientist Alice Chen and her quantum ghost sister Sarah lead a desperate mission into the conscious void to convince ancient cosmic Architects not to dissolve all dimensional variants, proving humanity's unique evolutionary potential justifies its continued existence..

https://ethanreeveswerewolfdetective.com/?page_id=373

Framework Genesis: From Concept to Creation - Book Eight in the Quantum Framework Series

In "Framework Genesis," researcher Alice must embrace her role as an "Architect of Reality" within the Interstice to save all conscious existence from meta-dimensional entities farming reality for sustenance, championing a revolutionary approach that transforms cosmic exploitation into an evolutionary garden for consciousness.

https://ethanreeveswerewolfdetective.com/?page_id=376

Also by Rae Stonehouse

Reality Unravelled: A Daybridge Chronicles Novel
Darkness Beneath Daybridge: Collected Cases from the Daybridge Archives
Fragments of the Veil: Daybridge Chronicles Trilogy #1 – Through the Rift
Shadows and Debts: Tales from the Nexus

Watch for more at https://liveforexcellence.com.